KEEPERS
of the
HIDDEN WAYS

B O O K   T W O

THE
SILVER
STONE

KEEPERS
of the
HIDDEN WAYS

B O O K T W O

THE
SILVER
STONE

JOEL ROSENBERG

AVON BOOKS NEW YORK

This one is for Elise, of all people.

KEEPERS
—— of the ——
HIDDEN WAYS

B O O K   T W O

THE
SILVER
STONE

PROLOGUE

~~~o~~~

War, and Rumors of War

The dusk is fully ended,
And remnants of twilight have fled.
Horses have been settled in their stables,
And children put to bed.
But before the day ends,
And before the day dies,
The Hour of Long Candles comes,
The Hour of Long Candles arrives,
The Hour of Long Candles appears,
The Hour of Long Candles arrives.

—traditional Vandestish chant,
used to announce the end of the day

Harbard swung the double-bladed axe with a slow, even rhythm, relishing the feel of the smooth handle against his right hand, the shock of the sharp, bright head biting into the wood, the spray of chips and the turpentine smell as he brought the axehead back, spun the axe half around, and then swung again, and again.

He could have called upon a fraction of his old strength and hacked through the trees as easily as he had more than once hacked through a battlefield full of enemies, but he had long since lost his taste for such things.

Amazing, really, for one who had waded through rivers of blood to now eschew even an easy slaughter of a tree.

He had started with the undercut, properly low, facing in the direction he wanted the tree to fall, and then walked around the base of the tree and started in on the other side. The old pine was stronger than he had expected: the final cut almost met the undercut before, with loud cracks of protest, the tree started to lean, and then to fall.

The butt-end of the tree kicked back against his shoulder, sending his axe flying end over end one way, kicking Harbard back easily his own length, knocking him flat.

With a swallowed curse—he had long ago learned to curse only deliberately—he rose, dusting himself off, working his shoulder, trying to pretend it didn't hurt. Had he been braced for it, he could have resisted, but he had been lazy and sloppy in his old age, and he hadn't expected it.

Old one, he thought to himself, it's as well you've long ago put yourself out to pasture. Even just a century ago, he wouldn't have stood in the way of a tree he was chopping.

Oh, well. He picked up the axe and walked to the base of the fallen pine, stripping off wrist-thick branches with quick strokes of the axe, only stopping when the trunk thinned out a few bodylengths from the top. He quickly severed the top of the tree, then set his axe down and stripped off the bark with his fingers, shoving them through the rough bark, peeling the tree like a banana. There was something pleasurable about chopping the tree the way an ephemeral would, but stripping the bark with the axe while avoiding cutting into the wood would be a tedious task, and Harbard drew a careful distinction between regularity and tedium.

In minutes, what had been a tree was a naked log and a

scattering of bark and branches that would have to be dealt with later, as when they dried they would become violently flammable tinder.

He found the center of the log and moved back a careful step toward the base to allow for its greater thickness, then stooped to pick it up by its balance, hefting it to his shoulder with a grunt. It was heavy. The trees seemed to get heavier each decade.

His bare feet sank ankle-deep into the packed dirt of the path that led downhill, past his cottage, toward the ferry landing. More than two dozen logs lay in a single row, crosswise across two short lengths of stone fence, aging and drying in the sun; Harbard set this one down on the newer end of the pile, using a series of small wooden wedges to separate it from the next one over, then set his hands on his hips.

Enough? It was hard to say. Maintaining his ferry barge was a matter of constantly replacing rotting logs, and while it was a certainty that the ones that now made up the floor of the barge would need replacement, it was not at all a certainty when.

Harbard allowed himself a grin. That was true for so much else.

High above in the blue, cloud-spattered sky, a raven slowly circled down, riding wind currents with its huge wings, never so much as flapping.

"Greetings, Hugin," Harbard said, in a language that was older than the sagging hills that rose behind the cottage. "What word have you?"

"War," the raven cawed. "War, and rumors of war."

Harbard sighed. There had been a time when such would have excited him, when the thought of the clash of axes and the clatter of spears would have aroused a fervor within him. Brave men facing other brave men, all competing for the honor of being noticed by Harbard and his friends, in life or in death...

But that time was long past, and Harbard preferred things quieter these days.

"Tell me," he said.

PART ONE

HARDWOOD, NORTH DAKOTA

CHAPTER ONE

Homecoming

"You want to try and land it, Ian?" the redheaded pilot shouted over the roar of the Lance's single engine.

Even after more than two hours in the air, Ian was still surprised by how loud it was.

Ian Silverstein shook his head. "Thanks, but no thanks." His chuckle was tight in his chest, and his hands clenched the steering yoke. It had probably been a mistake to ask if he could fly it a little. Ian had been joking, but Greg Cotton had said yes, then flicked off the autopilot when Ian put his hands on the steering yoke, well before Ian had put his feet on the rudder pedals.

Ian was surprised to find that flying really wasn't all that hard, but it was nervous-making. And it was one thing to try to hold the small plane steady and level—he kept having to push the nose down, or the plane would climb—but it would be another thing to try to line it up with the landing strip that was what Karin Thorsen had laughingly referred to as Hardwood International, and yet another thing to try to put the plane down.

Besides, Greg was kidding. At least, he *thought* Greg was kidding.

"Okay," Greg said. "I've got it."

"Eh?"

"I said, 'I've got it.' That means I'm flying now. You can let go. Honest."

The breath came out of him with a rush, and Ian let himself sag back in the right-hand seat as he wiped the palms of his hands on his pants.

Two thousand feet above Hardwood, North Dakota, the sky was clear and the air was smooth, with no trace of the turbulence that had marked the Lance's descent through the wispy layer of clouds now more than a mile overhead.

Greg put the plane into what he claimed was a shallow, one-minute turn, and while the turn indicator seemed to say he was telling the truth, Ian's stomach was sure he was lying through his teeth. It felt like he was laying the plane over on its side.

Still, through the bug-spattered windshield, it gave Ian a good view of Hardwood. What there was of it. A granary and a dozen or so stores lining Main Street on the western side of town; the municipal swimming pool—which probably got used all of two, maybe three, weeks of the year, given the weather—and the football field and school on the other, and between them perhaps a few hundred houses on the elm-lined streets.

"What's the population?" Greg asked. "About fifty?"

Ian chuckled. "Not quite that small. A couple of thousand." That was, maybe, a little misleading. Hardwood served the surrounding farms and tinier towns, as well, enough people that it had its own, albeit small, high school. The new clinic next to Doc Sherve's house had the only emergency room between Thompson and Grand Forks, staffed by overpaid doctors from a commercial service on weekends and during Doc's increasingly frequent vacations.

But the airport, such as it was, was little more than a pair of hangars, and an asphalt landing strip about a thousand yards long, broken in spots where weeds had pushed through.

It looked a lot shorter from the air than it had from the ground.

"How long is that?" Ian asked.

Greg glanced down at the Jeppson chart in his lap. "Twenty-three hundred feet. No problem."

"You can put it down there?" It looked awfully short.

"*Down?*" Greg sniffed. "Down is not a problem. I could look up in the manual what the specs are for landing this thing if you don't have to clear a fifty-foot obstacle, but it's not going to be more than a thousand feet. Landing's not a problem. Now, taking off's a different story . . . Might be a bit tight taking off on a hot day with a full load, no wind, and a full tank, but hey, it's cool out, it'll be just me in here, there's only about forty, forty-five gallons in the tanks, and I've got about five, ten knots of headwind. Easy."

He offered Ian an Altoid—Ian declined with a quick head-shake; they were too strong for his tastes—then popped a couple of the pill-like mints in his own mouth before closing the tin and dropping it to his lap.

"Two kinds of pilots," Greg said, as he reached forward and flipped the switch for the landing gear, nervously tapping against the three green lights until they came on. "The kind that's made a gear-up landing, and . . ."

"The kind that hasn't?"

"Nah. The kind that will," he said, easing back on the throttle and reflexively pointing toward first one dial, then another. "Which is why they charge more for the insurance on these retractable-gear jobs. Okay; looks good." He pushed the nose down, then up as he eased back on the throttle. "And we're . . . down." The plane bounced once, then settled down to a bumpy roll across the asphalt.

Greg let it almost come to a stop, then turned it around and eased it off the runway before cutting the power.

After the racket of the engine, the silence in the small cabin was deafening.

"Looks like we made it," Greg said with a grin.

Ian was already out of his seatbelt and opening the door. It was lighter than it should have been. That was the funny thing about these small planes—the metal skin was only about the thickness of an old-style beer can. It seemed too light, too flimsy to serve its purpose.

Then again, Ian thought, maybe that's true for me, too. He grinned.

He crawled out onto the wing and lowered himself to the tarmac. Greg followed, dropping to the ground with a practiced step-and-bounce off the mounting peg.

Ian took a deep breath as he walked around to the other side and the door to the passenger compartment, letting Greg open it. It didn't feel solid, like a car door; Ian was half afraid he was going to tear the door off if he handled it.

Greg reached in and handed out Ian's blocky black leather travel bags, a matched set, designed to fit underneath a commercial airplane seat or in an overhead luggage rack, and the cheap canvas golf bag Ian used for his fencing gear.

And for Giantkiller. Which you could call fencing gear, if you wanted to.

"You want me to watch the stuff while you walk into town and see about borrowing a car?" Greg asked. "You've got a fair walk if nobody shows up to meet you."

Ian shook his head. "Nah. I'll just stash the bags over in the shade of the hangar and walk into town." Amazing how quickly he was taking to small-town ways. Six months ago, he would no more have considered leaving his bags than he would have considered leaving his wallet. "There's no need to wait—unless you're going to change your mind and stay for dinner. Karin Thorsen's fried chicken and biscuits are pretty special." Ian's mouth watered at the thought of biting through that crunchy skin and into the moist meat beneath. Maybe it was that the chickens were grain-fed, and from the Hansen farm, or maybe it was the seasonings Karin used, or maybe it was just magic.

Bullshit. Her cooking was good, but the chicken could have been overcooked to tasteless rubberiness, and he still would be looking forward to dinner.

What it was, was that he was coming home.

"Wish I could, but I've got to get the plane back." Greg sealed the rear door closed, then gave it a friendly pat. "Next time, okay?"

"Fair enough." Ian reached for his wallet. "How much do I owe you for the gas?"

"Well . . ." Greg frowned. "We used about thirty-two, thirty-three gallons flying up. Figuring that the wind holds, it'll be about a hour and a half—maybe twenty-five gallons—back. I can use my company card and get it for about two bucks a gallon."

"Good deal. And thanks. You might as well top the tank off for Jake as long as you're filling up." Ian pulled eight twenties out of his wallet and handed them over. "Thank him for me, and I owe you dinner, next time I'm back."

"Sounds like a plan." Greg tucked the bills in his jeans and climbed back up into the plane, locking the door behind him.

"Take care," he said through the window. He belted himself in and shouted "*Clear!*" before closing the pilot's draft window and starting the engines.

Ian already had his bags in the shade of the main hangar; he dropped them and waved.

The little plane rolled toward the far end of the runway, slowly turned around, then accelerated down the runway and lifted off into the air before it was even two-thirds of the way along it, climbing leisurely into the blue sky before it banked away, heading back southeast, toward Minneapolis.

And then it was quiet.

The wind whispered through the grasses, and far off in the

west, past the windbreak of trees that must have been a half mile away itself, some distant farm machine was growling, but Ian couldn't have told what it was even if he was closer. What there wasn't was somebody noticing a landing at the airport and driving out to investigate.

No problem, though. Ian was back earlier than he had been expected. That was the plan, actually. There was no point in complaining when things turned out the way you wanted. Karin had asked if it was convenient for him to come home earlier than he had planned, and while she wouldn't talk about why on the phone, that was fine with Ian. Lying on the beach was getting boring anyways, and while he had been surprised to find a fencing club in Basseterre, none of the locals was much competition, except for one saber player who was particularly good at those silly flicking touches that were fine for scoring points, but nothing more.

Ian had to chuckle. It wasn't too long ago that he thought the purpose of a sword *was* to score points.

It was time to come home, and if that meant asking a friend to borrow a plane so he could arrive sooner, that was fine, and if it meant walking a couple of miles, that was no big deal, either. He had walked further than that in his time, and likely would again, although not soon.

Spring, maybe. Spend the winter studying swordsmanship with Thorian del Thorian the Elder, bowmanship with Hosea, and hand-to-hand with the deceptively fast Ivar del Hival, and come spring he'd be ready.

Preparing for it all was, well, it was fun. Getting ready is half the fun, Benjamin Silverstein used to say. Ian's father was an abusive asshole, but even a stopped clock was right twice a day.

He reached into his golf bag and pulled out the package that contained an épée, a foil, a saber, and Giantkiller's scabbard. It was a canvas sheet, tied at both ends with a length of soft cotton rope that also served as a sling. He slung it over his shoulder like a quiver. One thing to leave most of what he owned in this world out at the landing field, but another thing entirely to leave his sword there.

He started walking along the left side of the road, long arms and legs swinging to eat up distance quickly.

Hardwood International Airport—so read the hand-painted sign at the turnoff onto the dirt road; it wasn't just Karin's joke—was just over a mile outside of town, but the Thorsen house and Ian's own room at Arnie Selmo's were over on the far side of town, maybe half an hour away by foot.

The county road was slightly convex, with a broad shoulder leading to a steep drop-off down to the black soil of the fields below. It was hard to tell what had been growing here—at least it was hard for Ian, who was still basically a city boy. Not corn—there still would be cornstalks. Maybe potatoes?

A red-winged blackbird sitting on a post of the wire fence at the edge of the field eyed Ian skeptically as he walked by.

Somebody walking down the road wasn't a common sight hereabouts, he supposed.

"Well," he said, "I haven't seen a lot of red-winged black-birds, either."

The bird didn't answer. He didn't really expect it to.

A car whizzed by, pulling along dust and sand in its wake; Ian turned his head away and closed his eyes to protect them from the grit. It was doing at least seventy, fairly typical for this part of the world, what with roads straight as an arrow, running sometimes tens of miles without so much as a tiny bend.

It was out of sight before he heard another car approaching from the rear, and again turned away, but instead of it rushing by, he heard this one slow and pull over to the shoulder, sand crunching beneath its tires as it ground to a stop.

He turned to see a tan Ford LTD, the rack of flashers on its roof the only markings. That was enough.

"Hey, neighbor," a familiar voice said, as a broad face peered out the open window. "You need a ride?" Under a bristly mustache, Jeff Bjerke smiled broadly as he pulled off his sunglasses for just a moment, polishing them with a blue bandanna before replacing them on his face.

"Thanks, Jeff." Ian opened the rear door and slid his package onto the rear seat, then climbed in front with Jeff Bjerke, accepting a firm handshake in the process. Jeff was a head shorter than Ian's six feet, and even more so in the legs; Ian's legs were scrunched up uncomfortably.

Jeff was only four, maybe five, years older than Ian, but the air of authority that his pistol belt and khaki cop shirt gave him made him seem older, despite the incongruity of the jeans and sneakers. Ian wasn't used to policemen in jeans and sneakers, and there was something strange about the gun in Jeff's holster. It seemed smaller than a cop's gun should.

He didn't ask. He just knew that Jeff would say something about size not being important, but what you did with it, and Ian didn't really need to hear that. He was all too often the straight man around here.

"Where to? And what are you doing out walking?" Jeff frowned. "Car break down? I've been on this road since Thompson, and I haven't seen any stopped cars."

"Nah." Ian shook his head. "It's not that; I didn't come by car. I got dropped off at Har—at the airstrip. Left my bags there; figured I'd walk into town and borrow a car from Torrie or Arnie."

"You actually left your bags without anybody standing over them, did you?" Jeff grinned broadly. "Hey, Arnie and the Thorsens are turning you into a regular small-town guy, eh?" He threw the car into a quick three-point turn and headed back toward the turnoff, and the airstrip.

"Well, yeah," Ian said.

"Well, good," Jeff said. "Let's grab your stuff, and then we'll have you at Arnie's quicker'n grain through a goose."

"Can't beat that." Ian returned his smile. "How quickly does grain go through a goose, anyways?"

"Wouldn't know." Jeff shrugged. "I keep the peace, not the geese."

Ian dropped his bags on the porch of the small bungalow and waved goodbye to Jeff, who drove off slowly, the way people drove around town. It was one thing to speed down the country road, Arnie had explained to him, but in town you never knew when a ball was going to roll out onto a street with a pack of kids in hot pursuit.

Besides, so what if it took four minutes instead of two to get clear across town?

It was a quiet afternoon. Kids were still in school, although undoubtedly several packs of less-than-school-age children were prowling the streets and backyards of Hardwood, looking for some sort of minor trouble to get into, supervised only occasionally by the same sort of face that was right now peering out the front window across the street at Ian.

Ian waved a hello to Ingrid Orjasaeter, who returned his wave with a smile before vanishing into the relative darkness of her living room.

Ian knocked on the door twice, then twice again before turning the knob and letting himself in. No key was necessary, which was just as well; Arnie didn't have the slightest idea where the keys were, and that mean that Ian didn't, either.

"Hello, the house," he called out as he rubbed his feet on the welcome mat and dropped his bags to the floor. He let the screen door shut behind him, but left the front door open as he walked into the living room.

A vague musty smell hung in the still air, although the living room was neat and clean, no trace of dust allowed on the shelves of little knickknacks that Arnie's late wife had collected over the years. On one shelf, little porcelain cows and silver bells and little cut glass figurines surrounded an ordinary shot glass that Ian had meant to ask Arnie about, but never quite had remembered.

The overstuffed chairs and couch had probably been new fifty years before, and restuffed and slipcovered a half dozen times since then. They were comfortable, though, and that was nice. They were Ephie's, and that was important to Arnie.

"Yo? Arnie? Anybody home?"

He shrugged and walked into the small, tidy kitchen and pulled on the swing-out handle of the ancient Kelvinator refrigerator. It was three-quarters empty: a covered pot of something or other—probably soup or stew, almost certainly quite edible; Arnie was a not-bad cook—half a loaf of Master English Muffin Toasting Bread, half a bottle of dubiously dark Heinz ketchup, and half a six-pack of Cokes. Glass bottles, not cans. Arnie didn't like cans.

Ian twisted open a Coke, pitched the bottlecap into the garbage while he took a long swallow, then brought it with him, down the hall and past Arnie's bedroom on the left, to what had been Ephie's sewing room, and was now Ian's bedroom, on the right.

He opened the door and turned on the light.

The poster advertising the new Andrew Vachss book had fallen, again. The bed was stripped down to its striped mattress. Clothes lay scattered on the floor, a large heap of clean clothes near the foot of the bed, a smaller heap of dirty laundry over by the bookcase. An irregular heap of books covered the floor near the head of the bed, testimony to Ian's need to read himself to sleep.

It looked pretty awful, but it was just the way he had left it.

He forced himself to smile. Starting when he was four or five, every time he dared to leave his room messy, his father counted how many items were out of place, and hit him once for each item. Of course, at four or five, a kid doesn't have the idea of order, not yet; Ian could never get it right, and could never avoid his father's hard hand.

What would this add up to, Dad? A hundred things out of place? Two hundred? A goddamn million?

"Fuck you, Dad," he said, quietly.

Ian rehung the poster, pushing hard against the beads of gunk at the top, then gave a quick thumbs-up to Andrew Vachss's ungrinning face.

"Later, Andy," he said, slinging his canvas bag across his shoulders.

He drained the Coke and tossed it into the garbage can just outside the back door.

The street—it undoubtedly had a name on some map somewhere, but nobody ever used street names or numbers in Hardwood—ended in a T, rimmed by woods on all sides.

A short path through the woods broke on the yard of the Thorsen house. Two-storied, plus an attic that seemed to sprout dormers like a potato sprouted eyes, topped by a sharply peaked roof, the front cupped by a screened, U-shaped porch that stretched across the whole front and part of two sides; behind it, a red barn; in front of it, three cars parked on the grass next to Karin Thorsen's red Volvo, plus the shiny black Studebaker on blocks that it appeared Hosea had made some progress on restoring to service.

It still needed wheels, but Ian didn't figure Hosea would have finished the body until he had brought the engine back to life; the old guy believed in first things first.

Ian hadn't been in Hardwood long enough to recognize everybody by their cars the way the locals could—hell, Arnie claimed he could tell whether Karin or Thorian Thorsen had been driving their big blue Bronco from the way it was parked. Still, there was no mistaking the big maroon Chevy Suburban that Doc Sherve used as his traveling office—and, rarely, a makeshift ambulance—as well as his personal car.

Why would Doc be here? He could be just visiting—visiting seemed to be the major recreational activity in Hardwood—but during the workday?

Karin had asked him to come home early, and hadn't explained why.

Ian quickened his pace to a trot.

CHAPTER TWO

The Best-Laid Plans

Arnie Selmo was just warming to the argument when the kid rounded the building. These days, these quiet days, these too many long days without Ephie, arguing was one of the few joys he had left.

"The Garand," he had said, stretching out a hand for the bottle of Leinenkugel on the grass next to his chair, "was the best damn rifle the army ever had. Went to shit when they decided to trade it in on that those leetle twenty-twos." He took a sip from the bottle.

Doc Sherve chuckled, while Davy Hansen's natural glare darkened. Over by sliding glass doors that were open to their sliding screens, old Hosea Lincoln turned his attention from the file and piece of metal in his lap to flash a quick grin, his teeth ivory white in a face the color of coffee barely lightened by milk, not cream.

Davy grunted as he sat back in the chair, huddling into the olive drab army jacket that, shabby as it was, couldn't have been brought back from Vietnam. "I've carried a Garand. Heavy. Not the sort of thing I'd want to hump for twenty, thirty klicks a day, but have it your way."

"I'll be happy to go walking with—with my Garand any old time," Arnie said, cursing himself for an asshole. That sounded awkward, and stupid; Arnie hid his embarrassment with another pull at his beer.

Sure, he could walk Davy into the ground. Damn near any-body could walk Davy into the ground. From just below the knee, Davy's right leg had been blown off in some muddy field in Vietnam, and while Davy wasn't one to complain, it was clear that plastic leg they fitted him with hurt him when he walked too far on it.

Arnie hadn't meant any harm, but *shit* that had been a stupid thing to say.

It was just that that had always been Arnie's one talent, walk-ing. He had grown up on a farm a good six miles out of town, and it had felt like he had spent most of the Depression walking either to school or home from school, save only for those days that the Selmos were snowed in.

Even back in basic, closer to half a century ago than Arnie liked to remember, he would finish the thirty-mile hikes ready for more—although he would do his best to hide it; the second thing he learned in basic was to keep with the crowd, keep his head down.

And it hadn't left him, even with age.

Which had made it kind of funny, actually, when somebody as good at walking as Arnie had been was assigned to the cav-alry—Dog Troop, 7th Regiment, First Cavalry. Well, it hadn't seemed so funny when they'd shipped out to Korea; they'd fought their way up and down that fucking peninsula as infan-try, and while it was one thing to walk up and down the hills of Georgia, a Korean winter was something else entirely. Meaner than a North Dakota winter, somehow.

Maybe that had been because of the assholes who had been shooting at him.

Davy shrugged it off. "I'd just as soon carry any other twelve pounds of dead weight," he said, while Doc pursed his lips and shook his head.

Now, while Arnie had long since learned that you couldn't judge somebody by their looks, Doc looked like a country doctor, from the stethoscope sticking out of the pocket of the white doctor's coat now draped over the back of his chair to the small black doctor's bag that never was more than a few feet away from him, to the close-trimmed beard, now more gray than salt-and-pepper.

Doc took another bite of coffee cake, and washed it down with a sip from his mug. "Me," he said, "I try not to know anything about guns. 'Course, every year or so during hunting season, I learn about how somebody can shoot his foot off with one that he would have sworn was unloaded. Pretty dangerous, those unloaded guns."

"Well, at least I got a better excuse than that." Davy grinned and tapped on his own artificial leg. "You gonna come deer hunting with us this year, Doc?" he asked.

Doc bit on his lower lip, as though considering it, as though he hadn't been invited along half a million times. "Nah," he said, finally, the way he always did, "I never kill anything . . . on purpose." He raised a hand to forestall the usual argument. "Now, I'm not criticizing, mind, and I won't be one to turn down a venison steak or chop, should somebody find himself with some extra, but I don't fix my own car, and I don't kill my own food. I don't look down my nose at those who do, but I just don't. And as far as I am concerned—" He looked up. "And welcome back, Mr. Silverstein," Doc said, rising to his feet as Ian Silverstein rounded the side of the house at a quick jog. "What's the rush?"

The boy looked good for his vacation, Arnie decided. A light tan had taken some of that pasty, city-boy look from his face, and he had let his beard grow for the past month or so, which was all to the good. Ephie would have thought him too skinny, and tried to put some meat on his bony frame, but the kid was built along greyhound lines, not bull-necked and solid like a proper Norski-American.

Which was fine by Arnie; the world was big enough for all kinds of folks.

Ian eased a canvas bundle from his shoulders and lowered it to the ground as he accepted Doc's hand.

"Some sort of problem?" he asked. "I saw your car, and I hurried."

Arnie grinned. The kid was quickly turning into a real small-town type in what? Six months or so? Give him another few years and he might not wake up screaming in the middle of the night.

"Nah." Doc plopped himself back down in his chair. "Only problem is that I just finished my house calls for the day, and I'm taking the rest of the afternoon off, unless Martha and Katie run into something they can't handle, in which case they can either beep me," he said, patting at the pager he used as an oversized tie clip, "or call me on the bag-o-phone." He jerked a thumb at his doctor bag. "So instead of seeing what stale McGlynn's delicacies are waiting boxed at the Dine-a-mite, I decided to stop by and beg a piece of Karin's coffee cake and a cup of her coffee . . ."

"To which you are welcome, as always, Bob," Karin Thorsen said, emerging from the dark of the house, a tray balanced on the palm of her hand. Her eyes grew wide as she saw Ian, and she quickly set the tray down on the table and ran to him, giving him a quick hug and a peck on the cheek.

Something—her closeness, maybe?—seemed to bother the kid, and he tried to cover it by picking up the tray and setting it down next to Doc Sherve.

Better to do something than just to stand there looking like he didn't know what to do.

"Thank you. And welcome home, stranger," she said. "How was St. Kitts?"

"I had a good time. Quiet, but good." Ian stretched and smiled. "I spent most of the past month lying on a beach, halfway around the island from Basseterre, when I wasn't eating or sleeping."

"No fencing? Not a bit?"

He grinned. "Well, just a little. And I did a bit of snorkeling, but mainly I got some rest." He winced slightly, and his thumb touched his gut, just over his liver.

"Eh? What's this?" Doc frowned. "Indigestion? Or should I crank up for a quick appendectomy?"

"Neither." Ian shook his head. "Just an old wound, mainly healed up."

"I'll get you coffee," she said, turning away. "Black, as I recall."

Arnie suppressed a grin as he noticed the way Ian watched the tightness of Karin's jeans as she disappeared back into the house, but the boy caught him at it. Ian's cheeks burned red.

No harm done. Karin Roelke—shit, after twenty years of her being married Arnie still thought of her by her maiden name—looked a lot younger than her forty years, and it wasn't just Arnie getting old. The long legs in their tight jeans and the firm breasts pushing against the blue workshirt that was cut tight to emphasize her slim waist were enough to give even an old man ideas, and Ian was still a young buck, all full of piss and hormones.

'Course, the boy knew better than to make a pass at his friend Torrie's mom, and shit, if she didn't want to be looked at, she wouldn't dress that way. Nothing wrong with a young girl dressing to show that she was, well, built.

And hell, boy, when did you start thinking of a forty-year-old woman as a young girl?

Arnie caught Hosea's eye, and returned his broad grin. No harm done, eh?

Hosea Lincoln—well, that was what he called himself—gave a genial nod and smile before turning back to the piece of metal he was working on, taking another few rasps with a file before holding it up and examining it in the bright sunlight. Even sitting, he still looked tall and skinny, and the plaid shirt and faded, neatly patched Levi's overalls looked more like a costume than natural clothes on his long form.

His right hand gripped the metal firmly, if a bit awkwardly; it was his left hand that did all the fine work. "It's good to see you back, Ian Silverstone," he said, his voice slightly slurred, as though he had been drinking, although he hadn't.

"Silverstein," Arnie said, correcting.

Ian dismissed it with a shrug. "I don't mind. I've been called that," he said, and dropped a quick phrase in a language that had the lilt of Norski, but that Arnie couldn't even begin to follow.

Hosea answered in the same language, it sounded like. "I thought you were due to return in a matter of some days," he went on in English. "I trust you had a pleasant vacation?"

Ian nodded. "Just fine."

"And your injury is better?" Hosea asked, his brow furrowing.

"Well, as I always say, there's no rest for the weary." Doc grunted and set his coffee cup down and stood, pulling a packet out of his jacket pocket. "Okay, okay, off with the shirt, and let's see this injury," he said, tearing open the packet and pulling out a damp towelette-thingy, wiping his hands with it and then dropping the used towelette and its wrapping into a side pocket. He rubbed his hands together to dry them, and looked like Scrooge gloating over his money for a moment.

Ian shook his head. "It's just fine, Doctor Sherve, really it is."

"Yeah, right, and if I remember right, you're something like one year of college, four years of med school, and three years of residency shy of practicing medicine, so off with the shirt and pull up a seat," Doc said, pointing to the weather-beaten wooden chair next to him.

Davy chuckled. "Be glad you didn't tell him you have hemorrhoids, boy, or you'd be crouching on your hands and knees with your ass up in the air."

"Davy Larsen, shut up. Ian Silverstein, take off your shirt and sit down." Doc had been ordering people around over four decades that Arnie knew about, and probably more than that. Hell, he'd probably been bossy from the cradle on.

Ian unbuttoned the forest green cotton shirt and removed it, revealing a tanned and hairy chest, except for one spot on the right side of the belly, just below the rib cage, where bare skin surrounded a two-inch-long white scar, thicker at the top than the bottom. It reminded Arnie of an exclamation point.

"Let me guess," Doc said, "somebody tried to take out your gall bladder, but they figured it would be fun to start low and work their way up."

Hosea smiled. "You would likely not believe it if he told you what happened."

"I dunno. I've seen strange enough things around here. Performed an autopsy on a couple of werewolves not too long ago, as you'll recall." Doc grunted again as he poked at the scar with a blunt finger. "This hurt?" he asked, when Ian let out a groan.

"Yes, and it would hurt if you poked me in the *arm* that hard."

"Don't talk back, kid. I'm old enough to be your grandfather." Doc cocked his head to one side. "What happened?"

"Hosea's right." Ian spread his hands. "You wouldn't believe me."

Doc grinned. "Try me."

"Okay," Ian said, "I was in a swordfight with a fire giant who was masquerading as the Duke of the House of Flame, and he managed to get through my defenses, twice." Ian's lips whitened. "But I got through his. Once." He looked up defensively. "So call me a liar."

Doc shook his head. "Nah." His heavy brow furrowed. "Probably got a couple of adhesions in there, but it seems mostly healed up." He handed Ian's shirt back. "Any change in your bowel movements? Excess gas? No? Getting better, not worse? Yeah? Then you're probably okay. If it keeps giving you trouble, be sure to let me know, and we'll run a quick barium test."

"*Test*? Barium *test*?" Davy chuckled, again. "He means enema. Doc likes sticking tubes in you, and any damn orifice'll do in a pinch."

Doc grinned. "True enough. So stay out of the way of fire giants. It's not healthy."

Arnie had heard the story, most of it. And he would have thought that all of it was a tall tale, if it hadn't been for the Night of the Werewolves—which is what that night had come to be called even among the closed-mouthed in Hardwood—or Homecoming Day. Arnie himself had shot three, four of the Sons with deer slugs on the Night, and each one of them had gotten up, one of them finally mauling Arnie in a way that gave him a whole new set of scars to go with the three puckered ones that had gotten him his Purple Heart in a little unnamed village in Uijongbu and the one zipperlike one he had gotten from a grenade during the bugout from Taejon.

But on Homecoming Day, it had been the other way around. Just Arnie and Orphie—Orphie with a Garand, Arnie with a BAR—had nailed close to a dozen of the Sons, and hadn't gotten so much as a scratch. Silver bullets made all the difference.

Arnie's mouth grew tight at the thought. *Fuck with my neighbors, dog?*

Not twice.

After he'd lived through werewolves popping up out of the ground, Arnie hadn't had any trouble believing the kid about the Hidden Ways between here and Tir Na Nog, or about the Fire Duke, or even about the Brisingamen.

Shit, boy, after believing all that, you'd be a good mark for some con man, Arnie thought, grinning.

That could happen, even here. Somebody pretending to be a bank inspector had once conned old Addie Oppegaard out of her life savings, and would have gotten away with it if Ingrid Orjasaeter hadn't been such an insufferable busybody, always peering out of her window, and called her brother, John Honistead, about the strange car from out of state parked in front of the Oppegaards' house.

But it didn't hurt to believe, and if that wasn't so—if Ian and Torrie and that little girl of his and Thorian and Karin Roelke were all lying or crazy—then to hell with it, and to hell with everything.

You don't have to believe in everything, but Arnie Selmo believed in his neighbors.

Karin reappeared with a steaming mug of coffee just as Ian finished buttoning his shirt. It hadn't taken five minutes for her to pour a cup of coffee, and it would have taken more than five minutes for her to grind the beans and brew a fresh pot. She hadn't wanted to catch him with his shirt off.

"Arnie?" Doc cocked his head. "What are you grinning about?"

Arnie shrugged. "Nothing much, Doc."

Karin Thorsen had excused herself to go up to her office to do some work and Ian had finished his second cup of coffee and his third piece of coffee cake when car wheels crunched on the gravel out front.

Ian had wanted to take Karin aside to ask what was going on, but after being caught staring at her—and dammit, it was hard not to stare; Torrie's mom was spectacularly beautiful, and reminded Ian a bit of Freya, if the truth be known—he hadn't felt that he could sneak off into the house without drawing some sort of comment.

"They're back." Davy Larsen was already on his feet limping toward the front of the house, and Arnie Selmo, moving easier

27

than a man his age ought to, was right behind him, while Hosea slowly eased himself out of his chair.

Doc Sherve was suddenly at Hosea's elbow. "If you please, the others can see to this. I'll want a moment of your time, Hosea," he said.

"As you will," Hosea said.

Ian would have liked to have stayed and listened, but he didn't see a way to do it, not without seeming to be slacking on the unloading.

What was that all about? Hosea seemed to be a bit tired today, and his slight limp exaggerated, but he was older than most mountain ranges—he couldn't be aging right in front of Ian, could he?

The procession made it to the front just as Thorian Thorsen was backing the big blue Bronco up to the front porch, maneuvering it with a speed that Ian wouldn't have considered, but that Thorsen apparently could manage: he jerked it to a stop with the rear wheels a few scant inches short of the steps, and was out his door before Ivar del Hival had fully extricated himself from his seatbelt.

When he saw Ian, Thorsen's face broke into an easy smile that wouldn't have looked even slightly piratical if it wasn't for the scar that snaked down his right cheek, as though an acid tear had carved its way down his face before dropping off at the jawline.

Despite that, and the slight bend in the nose that told of an ancient break, there was something delicate about his face and the long fingers of his hands. Delicate, though, didn't mean weak; Thorsen's handshake was firm without being an attempted assault.

"I thought you weren't due back for another moon, perhaps," he said. "Along with Thorian and Maggie."

If his wife hadn't told Thorsen that she had called him back early, Ian wasn't going to mention it. "I missed this place," he said, finding that it was truer than he had thought.

It was kind of funny. Benjamin Silverstein, Ian's asshole of an excuse for a father, had kicked him out when Ian had stopped letting him beat him, and ever since then Ian had lived in college dorms during the school year—it was more expensive than living off-campus, but Ian couldn't afford the time commuting back and forth—and rented rooms during the summers.

And each time he had come back to any of those, it was just coming back to a familiar place, that was all. Just a place he knew.

But this felt like home, and that felt strange.

"How strange," Ivar del Hival said, echoing his thoughts. He was a big man, almost as tall as Ian and easily twice as wide, his smile white against a full, bushy beard that was so black as to be almost blue.

"Ah, so very strange, young Silverstone, that you should miss this little town," he said, his voice booming like the blare of a tuba. He looked funny dressed in the local uniform of jeans and a plaid flannel shirt, cut generously for his ample belly: Ian always expected to see him in the black and orange livery of the House of Flame.

"A place where you are liked and valued and welcome, and you would miss it?" Ivar del Hival laughed as he clapped a hard hand to Ian's shoulder. "How unusual. Next you'll be finding that when you haven't eaten for half a day, you're a trifle hungry, or that you find a soft warm bed not uncomfortable when your eyelids are heavy, or that if you haven't been properly swived in a twelve-day, your siitinrod gets somewhat hard at the mere sight and smell and touch and taste of a naked, beautiful, willing woman," he said.

Thorian Thorsen chuckled as he opened the tailgate, and selected a bag of groceries, handing it to Davy Larsen. "I couldn't find the plain Eucerine, so I picked up the Eucerine Plus for you," he said. "I hope that's acceptable."

"Just fine; I appreciate it," Davy said. He carefully set the bag down on the ground and took a step toward the Bronco, hands out.

"No need; there are plenty of us to unload," Thorsen said. "You'll want to get that hamburger meat in your refrigerator if you're not going to cook it today, and that ice cream is going to melt. Best to hurry home."

"I guess you're right." Davy nodded as he picked up the bag. "Thanks for picking the stuff up. Receipt in the bag? Good; I'll write out a check and drop it off later."

Thorsen nodded, dismissing the subject; he was already handing a couple of bags to Ian, who carried them into the kitchen, with Arnie, Ivar del Hival, Doc Sherve, Hosea, and Thorsen following. With each of them carrying two bags—except for Hosea, who settled for one—the Bronco emptied out almost immediately, and with Hosea supervising, the groceries were quickly stowed in cabinets, the huge fridge in the Thorsens' kitchen, and the coffinlike freezer down in the basement, except for the two repacked bags destined for Arnie's house.

Thorsen brought charcoal and lighter fluid out to the backyard and started up the barbecue, while Ian and the rest took to their chairs.

"So," Ivar del Hival said, sitting back down in his chair, his fingers laced over his ample belly, "what shall be your pleasure?"

"Eh?"

"You're back early, which I take it means you're eager to get back to Tir Na Nog, and continue the hunt." Ivar del Hival stretched out. "Now, if you were to ask me, I'd suggest you spend another half year or so taking fencing lessons from Thorian del Thorian, bowmanship from Orfindel here, and some hand-to-hand from me, but—"

Ian shrugged. "I'm in no hurry."

Closing his affairs here had turned out to be easier than he had thought. Unsurprisingly, D'Arnot had fired him when he hadn't shown up for work at the fencing studio, and arranging a leave of absence from school when he had already missed some weeks was just a matter of filing some papers. Ian felt bad about the hard feelings—but he could hardly explain the reason he'd been gone, so there was nothing to be done about it.

There were a few friends, in the loose sense, that he would have wanted to say goodbye to, but he could hardly tell them that he was planning on taking a Hidden Way to Tir Na Nog, to search for another of the jewels of the Brisingamen.

And, of course, there was that asshole of an excuse of a father, but Ian had nothing to say to him.

The complicated thing was converting four rucksacks filled with gold coins into cash, but he had simply dumped that on Karin Thorsen, and she had done that before, with her then-future husband's stolen gold. In the well-ventilated shop in the basement of the Thorsen house, the letters and the seal of the House of Fire disappeared, and the coins became anonymous small ingots that could be carefully, slowly disposed of, over a matter of years if need be.

Ian wasn't in a rush to leave. Torrie and Maggie were off knocking about Europe somewhere, while Torrie explained to Maggie that she wasn't coming along this time.

Ian frowned. Maggie wouldn't take that well, but there was no getting around it. Unlike Ian, Maggie had family connections, and simply couldn't quite literally drop off the face of the Earth without being missed. Unlike Torrie, Maggie didn't have family and friends who would cover for her.

Explain it to her family? Yeah, sure. *Hey, Daddy, I'm going to go wandering around Tir Na Nog, where what's left of the Old Gods are in retirement, searching for the jewels of the Brisingamen, in*

which are hidden the dark matter necessary to restart the universe.
Maggie's father was a clinical psychologist; he'd arrange with
a psychiatrist to have her committed.

And besides, it was dangerous.

Ian found his hand reaching down to touch the package con-
taining Giantkiller, the way he used to reach down and touch
his wallet when at a restaurant, as though if he didn't compul-
sively keep track of it, it would disappear—

"Well, when you're ready," Ivar del Hival said, "you can
count on me to go with you, at least as far as the Dominions."
He shrugged. "Not a bad place to start. Perhaps there's some
savant somewhere in the Cities with some clue as to where to
begin looking."

Thorian Thorsen snorted. "If it were easy, if there were clues
aplenty out, all of the jewels would likely have been found long
ago."

As it was, it was Torrie, not Ian, who had stumbled on the
hidden safe-within-a-safe that contained the ruby. Torrie,
having grown up with Hosea, had a better feel for the way of
hidden things than Ian did.

But to hell with it. "You're saying I shouldn't go?"

Thorsen shook his head. "Not at all." His smile was faint,
but it was there. "But I think that too much eagerness is . . .
unwise."

"I agree, Thorian." Ivar del Hival nodded. "I wouldn't think
of telling you what you should do, Ian Silverstein, even if I
thought I knew, which I don't. You're a stiff-necked fellow, and
I'd not want to match stubbornness with you." He bent over,
unlaced his heavy workboots, and removed them and his thick
socks, which he carefully folded before setting them aside. His
feet were short, no more than a size 7, but very wide. He was
missing the little toe of his right foot. There was probably a
story in that; for Ivar del Hival, there was probably a story in
damn near everything.

Ivar del Hival rose to his feet with a grunt. "But if you're going to continue your education, let us continue it now, while you have a chirurgeon in attendance, as you may soon have need of his services."

"Enjoy yourselves." Doc raised his cup of coffee in a toast. "Just remember, I'm a plain old country doctor, and if you yank his heart out of his chest or something, I won't be able to put it back."

Arnie Selmo grinned. "Aw, I bet you could put it back, Doc. Don't think it'd work, mind you, but I bet you could put it back."

Ian took his shoes off, rolled up his sleeves, and stood. "Light touches, only?"

"I think not." Ivar del Hival cracked his knuckles. "Nothing killing, nothing permanently debilitating, but I've been bruised before, and don't mind bruising my knuckles again." He dropped into a half-crouch as they sidled away from the circle of lawn chairs. "Let us see if your vacation has softened you, shall we?"

Thorian Thorsen was a duelist, and a wizard with a sword, but Ivar del Hival had spent his life in the service of the House of Flame, and that meant years of training as a soldier and warrior. The Middle Dominions were not what they had been in ages past, but an ordinary of the House of Flame was still expected to be able to lead a troop of peasant spearmen or archers in defense of the Dominions, and that meant that he had to be able to prove himself, if necessary, by fighting, peasant-style, either hand-to-hand or with weapons derived from farm implements. And in addition to the skill, Ivar del Hival was close to twice as heavy as Ian as well.

Ian dropped into a crouch and circled to the left, careful of his footing. One slip, and it was all over. His only advantages were youth and speed; reach was about a draw. If he could keep Ivar del Hival running around long enough, the old man would tire sufficiently for Ian to move in and score, but if Ian let those large hands fasten on him, even once, the match would be quickly over. Ian had lost to Ivar del Hival before, and didn't much like it.

Ian faked a lunge, ducked low under an outstretched arm, and came up around behind Ivar del Hival. The temptation was to move in and go for the choke, but Ian played it conservatively: he kicked at the back of Ivar del Hival's knee, and tried for a backhanded blow just above the kidney when Ivar del Hival stumbled.

He more felt than saw a thick arm sweeping toward him, and dove forward as Ivar del Hival fell behind him. An outstretched arm slapped hard against the ground to kill his fall, and Ian quickly skittered away on fingers and toes until he could get his feet under him.

"Nicely done, boy." Ivar del Hival rose again to a crouch, grinning crookedly. "Now it's my turn." This time, he closed in a rush that Ian was able to backpedal away from—

—until Ivar del Hival accelerated, faster than Ian had seen the fat man move before, and one huge hand fastened on Ian's right wrist.

It would have been pointless to pull back against Ivar del Hival; Ian had tried that before. So he went along with the pull, jerking his wrist up, working against the thumb of Ivar del Hival's gripping hand, smashing the edge of both hands down, hard, against the bigger man's biceps.

Ivar del Hival grunted, and his arms dropped, but as they collided, he managed a leg sweep, knocking both of Ian's legs out from underneath him, and landing on top of Ian as they both fell to the ground.

A hamlike fist deliberately pounded the ground next to Ian's neck. "Call that a strike to the neck," Ivar del Hival said, rising. He offered Ian a hand. "But nicely tried. Another fall?"

Ian was already trying to work out some stratagem for the next fall when Thorian Thorsen interrupted.

"No. It is my turn." Thorsen was on his feet, a palm outstretched. "I've been hearing so much talk of late about the incompetence of a House of Steel duelist when the competition doesn't involve swords."

"Very well," Ivar del Hival said, in between pants, with an expansive sweep of the arm. "He's all yours."

"No." Thorsen grinned. "I think not. I'll try heavier game. The game responsible for all the talk."

"Can't even trust an old friend, can I?" Ivar del Hival was still breathing heavily. "So you let the young one tire me, and then move in for the kill? Very well; have at you."

As the two closed, Ian heard a choking sound.

He turned. Hosea had risen from his chair, making a horrible gagging sound, his eyes vague and unfocused, his whole body twitching as though from an electric shock. He pitched forward to the grass, still twitching, his whole body spasming.

CHAPTER THREE

Decisions

Out of the corner of his eye Ian saw something tumbling through the air toward him; reflexively, he swatted at it, knocking the piece of metal Hosea had been working on to the ground.

Ivar del Hival and Thorsen had stopped, and were standing openmouthed, but Doc Sherve was on his feet.

"Shitshitshit," he said. "Not again." He pulled the lawn chair away from where Hosea was still twitching and knelt down, flipping him over easily.

Again?

"I need a hand here," Doc said, ignoring the way a flailing arm sent the contents of his shirt pocket flying. *"Karin!"* Another spasm sent Hosea's hand flying, loudly backhanding Doc across the face. Doc ignored it. Ivar del Hival, Thorian, and Ian surrounded Hosea, while Doc again called for Karin.

There was no response from the house. When Karin was up in her office working on a buy order, she tuned out the rest of the world.

Ian dropped to his knees next to Sherve. He reached out to grab at a flailing arm, then pulled his hand back. "What is it?"

"Grand mal seizure," Doc said, drawing a wrapped needle from his bag. "You're going to have to hold his arm still. Thorian—over here."

36

THE SILVER STONE

"Aren't you supposed to let somebody just have a seizure?" Ian said, feeling like an idiot as soon as the words were out of his mouth. If Doc was *supposed* to just let him have a seizure, he'd be *letting* him just have a seizure.

"Well . . . it depends." If Doc took offense, it didn't show in his voice or his face. "You let it go, if you think it might resolve by itself. Which most usually do." Doc managed to get hold of Hosea's flailing arm long enough to rip the sleeve up to well above the elbow—Doc Sherve was stronger than he looked. "And if it does resolve by the time we get the saline going, then we'll just leave well enough alone." His lips were white. "Thorian, Ian. I'm going to say this just once. You'll have to hold his arm absolutely still long enough for me to get the needle into the vein, and then tape it into place so I can get the drip started. After that, he can twitch as much as he wants—we'll just keep him from jerking on the tubing.

"Arnie, there's a phone in my bag. Pick it up, punch the send button—just the send button, or you'll have to dial the clinic from scratch—and tell Martha that Hosea's having another grand mal, and I want a chopper in Grand Forks standing by if pushing Valium doesn't work."

He shook his head, his hands never pausing in their quick, sure movements as he readied the syringe, then stuck it sideways in his mouth while he tied a rubber strap around Hosea's upper arm.

"Hell," he said, from around the mouthful of plastic, "I can push enough Valium to shut any seizure down, but I don't want to shut down his respiration while I'm at it, you know? Okay; grab tight—here goes."

Ian gripped Hosea's hand at the wrist, while Thorsen, on the other side of Doc Sherve, grabbed his upper arm with one hand, using his free hand to block the way Hosea's free arm was flailing away. It was frightening the way the old man was twitching, his muscles clenching and unclenching, his eyes all white, nothing but gasping breaths and horrid grunts issuing from his mouth.

"It's okay, Hosea. You'll be just fine," Doc said, wiping at a spot near the crook of Hosea's elbow. "Got good veins."

Ian hated needles; he closed his eyes and turned his head away until Doc grunted and said, "Got it."

Ian opened his eyes. A crooked crisscross of surgical tape held a needle flush against Hosea's arm. Ivar del Hival was standing over them, holding a plastic bag in his hands, and Doc had just finished connecting up a clear piece of tubing to it.

He started the drip, and quickly loaded a syringe and injected it into the tube.

"C'mon," he said, "just take it easy." Doc shook his head, muttered something under his breath, and filled the syringe again.

Almost instantly, Hosea started to relax. Doc put on his stethoscope and listened to Hosea's chest for a moment before he sat back, his breath coming out with a whoosh. He smiled. "Valium's wonderful stuff," he said, sticking the syringe point-first into the ground and reaching into his bag for another one. When he spoke again, his voice seemed more calm than controlled. "Which gives us about five, maybe ten minutes to push some Tegretol and see if that will keep things nice and quiet." He filled the new syringe, injected the drip bag, and frowned while he recapped the needle. His lips moved as though he was doing a quick calculation, then he adjusted the drip to a faster pace. "Okay, Arnie," he called out over his shoulder, "you can tell Martha that we'll be fine, at least for now; she can cancel the chopper."

He pulled the used syringe out of the ground, recapped the needle, and dropped both syringes into the coat pocket where he kept his garbage.

Arnie brought the handset over to Doc. "She wants to talk to you."

"Hi, honey," Doc said, lifting his shoulder, trapping the phone between his shoulder and the side of his head so he could keep his hands free. "I'd like you to get your nicely rounded bottom down to the lab; I'll be sending Arnie Selmo in with some blood—yes, blood levels, CBC, and liver function, for a starter, and dig out his chart. If you find anything else we haven't taken a look at recently, run it, too," he said, his eyes never leaving his patient or his gear. "Thorian, Ivar—stretcher in my car, and a metal stand for the drip—bring that here, and let's get him inside." He listened to the phone for a moment more, then bit his lip. "Yes, I know. But we do the best we can."

Supper had been a catch-as-catch-can buffet—leftover stew, sandwiches made from still-warm homebaked bread and paper-thin slices of salty ham from the pantry, some wonderfully garlicky potted goose, all washed down with pop and beer, then finished off with cups and cups of the local traditionally weak coffee and fresh coffee cake that had the whole house smelling of cinnamon—which had seemed to embarrass Karin Thorsen, although Ian couldn't see why.

It was fully eight o'clock before everybody had finished, and the dishwasher was loaded, and Ian could take an after-supper cup of decaf—for some reason, the locals brewed their decaf strong—out into the back yard.

Above, the sky was black as the oily surface of the coffee in his cup, scattered with stars as white as diamonds. He stepped out, away from the light of the house, until he moved out of the range of the motion sensor for the outdoor lights. It took a moment for his eyes to adjust, and he could make out the Milky Way. You never saw that in the city. Too much light pollution and probably too much air pollution.

One of the stars seemed to be moving, slowly, and Ian's sense of direction spun for a moment until he figured it was moving from northwest to southeast.

A satellite. You couldn't see those in the city, either. Wrong time of year, but every once in a while there was a meteor shower out here, too.

He sniffed the night air. Yes, there was a trace of skunk off somewhere in the distance, but that wasn't an unpleasant smell, not when it was this faint. It was kind of nice, actually.

The patio door slid open, and then closed, and Karin Thorsen stepped out into the darkness, her eyes searching for a moment until they locked on his.

"Ian—oh. I didn't see you for a moment." She took a few, tentative steps toward him, then stopped. The breeze brought the smells of Ivory soap and Obsession to him.

"Everything okay?" he asked.

She nodded. "Thorian says he'd like to see you in the basement in half an hour or so. Hosea took a little soup, and Martha Sherve's going to sit up with him tonight," she said. "Bob's talking about sending him into Grand Forks for some more tests in a few days, but—" She shrugged. "You know Hosea. He doesn't want to be handled by strangers."

"How long?"

"How long what?"

"How long has this been going on?"

She shook her head. "He hadn't had a seizure for ten years, not until . . . recently," she said, "although he's been on phenobarbital as long as I can remember." She tapped the side of her head. "He has some brain damage."

Ian's lips tightened. "I figured that out the day I met him," he said, remembering the slight slurring of words, the limp, the awkward way Hosea held his right hand. "I didn't know about the epilepsy. It's been worse since we got back from Tir Na Nog," he said, not really asking.

"Yes."

It figured. Hosea had quite deliberately damaged part of his brain. It had been clever and subtle and all, and Ian had admired his cold-bloodedness—although, as it turned out, Hosea would have been better off trusting in Ian's sword arm. This time.

"What's Doc Sherve say?"

"Say?" She smiled. "Mostly he doesn't say. Mostly he swears. Hosea has always been a problem for him."

Ian had heard the door opening and closing again, but hadn't thought that it would be Doc, Ivar del Hival with him.

"I thought you went home," he said.

"Just about to," Doc Sherve said. "Figured I'd give you an attaboy for helping out this afternoon. You did good, kid."

Ian didn't know what to say. He hadn't been told that a whole lot. "Thanks," he finally said.

Sherve produced a fat cigar from an inside pocket and unwrapped it with stubby fingers. "Do as I say, not as I do," he said, then bit off the end while he lit an old-fashioned kitchen match against the sole of his shoe. He puffed the foul-smelling cigar to life and considered the glowing coal at its tip. "And yeah, he's a problem." Cigar clamped in his teeth, he held out a hand and started ticking off fingers. "Normal body temperature runs just over ninety-six degrees. Resting heartbeat of forty-five, forty-six beats per minute, blood pressure one-ninety over thirty, which should make him a candidate for all sorts of problems, except that it seems natural for him, and on his stress test, his heart goes to one-twenty and his systolic pressure drops." The doctor spoke heatedly, in contrast to his words. It was like he was swearing, not just talking. "Liver enzymes are just about nonexistent, and his white cell count says that he has acute myelocytic leukemia, but there's no enlarged liver or spleen or lymph nodes, he doesn't hemorrhage, and in fact when he's cut he heals quickly, he's not weak, and he simply doesn't get infections, ever. Plus, he has neither an appendix nor an appendix scar—"

"Doc—"

"Shush. I'm not done. He has no appendix scar—nor an appendix, I was saying. Which is something I found during a contrast study I did a few years ago, which shows a gut that goes seamlessly, smoothly from small intestine to large intestine via some transitional structure I'm going to call a middle intestine—God knows what it does; I sure as hell don't. His bowel manifests what appear to be diverticula, even though there're no symptoms of either diverticulitis or diverticulosis." He sighed. "And then there's his brain. CT scan and MRI show literally dozens of damage sights—seizure foci—enough that he should be having seizures almost constantly, but until recently we've been able to keep him incredibly stable for years with a pathetically small regular dose of phenobarb, and I understand that when you were traipsing about Tir Na Nog," he said, "he did without his medicine without any difficulty at all." He nodded. "So yeah, he's a problem." Sherve puffed angrily at his cigar, the smoke immediately shattered and carried away in the breeze.

Ivar del Hival shrugged. "I do not see why you're angry, Doctor. That Orfindel should be different from humans is unsurprising. He's one of the Old Ones, after all. They're no more human than the vestri are, true enough. But why should this anger you?"

"Because," Sherve said, "I'm pretty good at what I do, and usually I'm very good at not worrying about what I can't do. Didn't bother me one bit when I used to tell Otter Larsen that if he didn't stop drinking his liver would give up on him, which it did, and it didn't bother me one whit that when Ephie Selmo's cancer was killing her slowly all I could do was make the pain go away, because I could do that. I don't care if the best thing I can do for where his stump chafes Davy Larsen is tell him to rub some Eucerine on it." He pointed with the cigar. "Because all of that makes sense to somebody, and when it doesn't make sense to me, I can refer it to some specialist in Grand Forks or even the Mayo if I have to. But the most Hosea will do is let me run a few tests for me to look at, and I don't have the slightest idea what to do. Operate? On what? His brain? And do what? Should I give him more meds?" He puffed on his cigar. "What I'd like to do is some combination therapy—maybe find the right mixture of Dilantin and Tegretol and some of the new drugs and hope that will keep him stable, but that's a job for a specialist, and I don't think there's any specialists in the Midwest with a lot of experience with a lot of Old Ones."

"All that is true, surely." Ivar del Hival nodded. "But that's not why you're upset."

Doc muttered something unintelligible. "It's getting worse. No physical change I can find, but more and more his seizure pattern is moving toward the way his tests say it ought to be, and it ought to be real, real bad." He spread his hands. "But there's nothing different I can detect—just about every test I run on him comes back with an anomaly, but they're the same damn anomalies that he's always had. The only thing that's changing are his seizures, and they just keep getting worse. And I don't have any bright ideas. Yeah, I could have called in a chopper from Grand Forks today—and I would have, if we couldn't have shut down his seizure—but I don't know that they'd be able to do anything, either."

Karin was pointedly looking away.

Ian sighed. So, this was why she wanted him back early.

Well, what did you expect? That she was going to bring you back so you and she could have an affair under her husband's roof?

No. She'd brought him back to Do Something. And he knew as well as she did what that was.

43

"There is another choice," Ivar del Hival said. "I don't think a vestri chirurgeon could do much for him, although that's always a possibility. But it's one thing to lick wounds, and another to pry open a head and stir the brains around until he's well. Still, his powers are probably still greater in Tir Na Nog, and that might be enough."

And there was more that could be done in Tir Na Nog. Hosea had a couple of friends at Harbard's Crossing, Ian thought, and both of them had a talent for healing.

Harbard and Frida, they were called. Odin and Freya, they were. Freya in particular had a healing touch; she had healed Hosea of the damage a köld had done to him, and she had healed Ian of the wear and tear that dragging an injured Hosea down the mountain had done to him. Perhaps it was her touch that had kept Hosea well in Tir Na Nog, and if so, likely it could again.

Ian rubbed at the palms of his hands. Dragging the sledge had left his hands not merely blistered, but bloodied and infected, and overnight she had brought him back to health, leaving no wounds, no scars behind.

"Makes my hands sweat, too, just at the thought of it," Ivar del Hival said. "I'd just as soon stay here until things settle down at home, and if I'm not going to stay here, I'd as soon go home. I wouldn't want His Warmth to think my villages can run themselves forever, and if I'm not going to run them forever, I need a new wife and enough time to produce a son or two." He made a face. "But I could take him with me, and see if the air and soil of Tir Na Nog works a miracle or two. It has before, and no doubt it shall again."

Ian liked Ivar del Hival; he couldn't help it. The larger man's loud laugh and easy, good-natured smile were infectious, and Ian appreciated, more than a little, the lessons in hand-to-hand and bowmanship that Ivar del Hival had insisted ought to supplement Thorian Thorsen's instruction in swordmanship.

But that was one thing. Leaving Orfindel in his hands was too much trust. Hosea's damage might have made himself less of a prize than he had been, but what if somebody didn't believe him? And what if his value wasn't zero? More than once, Hosea had been locked in a dungeon, imprisoned and tortured for the secrets he held, and Ian couldn't risk that again.

"It has to be me," he said, quietly. "Harbard and Frida wouldn't likely take to being disturbed by somebody they don't know."

Karin Thorsen's face was steady. "You were talking about going back, anyway."

Yes, he had been. Heading out on the road in search of another of the Brisingamen jewels, figuring that the trip was worth it, even if he never found what he was looking for. He had been expecting Torrie Thorsen to partner him, though. Torrie wasn't just better at freestyle—dueling—swordplay than Ian was; he was trustworthy in a way that Ivar del Hival never would be. Want to know Torrie's motives for something? Ask him, and he'd tell you. Ian liked that. Simple didn't mean stupid, but it did mean trustworthy, sometimes.

And then there was the matter of *her*. Ian shook his head. "I'll have to think about it," he said.

Sherve frowned. "Don't take too long."

Thorian Thorsen was waiting for him down in the fencing studio in the basement. "Good to see you back, Ian," he said, gesturing at the hooks and pegs where Ian's practice gear waited. "Take down your épée and let us try a little freestyle."

"But—"

"But nothing, young Silverstein." The older man's smile probably would have seemed friendly, if it wasn't for the scar that snaked down the right side of his face almost to the corner of his mouth. As it was, it seemed distant, possibly threatening. "Robert Sherve can watch over him better than can you or I, and the best thing for Hosea right now is rest." He held out a hand, palm upwards, blunt fingers spread wide. "The best thing for you now is practice."

Thorsen was dressed in shorts and a T-shirt, thick white socks cushioning the sneakers he seemed to prefer for sword practice. He dropped to a mat and launched into a series of stretches, and after a moment, Ian stripped off his own clothes to slip on a fresh jockstrap that smelled of chlorine—the damn things were an invitation to crotch rot if you didn't bleach them regularly—and then pull on a faded pair of walking shorts and a tattered T-shirt that read *I Know That Shit Rolls Downhill* on the front, and *But Why Do I Always Have to Live in the Valley?* on the back.

He took his time with his own stretches. If there was enough time to practice, there was enough time to stretch. Better to hurt a little for a moment now than to pull something.

Thorsen was waiting impatiently by the time Ian stood up and reached for his gear. "You would think that someone who wants to make the sword his profession would want to ready himself quickly for a lesson," he said.

He was like that, which always surprised Ian. It couldn't be his dueling training—a House of Steel duelist could spend *days* priming himself for an important duel, if he had to, and didn't need to sweat the minutes.

Ian put on his fencing jacket and trousers over the shorts and T-shirt, but left the gloves on a table. The new practice épée Hosea had made for him had exactly the same grip as Giantkiller, and even at the risk of injury to his hand or—much more likely—wrist, Ian found that he liked the feel of it against his hand.

After lacing on his shoes, Ian took the épée down from its pegs on the wall. Gripping it brought a little chill to him, but it wasn't unpleasant.

Ian came to attention. He brought his épée up in a salute,

quickly dropping his mask into place and bringing his point down and then back up when Thorsen charged, not bothering to mask himself.

Fuck you, Master Thorian, he thought, simultaneously deciding that he couldn't—No, that wasn't true. He *wouldn't*—take it easy on Thorsen just because the older man had refused to put his mask on. But Ian wasn't willing to blind him over a practice point or two.

They closed, and Ian started his favorite move, beating sixte, breaking it off to drop into a low lunge on the second sweep that went right past Thorsen's épée to score with a touch on the calf, then beat the older man's riposte aside as he retreated.

Thorsen grinned. "Nicely done," he said. "I was expecting you to try to begin with a beat, and you fooled me nicely." His voice was level and unaccentuated, although all the while he was probing for a weakness in Ian's defense, their blades ticking against each other with a rhythm that was almost musical for a moment, until Thorsen launched an attack on a downbeat that scored with a touch high on Ian's sword arm, just before a thrust of Ian's sword caught him on the left cheek before parrying Thorsen's blade.

That brought a grunt of pain from Thorsen, and Ian hesitated just a moment, a moment too long, as Thorsen redoubled his attack on Ian's blade, beating it aside, leaving Ian open from head to toe, off balance, unable to get a leg behind him to retreat on.

As Thorsen's blade snaked in for a touch on Ian's chest, Ian tried a last-ditch maneuver that had worked once before: he pushed himself backward, letting his feet slide out from him, and while it didn't stop Thorsen's blade from scoring with a hard slap against Ian's chest, right over his heart, as Ian's back slapped hard enough against the floor to knock the wind almost out of him, it did enable Ian to bring his own sword into line enough that Thorsen would have impaled himself on it if he hadn't halted his advance.

"A nice try," Thorsen said, setting his own sword down before he stooped to offer Ian a hand up. "I would have thought you'd be out of practice from your vacation, but if these old eyes don't mislead me, you've been working out—perhaps with a saber player?"

Ian smiled as he accepted the older man's hand. It was stronger than his would ever be, the wrist muscles thick and powerful, even for a fencer, but Thorsen's grip was only firm enough to help Ian to his feet, nothing more.

"I found a fencing club in Basseterre, played a few bouts," Ian said, as he pulled off his mask.

"I take it you didn't try to teach them freestyle," Thorsen said.

"True enough," Ian said, reclaiming his sword. He drew himself up. "Shall we begin again, this time with both of us masked?" A red weal was growing on Thorsen's cheek where Ian's blade had caught him. Had it been Giantkiller in Ian's hands, it would have cut him to the cheekbone, almost matching the scar on the right side of Thorsen's cheek.

"As you will."

Ian forced himself to settle down, but he won only one of the next few points, and Thorsen settled into teacher mode, forcing Ian to go over and over the bout in slow motion, move by move, stopping over and over to go over alternatives, and alternatives to the alternatives.

Thorsen faulted him constantly for a foot that was slightly out of line, a sweep that started an eyeblink too late or too eagerly, a moment of lost balance.

What Thorsen called "freestyle" in English translated literally to "strategy" in Bersmål. It was basically a continuous bout, with saber scoring on épée targets, and a prohibition on scoring a follow-up point immediately after scoring a point, emphasizing the necessity of protecting yourself even after you'd landed a blow.

Each formal style of fencing had evolved in its own way from dueling—foil from one-blow bouts by men who would not be satisfied with simply drawing blood; épée from a gentler era, when most duels ended at the first blood, and any touch would do. Freestyle—strategy—had evolved first to hone the sword-fighting skills that had made Middle Dominion warriors famous from one end of Tir Na Nog to another, and later from the bouts that men used to settle matters of law and honor in the Five Cities, in which any cut might well serve to slow an opponent down, to force him to bleed or surrender, and in which nobody would stop simply because he noticed his blood on another's sword.

But each style had its own flaws as a model of a real fight, and Ian thought he had worked out one of freestyle's. Best to save it for now. Besides, the older man had him in a sweat.

"I want to go with you," Thorian said. "Let it be me, instead of my son."

"With me?"

"It's clear that you're going to have to be the one to take Hosea. At least, it's been clear to him for some time, and to my wife for longer. You are welcome in . . . Harbard's house, and that may not be true of others, and would certainly not be true of me."

"Oh?" And what would Thorsen get out of it? Ah. Of course: he would be protecting his son.

"I'll not mislead you, Ian. I might well be of use, but not with Harbard any more than in the Dominions. I'm a forsworn man, Ian, and as crafty and devious as he is, the One-Eyed is known to have no use for men of such little honor. Young warriors find more of his admiration. Or are his preference, depending on how you look at it."

"I'll think about it," Ian said. "Let's see if we hear from Torrie over the next few days." He furrowed his brow. "*Wait* a minute. I've got an idea."

"Oh?" Thorsen's brow furrowed.

"Torrie uses a credit card when he travels, doesn't he? American Express Gold, right?"

Thorsen shrugged. That was a matter of money and finance, and by his raising and inclination, money and finance were women's work, and while not exactly beneath a man, sort of to one side of what he should notice. "That could be; if I wanted to know, I would ask my wife."

"Yeah." Ian nodded. "I think I will. Ask your wife, that is."

Thorsen shrugged again. "As you wish."

Ian found her in the kitchen, emptying the dishwasher.

It was Friday, which meant by the idiosyncratic Thorsen house schedule it was Hosea's turn to handle the cleanup, but the Thorsen house rules were flexible enough to handle a problem much less serious than Hosea being in bed recovering from a seizure.

"I need Torrie's Amex card number," he said.

Karin smiled at him. "You're welcome to borrow mine, if you don't have an American Express card—but, no, you *do* have an American Express card; I set it up for you myself."

Ian was grinning from ear to ear. "No, I don't want to charge anything to him. I think I can use it to find out where he is."

He was surprised to find her smile fade, and see her hesitate, just a moment. "I'll go upstairs and see if I can get it for you."

Ian set the phone gently on the cradle, and sat back in the overstuffed chair in Arnie's living room. Gently, gently; that was one of the rules: you controlled your own anger. It was yours, and not to be anybody else's problem. If you didn't start beating up on objects when you were frustrated, you would not end up beating on people.

Still, it was goddamn frustrating.

Arnie Selmo was in a pair of ragged-cuffed pajamas and an ancient plaid bathrobe. His slippers made flippity-flop sounds as he walked out of the kitchen with a pair of tall glasses. Ice cubes gently clinked as he set one down carefully on a doily on the table at Ian's elbow.

"Thanks, Arnie," Ian said, taking a sip. Rich and fruity, but with a familiar tang—"Red Zinger?"

The old man's lined face split in a smile. "And who says you can't teach an old dog new tricks? Makes a nice iced tea, and at my age, I can live without caffeine." Arnie lowered himself into an overstuffed armchair. "Any luck?"

"Nothing." Ian shook his head. "That's the trouble with the Eurailpass. They could be anywhere from Lisbon to Bucharest, and I don't have any way of finding them. Karin says she last heard from them in Paris, but I checked with the hotel they were at, and they left more than a week ago, and they're not due home for another three weeks." He frowned. "I'm surprised that Torrie would leave at all with Hosea in such shape."

"He wouldn't. Not a chance. Torrie?" Arnie snorted. "But Hosea wasn't doing badly. Oh, he'd had a seizure, but just the one. After being off his drugs for so long, that wasn't surprising, Doc said." His blunt fingers toyed with a tiny porcelain cat figurine from the end table, before setting it down in the exact spot it had come from.

Ian sighed. "Well, I thought I'd come up with a brilliant idea—I got Torrie's American Express card number from Karin, and I called them, to see if they'd tell me where it was last used. I mean, we're in a goddamn global village; they do verifications over the phone lines from anywhere."

"And he hasn't used it?"

Ian shook his head. "They wouldn't tell me. It's Torrie's own account, and nobody not on the account can get anything out of Amex without a court order." He gestured at the phone. "Even if it's an emergency."

"Well, think on it." Arnie's brow furrowed. "They won't give you any information, you say, but maybe they would take some?"

"Eh?"

"Call them up. You'll probably have to go to a supervisor, but explain that there's an emergency at home, and ask them to flag his account so that next time he uses it, the vendor has to call in for a voice verification, and when he does, have them pass on the message that he's to call home. Next time he uses the card, he gets the message."

"You think they could do that?"

"I don't see why not. And I sure as hell don't see a need not to ask."

He was reaching for the phone when it rang.

"Hello?"

"Ian? Bob Sherve here." Doc sounded too calm. "Hosea has had another seizure, and I'm pushing more Valium than I like to. Something's happening tonight, one way or another, and I frankly don't know what the hell the folks in Grand Forks could do with him, even if he was willing to let me call them in." There was some sound in the background. "He says he wants you to take him through, tonight. Now."

It was scary, but there was something good about being needed. "I'm on my way. Tell Mr. Thorsen to break out a couple of the emergency kits; I'll need them." The Thorsens had emergency kits packed at all times. "And have Ivar swipe the stretcher from your car, then bring him downstairs to the basement."

"The basement?"

"Just do it." Ian hung up the phone and stood. Well, he was used to traveling light, and besides, he wasn't even unpacked from his trip yet.

Traveling light could mean discarding the extras as he wanted. Start with the basics: Giantkiller, his boots, and clothes. Bring his bags along, and repack at the Thorsens', if there was time.

"I'll walk over with you," Arnie said. Arnie was already in jeans and a flannel workshirt that hung loose on his skinny frame. He stepped into a pair of heavy workboots and laced them up with more ease and dexterity than a man his age should have had. "Let me give you a hand."

"Don't mind if you do." Ian slung Giantkiller's belt over his shoulder, picked up a bag, and walked out into the night, Arnie Selmo right behind him.

By the time they made it down the path, through the windbreak of trees, and to the Thorsen house, the front door was standing open behind the screen door. The door off the front hall was open as well, leading to a set of broad, wide steps to the basement.

Basements, to Ian, had always been dank, damp places, but the Thorsens had a different idea. A central hall, lit by overhead fluorescent lights, opened on a full workshop to the right, a laundry room straight ahead, and the fencing studio and workshop to the left. Ian led the way into the fencing studio, where the rest were waiting.

Thorsen and Ivar del Hival were both dressed for the road, Ivar in blousy trousers and loose pullover shirt, Thorsen in jeans and workshirt, both in heavy hiking boots.

Doc Sherve, on the other hand, looked like he had just crawled out of bed, from the way his hair was all askew to the half-tucked-in shirt with the open button that revealed the knit collar of red pajamas.

Ordinarily, Ian would have paid more attention to how good Karin's legs looked when she was wearing only a short black robe, but Hosea's condition looked bad enough that he was privately embarrassed for noticing.

Hosea lay under a blanket, strapped at waist, chest, and ankles to the stretcher, his right arm strapped down, his left hand unbound. His face looked almost green, although some of that could have been from the whining overhead fluorescent lights. His eyes were glassy and unfocused, and his breathing ragged, although it steadied as he seemed to recognize Ian.

Ian knelt beside the stretcher. "You think it will help if we take you through?" Damn silly question. Ian knew that Hosea's powers were stronger in Tir Na Nog, and what the hell other choice was there?

"Through where?" Sherve's voice was almost a snarl.

"Be still, doctor," Ivar del Hival rumbled. "The young Silverstone knows what he does in this, just as you do in matters of chirurgery and medicine."

Hosea's mouth worked, but the only sounds that came out were grunts.

"Well, whatever you're going to do, you'd better do it," Arnie said. "Sure as shit he can't get a hell of a lot worse."

"Yeah." Ian was on his hands and knees next to the fencing strip. The other time they had gone through this Hosea had been the one to operate it, not Ian, and Hosea had a way with hidden locks and catches that Torrie understood better than Ian. "Tell Torrie I'll blaze our way, Boy Scout style, if and when he comes after us."

"If you wish, but I don't see the need," Thorian Thorsen said, squatting to help him. "I've left a map of the way to Harbard's Landing for him."

Ian nodded. "Two steps ahead of me, eh? Good."

"Don't you think—" Karin Thorsen caught herself. "I need to speak to you privately for a moment, Ian. Please."

Feeling the eyes on his back, he followed her down the hall into the laundry room.

She opened her mouth, then closed it. "I have to ask you a favor. Please don't let my husband go along with you."

He didn't quite know what to say. "It's not my decision. Hosea is—I mean, he's been with—"

"Hosea's been dear to me for longer than I care to think about," she said. "But I'm scared, and I . . . I am afraid of being left alone here, without Thorian."

It would have been easier to argue with that fear if a pack of Sons hadn't broken into her house and dragged her half-naked and bloody off into the night and to another Hidden Way to Tir Na Nog not too long ago.

Ian was wondering why he wasn't afraid. It wasn't that he was looking forward to Tir Na Nog—or maybe he was. It had been half a year since he had been back, and maybe that was what was wrong. Well, there was a quick cure for that, and he didn't really need Thorian Thorsen's help to scratch that itch.

His hand found the hilt of Giantkiller. "It'll be okay. I'll ask him to stay here."

"No. He won't listen if you *ask*; you have to *tell* him." She took a step toward him. "Please," she said. "Don't let him leave me alone. I don't pretend to be some sort of hero; I'm not, Ian. All the while we were in Tir Na Nog, it was all I could do to hold myself together, it took everything I had . . . I'm no use in this sort of thing, and I don't pretend to be. I can't—please. *Please.*"

That wasn't how Torrie and Maggie had told Ian about it, but Ian wasn't disposed to argue. Karin would know better than he would how scared she had been, and Ian didn't blame her one little bit.

"Well . . ." He spread his hands. "I'll—"

He didn't remember making a move toward her—he certainly wouldn't have made a pass at Torrie's mom, Thorian's wife, would he?—but somehow or other there she was, warm in his arms, crying on his shoulder, the nearness and warmth of her making him more aware than he was comfortable with that she was wearing little if anything under her short robe.

He stopped his hands from reaching for her. He'd long found Torrie's mom awfully attractive, but what the hell was going on?

"Okay, okay," he said, clenching his hands into fists. "I'll tell him. We'll do it your way."

She pulled back. "Thank you," she whispered, her voice barely above a trembling murmur.

She didn't seem to notice that he was trembling like a leaf.

Ian strode back into the fencing studio, trying to make himself stop shaking.

Idiot, he thought to himself, the idea of crawling through a Hidden Way between worlds doesn't frighten you, and you're half falling apart because a pretty woman grabbed you. If she'd kissed you, you'd probably have pissed yourself.

Shut up, he told himself. Save it for later.

"Karin makes a good point," he said, *that if a pretty woman in a short robe cries on my shoulder, I'll do whatever the hell she says,* "that there are some problems in bringing Thorian along."

He was making it all up as he was going along, but nevertheless, it sounded right. "With him as part of the party, we're automatically in trouble with the House of Steel, and even if Thorian del Orvald wants to help out the friend of his grandson—and he might want to; he seemed to like Torrie—he's still the Duelmaster. He's still got to send his men after Thorian the Traitor."

Thorsen opened his mouth, then closed it, then opened it again. "You've spoken of traveling to Harbard's Landing, not to the Cities of the Middle Dominions."

"And if we can't find what we need at Harbard's Landing?" Ian shook his head. "No. And then there's the matter of the Sons of Fenris. They've visited here once, and—"

"That was a surprise. It wouldn't be, not again." Arnie Selmo's lips twisted. "I don't think anything'll get past Davy Larsen and his partner, not right now. And we are keeping watch—"

"But only on an entrance that you know," Ian said. "There's an entrance to the Hidden Ways right under your feet that you don't know about, that none of you would ever have known about if Hosea hadn't shown me." Entrances tended to keep themselves hidden; it was part of their nature. Unless you knew where to look, and intentionally looked there, you would find yourself making an excuse to look elsewhere, and never know it.

Ian had expected an argument, but Thorian Thorsen drew himself up straight.

"As you would have it," Thorsen said. "But I—"

"Besides," Ivar del Hival said, quietly, leaning over toward Thorian Thorsen, "it's the champion's to decide, not yours, old friend." He drew himself up straight as he turned to Ian. "Will you have me as your companion, Ian Silverstone? You'll need another pair of hands to carry the other side of the stretcher, at least."

Ian nodded. "I was hoping you'd volunteer." He would have liked to have Torrie with him, either instead or in addition, but so be it; there was no time to waste. He turned to Doc Sherve. "Shoot him full as you can of whatever you think he ought to have," he said. "And do you think I ought to take anything with me?"

"Drugs?" Sherve smiled crookedly. "My license is limited to North Dakota. We don't exactly have reciprocity with Tir Na Nog," he said. He shrugged. "I know things work differently there, but how? Will Valium be more likely to suppress respiration, or less? How effective would Tegretol be?" He had opened his bag and had started to remove items, then sighed. "Shit," he said, as he started to replace them. "In for a penny, in for a pound. Take it all. Better you have stuff you can't use than you don't have what you need." He closed his doctor's bag, latched it, and held it out. "Use the Merck manual and your best judgment."

"Take me," Arnie Selmo said, quietly.

Ian turned, shocked.

"Take me," Arnie repeated. "My pharmacist's license is out of date, but Ephie and I ran Selmo's Drugs for more years than I care to think about. I'm no young buck, but I don't wear glasses, and I can still walk the legs off most men, and there might be something to having somebody expendable watching your back."

"Huh?" Ian didn't understand. "Expendable? Who is expendable?"

Arnie looked him in the eye. "I am," he said, quietly. "Have been, for—shit, boy, I could tell you how many days it's been, but you never had the—" He stopped himself, then started again, his voice low and husky. "But you never knew her, and it wouldn't mean anything to you," he said. "I'm tougher than I look, and I didn't promise her not to . . ." He closed his eyes for a moment. "I didn't promise her not to do this. For something worth doing, I'm as expendable as a piece of Kleenex." He looked over at Thorsen. "I'm about your boy's size, if a bit narrower in the shoulders. You think he might have something that could fit me?"

Tilted on its side on hidden hinges, the fencing strip was a too-long door, opening into blackness.

Not darkness. No trace of a probing flashlight beam bounced back.

Ian finished bolting the pulley to the overhead beam, then checked the knots on the improvised sling that would hold Hosea's stretcher. Ian remembered the demonstration Hosea had given him; this entrance would only go one way.

Had Hosea found it here or made it here? Ian hadn't thought to ask, then, and it hadn't come up since. He should remember to ask, later.

He took a piece of inch-thick dowel stock from a bin by the workbench and poked one end into the darkness.

It slid into the blackness silently, but when he pulled it back, the part that had gone into the darkness was gone. Ian held up the end. It had been cut cleanly, at an angle, leaving the dowel with an oval end as smooth as the finest sandpaper could have left it.

Eyes widened as he looked from face to face. "Don't hesitate, either of you. And for God's sake, don't hesitate when you drop Hosea through." He tried to visualize it. "The hole only goes one way—any rocking that sends part of him back up will slice off what's through. Don't try to lower him or anything. Just steady him over the opening, then drop him right through; we'll catch him."

Ian's mouth was dry and tasted of salt and iron, but he forced a calm smile. That was one thing that the Fire Duke had taught him: it was just as easy to do something dangerous with style and bravado as it was to do it knock-kneed and trembling.

He drew Giantkiller slowly, and brought the sword up in a quick salute, then sheathed it with a loud snap, and stepped off, into the darkness.

CHAPTER FOUR

~o~

Another Homecoming

Torrie and Maggie were having a final drink in the lobby of the Algonquin when he had the trouble with his American Express card.

It was strange to feel so comfortable here. Torrie had never thought that he could possibly have the feeling of homecoming in—shudder—New York City. Yechh.

But he did. It was nice to be able to read the headlines on a newspaper or the label on a tube of toothpaste; it was a treat to be able to get into a taxi and let it be the problem of the Iranian in the front seat to figure out what Torrie said. It was nice to be able to plug in his razor, to know exactly what it was that sidewalk vendors were selling, to think of a policeman walking down the street as friendly instead of hostile.

He liked the professionally genial staff of the Algonquin, although after the sullen surliness that passed for service in Paris—a surliness that had been tinged by more than a trace of contempt when Torrie had trotted out his high-school French—he probably would have liked any American hotel.

It was wonderful to be home, even if the substitute home was that grimy, crowded, noisy, crime-ridden icon called New York City.

A couple of days here, a quick stop in St. Louis—Torrie was not looking forward to meeting her parents, but Maggie was insistent on the subject, and it was in the long run better to humor Maggie than to argue with her—and then home for a couple of weeks before school started up.

Which was another problem entirely. School or Tir Na Nog? In the long run, of course, the answer was Tir Na Nog. His father and Uncle Hosea had been training him for his entire life for that, even if they had never quite admitted it to themselves, and even if Dad would never for the life of him have sent his son off after the Brisingamen jewels.

Was there more important work than making sure they got into safe hands? No; it simply wasn't possible.

"Eager to get back?" Maggie asked.

"Well, yeah." He nodded. A small-town kid never quite loses it, he decided, the expectation that everybody you run into is somebody you know, and that people you don't know are strangers, the word laden with overtones of alien and different. And New York was full of strangers. "Be it ever so humble, and all that."

She snickered. "Yeah, right. Humble." She had seen the Thorsen house. Not a showy place, but a deucedly comfortable one. It was amazing what a lot of work and a lot of money could do, even when you were constrained to not make it showy.

He smiled. "Okay. But it's mainly that it's familiar, okay?"

"Well, country boy, if you were to take your feet out of the furrows every now and then and put your nose in a book, you might learn enough about other places to feel comfortable in them. Like here, say."

"Here, say, is the lobby of a hotel. It's nice, but . . ." It was light and airy, and an airflow coming from the direction of the hotel restaurant brought a trace of beef and garlic, but it was still a hotel lobby.

"This isn't just any hotel. This is where the Algonquin Round Table used to meet, every day," Maggie said, probably for the dozenth time, as she sat back in her chair and looked at him over her Virgin Mary. She had offered Torrie a taste, but he had passed; if it was hot enough for Maggie Christensen, it was too hot for him. Where the girl had gotten her taste for pepper was a mystery to him; it wasn't like Maggie was from New Orleans or somewhere near what a Texan friend of Torrie's always called the "Meskin" border.

"You've mentioned that." Torrie shrugged. "Not a big deal to me."

"Robert Benchley, James Thurber—"

"The cartoon guy?" he asked, mainly to tease her. He enjoyed playing the uneducated hick at times.

"—Dorothy Parker not a big deal?" she asked. He couldn't tell whether or not her indignation was slight and real or faked—Torrie had never quite figured Maggie out, and probably never would.

"Dorothy Parker?"

Her mouth pursed into a frown. "You know:

> " 'Oh, life is a glorious cycle of song,
> " 'A medley of extemporanea;
> " 'And love is a thing that can never go wrong;
> " 'And I am Marie of Roumania.' "

He sipped at the bottle of Sam Adams, ignoring the glass near him. "Cynicism looks cute on you." Hell, everything looked cute on her. Even now, although she was dressed sensibly for travel in an oversized navy raw silk shirt over a cotton tee and leggings, her hair, now grown shoulder-length, pulled back into a bun that she tucked under the black beret she had bought from a street vendor in Paris.

Torrie had idly picked it up from a nightstand a few days later, and noticed that the tag read "Made in the Philippines." Rather, it *had* read that way—a few cuts from the tip of the sharp knife blade of the SOG Paratool that Torrie always carried had taken care of that problem.

Better to protect an illusion or two than disappoint Maggie over something trivial; Torrie valued kindness over truth.

Torrie beckoned for the waiter, then handed over his American Express card. He had relied on cash and traveler's checks, which he had bought for cash before leaving the country—it was a Thorsen family habit to avoid leaving a paper trail whenever possible—but carrying too much money might have drawn unwanted attention at any port of entry, and he had stretched out the money supply by using his credit card for things that would have left a paper trail anyway, like paying for hotels. Keeping family money as a private matter was something he had been raised to do, and only recently had it been explained to him why it was necessary. The last thing Mom and Dad needed would be for some busybody at, say, the IRS, to look into the origin of the Thorsen family fortune, and while Mom had carefully laundered almost all of it over the years—and multiplied it severalfold by careful investing and trading—it was best to keep a low profile.

Particularly now, particularly since Torrie and Ian had dumped close to a million dollars' worth of gold on her, in the form of golden coins hauled back in their packs from the Middle Dominion City of Falias. It would take years for her to safely turn all that into cash and investments—if she was left in peace.

Still, Torrie thought with a smile, it wasn't just any twenty-year-old who was able to split his share of a million dollars with his girlfriend, and not worry about it.

Mom and Dad's money made that possible, and while Mom clearly hadn't liked the idea, Dad couldn't have cared less. He hadn't gotten over all of his upbringing, and couldn't see money matters as something that properly ought to concern a man.

That was a nice thing about being brought up by a father of Middle Dominion origins.

"Excuse me, Mr. Thorsen?" The waiter was back, a look of

studied casualness written across his face. "There appears to be a small problem with your credit card, sir."

Torrie didn't quite snort. Sure, they had been gone for months, and sure, there had been a couple of bills during that time—the credit card people billed monthly, didn't they?—but Mom would have paid it, on the day it was due, neither one day earlier (no sense in giving up even a tiny bit of interest) nor later (always best to have a perfect credit rating).

"Really." Maggie leaned forward. "They declined your credit card?"

"Nonono, sir," the waiter put in quickly. "When I put your charge through, a code came back to call American Express, sir. The supervisor asked me to emphasize that they were approving the charge, and that there's nothing whatsoever wrong with your account, and that they're sorry to disturb you, but that she would like to speak to you." He gave a professional smile.

Maggie frowned. Torrie got to his feet. He didn't like this at all. He forced himself to keep to the waiter's leisurely pace as he followed him across the thick carpet of the lobby, and to the front desk.

An old-style rotary phone lay there, the receiver off the hook.

"Hello?" Torrie said.

"This is Madeleine Alessi; I'm a supervisor at American Express customer services. Am I speaking with Thorian Thorsen?" a woman's voice asked.

"Yes. That's me."

"Purely for purposes of identification," she went on smoothly, "could you please give me your mother's maiden name?"

"Roelke," he said. "R-O-E-L-K-E. Now, what's going on, please?"

"There's nothing wrong with your account, sir—it's entirely current—I apologize for bothering you. But we have been asked by a man identifying himself as your father to ask you to call

home immediately, on a matter of some family emergency—
your Aunt Jen has been taken to the hospital, he said."

"Thank you. I'll do that immediately."

"Thank you for using American Express."

Shit. Torrie hung up the phone and hurried across the lobby
toward the bank of pay phones.

He didn't have an Aunt Jen, or any aunts or uncles at all.
Uncle Hosea wasn't his uncle; his mother had been an only
child, and as far as he knew, his father's family consisted only
of Thorian del Orvald and his wife.

But he understood the "call home" part.

His fingers were already dialing, punching up MCI and then
his home number. His mother answered it on the third ring.
"Hello?"

"Torrie here, Mom. What's going on?"

She was silent for so long that Torrie opened his mouth,
about to ask if she was still on the line.

"It's kind of . . . complicated to talk about over the phone."

It was a rule that you didn't discuss Family Business over
the phone. "Anything I can do?"

Again, a long pause. "You can come home as soon as possible."

He nodded. "Okay." Then a thought hit him. Two thoughts,
in fact. "Can I talk to Dad?"

No pause this time. "Certainly."

His father was on the line almost instantly; clearly, he had
been waiting by the phone. So much for the worry that his
father had vanished.

"Yes," Dad said.

"*Havadh er derein isti vejen?*" Torrie asked, then continued in
Bersmål: "Is there some danger?"

"No," Dad said in the same language. "Not for us, here, now.
If there were a knife held, say, to your mother's throat, surely
her captors would not let me mention it, not even in Bersmål,

an' they spoke it." Torrie heard a chuckle; he wasn't sure whether Dad was amused or impressed. "But there have been some difficulties with Hosea, and he and a friend of yours have left."

Left? That meant— "Shit," Torrie said. Ian was impulsive, sure, but Uncle Hosea was anything but that. It must have been awfully important. "Okay, we'll grab the next plane out," Torrie said. "Can you pick me up in Grand Forks?"

"Call when you know when your plane lands; you'll be met. Is there anything more we need discuss now?"

"I don't think so."

There was a click on the other end. Dad had been raised in a society where saying good-bye was a matter requiring some formality. Twenty years in Hardwood had made some changes, but he had never quite gotten the idea that any leave-taking convention could possibly apply to something as strange, artificial, and exotic as a telephone call.

Maggie was at his side as he hung up the phone. "What's going on?" she asked.

"Ian and Hosea have left," he said, quietly.

"Left, as in—" Her eyes got wide. "Oh."

"My father wants me home immediately." Which meant that Dad either wanted to hare off after them, or wanted Torrie to. No question which way made more sense: Dad could protect the home front better than Torrie could, and Torrie's head wasn't wanted by the House of Steel. Dad was protective, but that applied to Mom as much as it did—no, more than it did—to Torrie, and Dad was nothing if not sensible.

"Us," Maggie said, looking thoughtful. "I'll have to figure out some story to tell my parents, but . . ."

"No," he said, shaking his head.

She nodded, once. "I was your father's ace-in-the hole with the Sons, and that made the difference in the end." Her face grew grim. "And the simple truth, Torrie, is that while there are things you could do that would stop me, you wouldn't do any of them."

Well, truth to tell, while Maggie wasn't as good as Torrie or Ian with a sword—then again, she hadn't been at it a quarter as long—she was a fair-to-good épée player, and according to Dad's report, no slacker with the edge, either. That had made the difference when the Sons had finally cornered Maggie and Mom and Dad in the Hidden Ways: the Sons had written Maggie off as just another helpless female . . .

"Jealous?" she asked.

"Eh?"

"I seem to recall one Branden del Branden showing some interest in me." She smiled.

That was true enough. Branden del Branden had tried to have Torrie killed over Maggie. That showed a certain amount of interest in her.

"Are you planning on keeping the two of us apart?" she went on. The light tone was gone from her voice. "I don't recall having agreed not to see anyone else. Or did I miss something?"

Torrie's lips tightened. Dammit, she had him on the defensive, and all he had been trying to do was to keep her out of danger.

There was really no point in arguing with Maggie. She was like Mom: one way or another she would get her way. He sighed as he beckoned to the desk clerk. "Would you get our bill ready, please? We have to catch a plane."

Maggie barely broke a smile.

"My turn to pack us up," he said, handing over his American Express card. "Why don't you get us a couple of seats on the next flight to Grand Forks?"

As he headed for the elevator, she already had her battered datebook open, and was punching a telephone number.

PART TWO

TIR NA NOG

PART TWO

TIR NA NOG

CHAPTER FIVE

Avoidance Play

The long tunnel stretched out in front of Ian, vanishing in the darkness ahead. He walked, surrounded by the dim, directionless gray light that was without heat. The air was flat, tasteless, odorless.

Clearly he should have been hurting, probably he ought to be dog-tired, but for sure he should have felt something—shit, *anything*—but he didn't. It was as though he wasn't really there; it was like watching a dull silent movie projected into his eyes.

It should have felt like something. His heavy woolen cloak covered his shoulders, but he had thrown it back to keep his arms free, leaving his upper chest open to the air. Either the covered part of him should have been warm and sweaty, or the uncovered part chilly, but neither was either. The unyielding surface beneath his boots should have made his feet ache, but they didn't. It wasn't that they were numb; he could feel the weave of his thick socks by wriggling his toes.

His hands and shoulders should have hurt, too; he had been carrying the back of the stretcher for thousands and thousands of steps, long enough to lose count. There was no cramp in his fingers, no blisters or pain on the palms of his hands.

Long enough, certainly, to be hungry and thirsty, to need to stop and take a meal and a piss. But his stomach didn't feel empty and his bladder didn't feel full; mainly he just plain didn't feel.

Ian walked through the endless grayness without pain, without pleasure, without hunger, without time. It was hard enough to think about, and would have been impossible to explain. It was almost as though it was happening to somebody else.

On the stretcher in front of him, Hosea lay sleeping in his straps, his chest slowly, evenly rising and falling, his eyes never twitching, his head bobbing in time with their steps, as though nodding in lukewarm agreement. Ivar del Hival's bulk at the front of the stretcher gave Ian only occasional glimpses of Arnie Selmo beyond him; the two of them trudged silently, constantly, unchangingly.

Nobody had spoken in that endless time. Ian thought he should, could, might, ought to say *something* to break the silence interrupted only by the sounds of footfalls, but he was unable to.

It was as though part of Ian had been turned off.

He had walked that way for an endless time beyond time through the Hidden Ways, until the tunnel slanted upward and in mid-step, in mid-blink Ian found that the ground beneath his feet was dirt, not the rippled gray stone of the Hidden Ways. The tunnel had widened, too, and the walls were of dirt, supported every dozen or so yards by an upside-down U of timbers that made Ian feel as though he was emerging from the world's esophagus.

The smooth wood of the stretcher poles weighed heavily in his hands, and the straps of his rucksack had started to cut into his shoulders. A distant reek filled his nostrils, and even before Arnie Selmo, in the lead, stepped through a curtain of ivy, a chorus of twittering birdsong filled Ian's ears.

The nice thing about being the back man on a stretcher is that there aren't a lot of decisions to make; Ian shut his eyes and ducked his head as he followed Ivar del Hival through the leaves, and out into coolness that was fresh and bracing, with no trace of the tunnel's dankness.

They had exited through an arch in a curved wall, a wall so overgrown with vines that—

No. That wasn't wall peeking through the gaps in the greenery: it was bark. The tree above them was by far the largest he had ever seen, so much so that for just a moment, Ian felt like he and the rest of them had shrunk.

But no: the brown, rotting leaves that lay on the ground around them were normal oak leaves, and the other trees off in the distance were simply large and leafy, not immense.

The opening they had walked through was an upthrust loop of root, overgrown with vines and moss, of the largest oak tree Ian had ever seen. Its girth was easily as grand as one of the great sequoias. Although it was impossible to tell how tall it rose. Thick branches sprouted from the trunk only a few yards overhead, a green canopy arching out over the forest.

Ivar del Hival grinned as he and Ian set the stretcher down on the forest floor. "I've heard it said that a native-born draws strength from the very air and soil of Tir Na Nog," he said, crouching, and grabbing up two fistfuls of rotting humus from the forest floor. "And I can swear it to still hold true for Ivar, the son of Hival." He rubbed his hands together, as though to grind the blackened rot into his skin.

Arnie Selmo had already walked a couple of yards up the mostly buried root and seated himself. "I don't know about you two, but I don't feel near as tired as I ought to be." A corner of his mouth twitched, deepening the creases in his lined face. "Matter of fact," he said, "I feel kind of good."

Ian nodded. "Same as last time; the Hidden Ways don't seem to tire you. It's as though—"

He caught himself. Hosea's brown eyes were looking up at him, a thin smile on his face.

"Hosea!" Ian dropped to the ground next to him. Arnie Selmo was already half-climbing, half-tumbling down the side of the root, Doc Sherve's black bag in his hands.

Hosea licked his cracked lips, once, then swallowed.

"Thank you," he said, his voice thin and reedy, slurred. "Thank you, Ian." He started to work his right arm free of the straps that bound him, waist and chest, to the stretcher; Ian knelt and released the catches.

Hosea's fingers reached down through the humus, the shaking of his hand and arm rattling the dry leaves. And then, with his hand buried up to the wrist, the shaking stopped. "It's good to be back," he said, his voice stronger.

Ian couldn't speak for a moment, and neither could Arnie. It wasn't like it had been in the Hidden Ways; it wasn't that he found himself unable to speak or unwilling to form the thought. But deep in the back of his head, he had been sure that this undertaking was doomed from the start.

So much for his intuition; Ian had never much trusted his intuition anyway. Shit, intuition was mainly wired-in experience, and what had been wired into Ian's head was that anybody you love is either going to beat the shit out of you and then kick you out of his life, the way his father had, or fucking die on you, like Mom.

You couldn't win, not even for a moment.

Ian stood and stretched. *Well, fuck it; this is a win, at least for the moment.*

Ivar del Hival broke the spell with a grunt. "Let's get moving. The day gets no younger, and neither do I."

"Yes," Hosea said, nodding, as he let himself sag back on the stretcher. "We perhaps can make Bóinn's Hill by nightfall, and sleep well."

"I don't see the need." Ivar del Hival frowned. "That place? It's said to be hagridden." He shook his head. "So much so that I'd not want to use the name, not out in the open."

Hosea smiled. "Hagridden is such an unkind word. Let's just say that it's . . . unempty. Eh?"

He tried to push himself up to a sitting position, but he

couldn't, and before he could hurt himself trying, Ian laid a
hand on his shoulder and eased him back to the stretcher. "I
think you'd best let us carry you, for a while at least. Rest,
Hosea. Please."

Arnie Selmo had put the medical kit away, and was already
on his feet. "Anybody got a direction?"

They weren't more than three, maybe three and a half hours
out of the hidden exit from the Hidden Way when Arnie Selmo,
walking point, froze just short of the crest of a ridge.

"Down," Arnie Selmo hissed from up ahead, dropping three
steps back, then following his own order.

By the time Ian and Ivar del Hival had lowered the stretcher
to the green strip of moss that edged the dirt road, Arnie had
shed his rucksack and gear, and was down on his belly, snaking
his way back uphill, toward the crest of the ridge, moving easier
than a man his age should.

Ian wanted to crawl up to where Arnie lay, but decided he
had better check on Hosea first.

Hosea was sleeping again—the jouncing of the stretcher
seemed to put him right out. But his dark skin had an ugly
grayish pallor, and his breathing was slow and ragged. Torrie
felt Hosea's throat for a pulse. The skin was cold and clammy,
but the heart beat slowly and regularly.

This was good; Hosea had refused Arnie's offer of medicine,
and Ian was relieved that Hosea seemed to be improving, although slowly.

One good thing for sure: he hadn't had any seizures since
they had entered the Hidden Way.

Hosea's eyes fluttered, then opened, and he looked up at Ian,
glassy-eyed. He licked his lips, once, and tried to speak, his
mouth moving wordlessly, until Ian silenced him with a finger
across the lips.

Not now, Ian more mouthed than whispered.

Hosea gave the slightest of smiles, and let his head loll back. But the eyes kept watching Ian. There was always something special, something strange, about those eyes. The eyes of a judge maybe, constantly evaluating everything they saw, and behind them an intelligence that was neither warm nor cold, completely comfortable with what was, no desire to control or change anything.

Rest, Ian mouthed, then, with a quick nod from Ivar del Hival, Ian made his way up the ridge toward where Arnie lay, first ducking down, then dropping into an awkward crouching walk, and then to all fours and finally snaking his way the last few feet on his belly.

"Easy, boy," Arnie whispered. "We've just missed bumping into a troop of horsemen moving east, all, er, dressed to kill." The smile in the lined, homely face wasn't warm, or particularly friendly. "Don't know as we don't want to meet them—but I don't know as though we do. Want to take a look?"

Ian started to creep up toward the crest of the ridge, stopping when Arnie tugged at his foot. "No. Not the top." He jerked his thumb toward where a patch of gorse sprawled across the crest of the ridge. "You don't want to show an outline. Give yourself some cover."

Arnie's sureness wasn't only making Ian feel his own clumsiness at this; it was beginning to be irritating. "And if there hadn't been some cover?"

Arnie smiled. "Then, say, you tie a headband around your head, and stick some small branches in the back of it. Just a few, now—the idea is to break the outline of your head. Or, if you don't have branches," he said, the smile on his lined face suggesting that he had anticipated Ian's objection, "a few sheaves of grass." His mouth twisted. "You want another lesson, or you want to go look?"

With a frown and a nod, Ian dropped to his belly and snaked his way over to the gorse patch, careful of the spines. It wouldn't have been possible to make his way into or through the patch without getting scratched all to hell, but the edge of the patch broke on a low cairn of stones, and Ian was able to work his way to a notch without getting too badly scraped.

The ridge dropped to a small, silvery stream twisting through the valley below; the stream separated the grasslands from forest beyond, as though something or someone had decreed that no trees were to grow on the western side of the stream. Which was possible, Ian decided.

Beyond the stream, a narrow road rimmed the edge of the forest, probably wide enough for one car—or one horsecart, as was probably more relevant. A line of horsemen plodded along the road in a double column.

The front of the column had passed around a bend in the stream; Ian counted fifteen pairs of horsemen before the final pair disappeared, leaving a thin haze of dust in their wake.

"Not good." Ivar del Hival was suddenly at his side. Ian hadn't been paying attention, and that was bad.

Ivar del Hival grunted. "Best to wait a while. Can't see what standard they're carrying, but the armor is Vandestish—and that doesn't bode well for anybody."

"This *is* Vandescard." Why should it be a surprise that there would be Vandestish soldiers in their home country?

Ivar del Hival nodded. "But why is there a troop of veteran cavalry patrolling *here*? Off in the south, surely; they'll be campaigning against the Beniziri forever, perhaps." His thick lips pursed. "But here, in the East? Could be they're relieving some town outpost, but if so, where's their baggage train?" He shook his head. "Let's give it a little while, and head on down." He jerked his chin at the road below. "We'll not only avoid some of the dust, but we'll miss having to explain ourselves to any stragglers."

Ian frowned. "We've got something to hide?"

Ivar del Hival's smile was a trifle too broad for Ian's taste.

"Well, truth to tell, I don't feel like explaining what a minor noble from the House of Flame is doing in Vandescard with three strange-looking folks—no offense intended. If I'm on a trade mission, where are my trade goods? And if I'm after a word with, say, the local margrave, where are my letters-of-commission?" The big man pulled a flask from his rucksack and took a measured swig, offering one to Ian with a quick raising of the eyebrows; Ian declined.

"So," Ivar del Hival said, "that might make me a spy, and while I could likely be ransomed or just pardoned, there are those soldiers . . . and even possible spies can be hoisted on the all-too-certain end of a lance, apologies to come later, if ever."

Ian nodded, and turned to go back down the ridge, toward Hosea, rising to his feet only when he was sure that the crest of the ridge hid him.

His breathing had slowed, and Hosea had gained enough strength to turn on his side; he had taken the canteen strapped to the rucksack Ian had dropped next to him.

"Are we winning?" Hosea asked, his smile crooked.

"So far, so good. Arnie spotted some local cavalry, and Ivar del Hival seems to think that's strange."

Hosea rose to one elbow. "Cavalry?" He nodded. "He's right. That is strange. Horse-borne soldiers are usually minor nobility—and there's little glory and less gold to be won hereabouts, near the Dominion border." His face was somber. "These days, that is."

"It's perhaps worse than that, although it's hard to say." Ivar del Hival pursed his lips. "For a moment, I thought the foremost of the lancers was wearing an enameled armored glove, but—"

Hosea's brow furrowed. "Enameled?"

"Which couldn't be. That would be pretentious, and in Vandescard, pretension is dangerous."

Ian didn't understand any of this. "So one of them was wearing a decorated metal glove—why is that important?"

"It means that the patrol is being led by a Tyr's Son. It's the elite Vandestish military society, and they tend to delegate the routine to others."

"And they're the only ones allowed to wear decorated gloves?"

"It's not a glove. It's a ... prosthetic hand, I guess you'd call it." Hosea pursed his lips. "It could be worse; at least it wasn't an argenten."

"Small benefit." Ivar del Hival straightened. "Well, we'd best be on our way. The sooner we make Harbard's Landing, the sooner I can bring word to His Warmth that there's something curious going on in Vandescard."

Ian grunted. "You seem to be making a lot of one troop of cavalry, and one guy missing a hand."

Ivar del Hival shrugged. "Perhaps."

The stretcher was getting heavier, but that wasn't the worst part of it: Ian's nose itched, and he could hardly stop every few moments to scratch at it. Twitching it didn't help, and neither did screwing up his face.

Arnie had insisted on taking a shift at the stretcher, and was bringing up the rear while Ian carried the front and Ivar del Hival took the lead, ranging anywhere from twenty to fifty yards or so in front of them, often disappearing around a bend for a few moments.

Hosea was clearly feeling stronger; he was talking about walking, although that was, at best, premature.

What had appeared to be a trail along the edge of the forest had turned out to be a stone road. An ancient road, at that—only the stones along the side near showed any bulge at all; the rest had been worn flat in their beds of mortar.

Ian frowned. That didn't make sense. The mortar should wear out much more quickly than the stones. He said as much.

Arnie chuckled. "I was thinking about that, too. Next time we take a break, take out a piece of metal what don't owe you no money and try and scratch at that mortar—bet you dollars to doughnuts all you'll get is a scratched piece of metal."

Ian's brow wrinkled. " 'What don't owe me no money?' "

"Old expression. From World War Two—Bill Mauldin did a cartoon of a sergeant saying something like 'I need a coupla guys what don't owe me no money for a little routine patrol.' "

Ivar del Hival's face split in a grin. "It should be worn away by now, shouldn't it? Mortar being such a weak thing, and all." He produced a short piece of metal: a wire tent peg. "Give it a try," he said. "It's my turn to carry."

Gratefully, Ian set his end of the stretcher down and scratched at the mortar between a pair of flattened stones. Nothing.

It wasn't the hardest metal, granted, but it should have left some mark. He scratched harder, and the point of the peg came away blunt, leaving a dark streak behind that lay on top of the mortar. Ian tried stabbing down at it, but only succeeded in bending the peg.

"The ancients knew how to build, eh?" Ivar del Hival had taken Arnie's place at the rear of the stretcher, while Arnie squatted in front and gripped the poles before counting to three and standing.

A man Arnie's age shouldn't have been able to do that so easily, but Ian was getting used to things not being the way they were supposed to be. Shit, he'd had years of practice with it—his father had been a good teacher of how things weren't as they should be—but he was used to it being a curse, not a blessing.

Ivar del Hival nodded. "Your turn on point. We take this road for most of the rest of the day." He looked down at Hosea.

"I'd rather stay clear of Bóinn's Hill, Orfindel, but if you insist . . ."

"I do."

The sun lay on the horizon, the darkling western sky splattered with apricot and crimson, a casual finger painting by a baby god.

Ian sat, leaning back against an upthrust column of rock. He shivered, and gathered his cloak about himself, not sure whether the shivering was caused by the cold or the oncoming dark.

Or misgivings.

The trail had exited the forest a couple of miles back, and ran up a shallow saddle between two hills. At Hosea's direction, they had left the trail, and made their way up the tall grassy side of the larger hill, up to the summit, where a row of four ancient stone pillars poked their way out of the grass and the brush. They reminded him of an ancient British menhir, a megalith he had seen in some book, a long time ago, but these seemed too irregular to be carved, perhaps too regular to be natural.

From a distance they had looked like the fingers of some fossilized giant reaching out of the bowels of the earth. Close up, they were just big rocks.

It was cold on the top of the hill, but a fire would have been a bad idea while they were still in Vandescard.

"Tomorrow," Hosea said, huddled in his own cloak and blankets. "Tomorrow night we may well make Harbard's Landing. If not, we'll be close. Close enough to risk a fire."

Arnie Selmo had already turned in. He lay sleeping on a bed of grass sheaves he'd cut.

Ivar del Hival coughed politely off in the distance, announcing his return. He had a small shovel in one hand, and a roll of toilet paper in a ziplock bag in the other.

"I'll take first watch, if you'd like," he said.

"Nervous about sleeping here?" Ian asked.

Ivar del Hival shrugged. "When you reach my age, young Ian, you'll understand that there's a difference between cautious, nervous, and scared. In fact, I'm all three." His grin gave the lie to his words, or perhaps the grin itself was a lie. Hard to say. "I'll wake you," he said.

As a child, Ian had been subject to insomnia, but he had managed to ruthlessly purge that problem during his last semester in high school, after his father had kicked him out with nothing more than a suitcase and a gear bag. When you were working full-time and going to school full-time, insomnia was a luxury. Ian couldn't afford many luxuries, not until recently.

He lay back and closed his eyes, and willed himself to sleep.

He sat up suddenly, his muscles tense, reaching for Giantkiller. His fingers couldn't find the hilt of his sword, and when he looked down, it was gone.

"Be easy, Ian Silverstone," came a whisper somewhere off in the night. "There's nothing to fear."

The others lay sleeping under the canopy of stars. Or at least motionless.

Where was Giantkiller?

"It's not here." A distant chuckle. "I'd not like to see what that could do to me, even . . . here. But worry not, young one; you will find it lying by your side when you awake."

The air in front of him seemed to gather substance, weaving the flickering starlight into wisps of white and red light. The wisps gathered themselves into threads, and the threads wove themselves into a dim, airy fabric that took form, an outline of a woman, slim and erect. She was wrapped in a gauzy fabric that covered her body from just below the arms to just above the knees, leaving long, slim arms bare to the shoulder, tiny feet with toes pointed, just barely touching the grass. One of the feet was bent in at the ankle at a funny angle. Her left arm lay folded across her chest, the hand concealed under her right forearm.

"Let me guess," he said, surprising himself with his own calm. "The ghost of Christmas past, perhaps?"

"No." Her face was masked in shadow, but he could hear her smile as she spoke. "Ah, to be that young again," she said. "It has been a long time."

"And it has been a long time since other things, as well." Ian hadn't heard him move, but Hosea was standing next to him. "How are you, Bóinn?"

"Well enough, I suppose, my love." Her form did something halfway between a waver and a bow, perhaps. "Old. Tired," she said. "Though not lonely, by and large. The rocks, trees, and grasses are good company, even if the rocks tend to the taciturn, and the grasses to chattering."

Hosea smiled again. "I've always preferred to talk to trees, myself. They're very good listeners." He clasped his hands together, and stretched them out in front of him.

Her image wavered for a moment, like a distant mirage on a hot road, then solidified into that of a young woman, the left side of her face brightly lit, the right hidden in black shadow. Her pixyish face was framed with curls of blood-red hair and covered with freckles. Her shift was of clouds woven with light, and her bare feet, toes pointed like a ballerina, still didn't quite touch the ground.

Her expression grew somber. "Have you brought a gift for me?" she asked.

Ian was waiting for Hosea's answer when he realized that both Hosea and Bóinn were looking at him.

A gift? Er—

Check the cuffs of your jeans, said a distant, directionless contralto.

He bent to do so, and found nothing in them except for a some dirt, a few strands of grass, and an acorn.

Acorn?

He was about to toss it aside when she spoke. "And will you plant it for me, come the morning?"

Ian nodded. "That I will. And water it."

She nodded somberly. "A fine gift, indeed; it will be a lovely tree." She waved her hand, and a huge oak tree stood in front of the megaliths, its gnarled branches spread wide, an aged grandmother watching over a beloved grandchild. "Perhaps you or your children shall someday sleep beneath it, for you shall always be welcome in its shade. Now what is it that you ask of me?"

Ian didn't know quite what to say.

"Sleep," Hosea put in, "and safe rest, for all of us. That's all."

She nodded. "That much I can do. For tonight." She shook her head and sighed. "And it's little enough."

"Bóinn," Hosea said, stepping forward, resting one hand not quite on her shoulder. "Thank you."

It finally hit Ian. Hosea's lisp was gone, and he was standing upright easily, no trace of a limp. The hand near her shoulder was Hosea's right hand, the one that barely worked, the one Hosea would never have used.

"It's all I can find the . . . desire to do, these days," she said. "There was a time . . ."

"Yes," Hosea said, "there was, Bóinn." He touched two fingers to his lips, then held it near hers. "And I miss them, too."

She turned to Ian. "All I can offer you is rest," she said. "Safe rest."

She stood silently, as did Hosea, until Ian decided that some response must be required. "I'd . . . like a night's rest, at that," he said.

"And that would be fair recompense for your gift of such a fine tree?" She didn't sound puzzled; it was more like this was a formal question, like *Do you understand these rights that I've explained to you?*

"Er, sure. Yeah," Ian said.

"Then so be it." She passed her hand across his eyes, and the world spun away into a deep blackness that was filled with nothing but warmth and ease.

He sat up suddenly, his muscles tensing, his right hand reaching for Giantkiller, as though with a mind of its own. His fingers found the hilt of his sword, and he sprang out of his blankets and to his feet, a shout coming to his lips as he freed the sword with a quick flick of the arm that sent the scabbard tumbling through the crisp morning air, only to bounce off the nearest of the megaliths, and then fall, silently, to the grass.

Ian found himself standing, barefoot and cold, on the dewy-wet grass in the dawning light.

Bóinn was gone, and so was the oak tree.

While Arnie Selmo was tugging on his boots, Ivar del Hival, his hair mussed from sleep, was already on his feet, his own sword drawn, his other hand clutching a forked dagger. "By the brass balls of Benizir!" he said. "What is it?"

"Be still; all is well." Hosea sat leaning against the nearest of the megaliths, wrapped in his blankets like a mummy, only his head peeking out. The slur was back in his voice, and his right hand lay limp in his lap. "Ian simply woke up a trifle suddenly. Did you sleep well?"

That was a silly question, but—well, yes, he had slept well; he was more rested than he had felt in years. Ian was more embarrassed than anything else as he looked around. The sun was just peeking over the crest of a hill in the distance. Above, the blue sky was dotted with cottony clouds.

Just a normal, peaceful morning.

Had it been a dream? Or was it something else?

He stooped to pick up his scabbard, and slid Giantkiller back in, then reached for his jeans. Could it—?

His left cuff had unrolled somehow or other, but his right one contained dirt, some strands of grass, and an acorn.

He stood, squinting at the acorn in his hand, when he realized that there was no early morning muzziness in his head, and the adrenaline shock of his awakening faded into a feeling of eagerness to be about the business of the day.

"Well, as long as we're all up, we ought to be going," Arnie Selmo said, as he started to roll up his bedding. "No need to waste daylight. A quick piss and let's be on our way."

Ian nodded. "Just as soon as I plant and water this."

Arnie probably would have argued, but Ivar del Hival nodded.

As did Hosea. "That would seem fair enough."

CHAPTER SIX

 ⏜

Harbard's Landing

The golden light of early morning gave way to the brighter light of midmorning; midmorning surrendered to the warmth of the noonday sun; noon submitted to the afternoon; and afternoon was starting to face the inevitability of sundown when the road crossed a saddle along a ridgeline, and started down the road to Harbard's Landing.

Ian half-suspected that the road had been laid out deliberately to dump travelers out onto a view of the panorama below, where the gray river Gilfi twisted through the patchwork valley floor, the fast-moving waters catching and shimmering in the golden light like the scales of a writhing fish.

It was all in green and black and gold: The green of the forested land that rimmed most of the valley, broken only in places where roads cut through and wound their way down toward the river, as though they were streams of brown that had been frozen; black, where the inky soil spoke of fresh plantings; and golden, where fields of grain rippled in the breeze, like lakes of gold.

"Well," Arnie said, setting the front of the stretcher down in now-practiced timing with Ivar del Hival at the other end, "I'd have to say that was worth looking at, all things considered," he said, nodding in agreement with himself. "And I'd also have to say that it looks a bit clearer, a little brighter than colors ought to be." He ran stubby fingers through his thinning gray hair, his mouth twisted into a frown.

Perhaps a mile down the slope, the river curved around an outcropping where several log buildings stood, like something made from a Lincoln Logs set—the old, good wooden kind, not the modern plastic ones.

One of the buildings stood almost at the water's edge, and from it a dock projected out to where the flat barge rocked gently, held by its hawsers against the current; to one side, the corral, with its horse-drawn windlass, stood empty.

Ian almost fancied he could see the ferry's cable that ran across the river to the far shore, but probably not.

"And why are you smiling so?" Ivar del Hival asked. He rubbed his thick hands together, as though to clean his palms.

"I'm . . . rather fond of the ferryman's wife, Frida," Ian said.

"Ah," Ivar del Hival said, and made a sound halfway between a grunt and a groan. "Ah, to be young again, and to have no greater concern than seeking a quick dance in the bedding with a ferryman's young wife."

"It's not that."

Her name wasn't really Frida; it was Freya. It was her gift that had given him the courage to face off against the Fire Duke, and her blessing that had given Ian the clue as to how to beat him. And it was Freya to whom he had entrusted the Brisingamen ruby.

But he couldn't say that. You didn't just go and bare your soul in front of people.

"She makes a great stew," Ian finally said, "and a better pie."

Arnie Selmo kept his rucksack on his back while Ian knocked again on the old oak door, this time more loudly.

No answer. Arnie shook his head. There was something about this place that he just plain didn't like, and he couldn't put his finger on it.

Shit, boy, he thought, *you're just getting old.* That wasn't it, though. Truth to tell, he felt younger than he had in twenty, thirty years. He had woken in the morning with little stiffness and no pain, and he couldn't remember how long it had been since he had felt that way. He could remember not caring on those mornings when he would wake up next to Ephie during her last months, watching her toss and turn in what little sleep the Demerol/Vistoril cocktail could give her. His pain just plain didn't matter then.

But here, it didn't just not matter; it was gone.

Here, he had slept on a couple of blankets on the cold ground all night, and then walked for hours, more than half the time carrying half of Hosea's stretcher, and he felt . . .

Just fine. Shit, he hadn't even thought about how much he missed Ephie for a couple of minutes after waking. That thought made him feel vaguely guilty.

"Hello," Ian called out. "Anybody home?"

No answer.

"Could try the door, I suppose," Arnie said, only half-seriously. He wouldn't have opened that door uninvited for anything.

"No." Ian shook his head.

Back home, no answer at a closed door might mean there was a problem. Back home, he would stick his head in and shout, "Anybody home?"

Different place. This wasn't Hardwood, where almost nobody ever locked their doors—what if a neighbor needed to get in? "I guess that wouldn't be a good idea," he said.

Ivar del Hival nodded in quick agreement. "Enter a house of an Old One without permission? Surely there are cleaner ways to kill oneself."

He had finished unstrapping Hosea from the stretcher, and helped him to his feet. Hosea stood unsteadily, rocking gently, as though he was compensating for the ground moving underneath him. He reached out his good hand, rested it against the wall of the cottage.

"No," he said. "There's no one home." His eyes seemed to have trouble focusing. "Ian—please check the corral; you can see if Silvertop and Sleipnir are there."

"Sleipnir?" Arnie grinned. Now, that was funny. "You mean this Harbard guy named his horse after Odin's horse?"

"Not exactly." Ian said, grinning. "But close."

"This I've got to see."

He followed Ian as they took the path from the house, down-slope to where the arc of corral curved against the riverbank.

"Pretty silly thing—open on the river?" he said.

"It wouldn't stop either Silvertop or Sleipnir from escaping by river, but, then again, it's not there to keep either of them in. Not that it could."

The ground inside the corral was hard-chewed by dinner-plate-sized hoofprints, except for one area near the river's edge that looked freshly raked but for a few hoofprints and a few piles of suspiciously large pieces of horse shit that were draw-ing flies.

No horse was visible, but there was a cave down the shore-line, hidden by the riverbank; perhaps—

"Silvertop, Sleipnir!" Ian called out, rewarded almost im-mediately by a chorus of clopping hooves that sounded like a stampede.

But it wasn't a herd of horses. It was just one animal, huge, easily larger than a Percheron or Clydesdale. Its coat was dark gray mottled with darker gray, and its long mane was un-combed and uneven, knotted beyond combing.

And it had eight legs. They should have been all tangled up with each other, but somehow or other, they all seemed to work together, in a funny four-staged rhythm. It cantered towards them, coming to a stop just feet away from the corral fence.

Arnie had already taken one step back; he took another. "Holy *mother* of *Christ*," Arnie said.

"Yeah." Ian turned to the horse. Its huge eyes weren't gentle and soft, the way a horse's eyes were supposed to be. They were too active, too cold, too knowing.

"Hello, Sleipnir," Ian said, trying to sound more relaxed and confident than he felt. "We've come to see her—and him, too. But mainly her."

The horse snorted; it sounded like a thunderclap.

"So?" A voice screeched from behind him. "Should that be a surprise?

"Should I question my vision,

"Should I doubt my eyes?"

Arnie spun around.

A raven sat on a tree stump, glossy wings folded back, eyeing them skeptically.

Ian just smiled at the raven, as though recognizing an old friend. "Hugin or Munin?" Ian asked.

"Munin," the bird said. "Memory.

"Munin I have always been, and

"Munin I shall ever be.

"Are you Ian Silver Stone,

"Or are you Ian Silver Stein?

"Answer in your language,

"Or tell me in mine."

"Either," Ian said. "*Jeg står till dinab Deres t'jenest.*"

And why the hell would Ian put himself at the service of a raven? And—

It hit Arnie like an electric shock—Ian had spoken in a language that had the lilt, the music of Norski, perhaps, but it wasn't a language Arnie had ever heard before.

And how had Arnie known that the bird's name meant Memory?

And waitaminute. The bird hadn't spoken in English; it had

been Bersmål. Arnie had understood it without having to think about it.

Ian was watching him, head cocked to one side, perhaps in unconscious imitation of the raven. "It works, I see," he said.

"And even if it didn't work for you, it worked for me," the raven cawed—this time in English, with an accent that sounded vaguely British.

"I have heard the words before,

"And if not for the remembering,

"What is Memory for?"

At a sound from behind him, the bird turned; Arnie followed his gaze to see Ivar del Hival and Hosea at the top of the path, Hosea's arm thrown over Ivar's broad shoulders, Ivar half-supporting him.

"I see you, Orfindel," the bird said. "I can remember you fatter;

"Has age finally caught up with you,

"Or is something else the matter?"

Hosea nodded. "And I see you, Munin. We've come—"

"I know why you've come," a voice boomed.

There had been no sound of footsteps on the gravel path behind them, or if there had, they had been covered by the rush of the river.

But a man stood there, leaning on a spear.

His age was impossible to guess. His hair and full beard were gray—a dark and threatening gray, the gray of a thunderhead, peppered with strands of black, not a cottony Santa Claus beard—and his face was weathered and creased like old leather. But his shoulders were broad, and his back was straight and unbowed, and he stood with a young, strong man's ease.

He wore heavy calf-high boots, laced with leather, his trousers bloused, and his shoulders and torso covered by a cloak that rose into a hood that covered half his face, leaving one unblinking eye watching them all.

He was a big man, perhaps six feet tall, but somehow he seemed taller.

"You've come to see to the healing of Orfindel," he said. His voice was a rumble of distant thunder. "For the second time, Ian Silverstone," he said to Ian, ignoring the rest of them as though they weren't there. "You've come unbidden. But I do give you greetings, even though I do not give you welcome."

"G-greetings, Harbard," Ian said. His lips tightened, and he swallowed once, hard, and then spoke quietly, with only a small stutter in his voice. "I seem to recall having sent something of value this way," he said.

"This way, you did," the bird cawed, loud and piercingly.

"And this way it came,

"But you bound Hugin to give it to *her*, not to him.

"They argued, but he claimed it was your decision, and not merely your whim.

"But as much as they argued, it all was the same."

Harbard reached out a hand in an odd gesture, his fingers spread, but not far, vaguely curled, as though pointing with them. His fingers were long and thick, and his arm was covered with thick gray hair from the root of the fingers up to where it emerged from his shirt. A round, puckered scar on the back of his hand was almost hidden by the hair.

"And now, she is gone," Harbard said, "at least for a time, putting it somewhere for safekeeping, she says." He let the arm drop by his side. "She climbed aboard Silvertop's broad back, and rode off without a backwards glance."

That was something Arnie could understand, at least the gist of it: Harbard's wife had left him to hide the Brisingamen ruby that Ian had spoken of, and he was lonely.

Arnie nodded in silent commiseration.

Harbard looked him over, penetratingly. "And who would you be?" he asked.

"My name is Arnold Selmo," Arnie said, drawing himself up

straight. He might be feeling young and more bouncy than he had in a quarter of a century, but he wasn't a kid, to be sent stuttering by a glare.

"Ah." His face was still half-hidden by the hood. "I remember you. You were a brave man in your youth. There was a time—" He stopped himself and raised a palm, fingers widespread, a sign of stopping, of apology. "That is the trouble when you get old. You let your mind stray towards the what that was, and not the what that is."

"Look," Ian said, "Hosea's got trouble, and—"

"As do I," Harbard said, sharply. "As do I," he repeated, slowly, carefully. "I will try to ease his trouble if you will ease mine."

Ian's smile looked forced, and his voice sounded strained. "Sure. What do you need, the broomstick of the Wicked Witch of the West?"

For a long moment, Harbard stood silent. Then his mouth opened, with a broad smile that was accompanied by a deep laugh that shouldn't have sounded as threatening as it did.

He threw back the hood of his cloak, revealing a black eye-patch that covered his left eye. "We shall go inside and talk about it, while we eat," he said. "There is much to talk about, Ian Silver Stone."

"Yes, yes, yes," the bird cawed. "There is much to discuss: what we'll do for you, and what you'll do for us."

Arnie didn't like this one bit. But shit, there was a lot he didn't like, and he was used to it.

Well, Harbard's cooking sure wasn't worth a trip, Ian decided. Not a trip through the Hidden Ways, and barely a walk across a room. The stew was probably just venison that had been boiled until it fell apart, seasoned with a handful of crushed wild onions, although a bit of salt and pepper from Ian's kit improved it considerably.

On the other hand, the apples from the apple barrel just inside the door were incredibly sweet, with a quiet tartness that lingered on the tongue. It was like biting into perfectly aged cider, perhaps, except that there were rich, creamy overtones to the taste. And maybe a hint of blackberries? It looked like an ordinary enough apple, with more Macintosh than Delicious in its ancestry. But the vaguely golden flesh was firm without being hard, crunchy to the bite.

The strange thing, though, was how filling it was. The smell of the stew had reminded him painfully how long it had been since their sketchy breakfast, and he was certain he could empty the bowl of stew and eat a dozen of the apples, but after wolfing down a moderate bowl of stew, it was all he could do to nibble one apple down to the core.

Hosea lay behind him, stretched out on a cot near the stove, propped up with pillows improvised from sacks of cornhusks, while Arnie and Ivar del Hival flanked Harbard, who sat on the other side of the table, having sat down to his own meal after serving them with surprising grace and goodwill, considering.

Ian finished nibbling at the core of the apple, and started to set it down on his plate.

Keep the seeds, Hosea murmured, his voice pitched too low for anybody else to hear. *Plant them, somewhere, some time. The fruit of their trees will not have the same virtue as those which were tended by Idunn and now by Freya, but they will grow in any soil.*

"You have been made welcome," Harbard said in fluent Bersmål that had a hint, perhaps, of the lilt of an older language, "with water, food, and fire, and now, perhaps, it is the time to discuss a matter of . . . 'business.' " He said the last word in English, perhaps because the same word in Bersmål didn't quite have the same neutral connotation.

" 'Business'," Arnie Selmo said. "What business do we have?" He had clearly been following the discussion in Bersmål, but spoke only in English. Deliberately, or couldn't he manage in Bersmål? Ian couldn't tell.

"I . . ." Harbard said, slowly, "have need of a herald, a messenger, to one of the Vandestish. He—or they—seem to be intent on provoking a war with the Middle Dominions. You spoke earlier of seeing a Tyrson on patrol."

Ivar del Hival nodded. "Well, that's an obvious enough explanation for the Vandestish patrol we spotted." He took another bite from his apple. "The Margrave of the Hinterlands, perhaps?"

"He . . . appears to be involved. And that war must needs be stopped," Harbard said, "before it ever begins."

"Well, that would be nice," Ivar del Hival said, "but who will go to bind the wolf?"

"*You* cannot," Harbard said. "No matter what token you carried, you are still fealty-bound to the House of Fire, and would not be accepted; your oath is to the Fire and the Sky, not to me."

"Well, yes, it is." Ivar del Hival nodded. "True enough. I was nervous about being even on the fringes of Vandescard. And still am, for that matter." He spread his hands. "But be that as it may, what can one do?"

"Ian Silverstone will carry it. You will fall under his protection. That is likely to save you."

Ivar del Hival frowned. "I've always preferred better odds than 'likely,' but so be it."

Ian was puzzled. Why would Odin—or Harbard, or whatever he called himself these days—want to have a war stopped? And what did Ian and his friends have to do with that?

"Why?" Arnie Selmo's lined face was unreadable. Ian wouldn't have wanted to play poker with him, not now. "Why," he said, choosing his words slowly, "would redhanded Odin, the carrion-god, want to stop a war? Why would he not want to see yet another field fertilized with the blood and shit of dead young men?"

Ivar del Hival started to rise to his feet, but dropped back to his chair. "Odin?"

Shitshitshit. The last thing they needed to do was aggravate Harbard, particularly with Freya gone.

"If I had cared to be called Odin," Harbard said, his voice the roar of approaching thunder, "I would have so named myself." Harbard rose slowly, the tips of his broad fingers pressed gently against the surface of the table. "There was a time, youngster," he said, his voice husky, "when I would have slapped your head from your shoulders for such impertinence."

Ian considered the grip of Giantkiller, next to his left shoulder, as it hung in its scabbard on the back of his chair.

He didn't like his chances much, and besides—

"But old men have to learn patience," Arnie said, not backing down, his eyes on Harbard's, "and they can't let themselves have the recklessness, the impetuousness, the go-to-hell of youth. They have to learn how to balance what they want with what they can do, and they have to, perhaps worst of all, learn how to let others do for them what they could once do for themselves.

"They have to learn that foul, horrible word: settle. They— no, we. We have to learn how to settle." His lips were tight, but his hands were loose on the table in front of him. "If you could do for yourself what you need to have done, you wouldn't be negotiating with us. So, old one, if you are going to negotiate, then sit down at the table and tell us what you offer, and what you want. *Settle*, Harbard."

Harbard stood silently for a moment, his massive hands clenched at his sides, visibly fighting for control. "So be it," he said. He reached into his pouch and brought out a ring, and slipped it over a thick knuckle. It was plain and unadorned, a simple gold band, gently rounded, too thick to be a wedding

97

ring. It reminded Ian of another ring, of a ring he had come to hate, but this looked only vaguely similar. This one was plain, uninscribed, and it didn't have that red stone with the nauseating symbol on it.

"Try this on," Harbard said. He rolled it across the table to Ian, who reflexively picked it up. It felt warm, body-temperature or maybe a little warmer, and was heavier than it ought to be. It was obviously too large for Ian's ring finger; he tried the index finger and then the middle finger of his left hand, with no success; he tried the thumb, and there it fit comfortably, if a trifle snugly. Ian slid it off and held it on his palm for a moment—it still seemed heavier than it ought—before setting it down in front of Harbard.

"Draupnir?" he asked. "Odin had a ring called Draupnir. Every eight days—"

"Yes, yes, yes," Harbard dismissed the idea with a wave. "Dropper. Yes, every eight days it would drop eight rings. The vestri can be blamed for that silly tale; they've always been overly fond of gold. It never existed. Call this Harbard's Ring, if you like."

"And they're going to believe me because I have a gold ring on my thumb," Ian said.

Harbard's unblinking eyes stared at Ian from under heavy brows. Ian couldn't tell what color the eyes were, though, even though he was looking right at them, a bird hypnotized by an unblinking snake.

"They will believe you because you are my herald, my messenger, my spokesman, Ian Silverstein," he said, the rumble in his voice making the dishes dance on the rough surface of the table. "That is enough." He was silent for a long moment, then dropped his gaze to the surface of the table. One blunt finger played with a small pool of spilled cider as he spoke. "I'm old and tired, Ian Silverstein," he said, his voice no longer the rumble of a god but the high, quiet one of an old man, "and that's the truth. I am not now what I was, and I will be even less as the millennia spin by, out of control. My wife has left me, and while I think she shall return, I don't think she'll return to a war-torn land."

He looked at Arnie Selmo. "I would hope, young one, that you would understand how horrible it is to grow old alone."

"Yeah, I know something about it." Arnie's expression was cold granite. "Too much about it. So what do we do now?"

Harbard stood slowly, an old man whose every movement was painful. "I now shall take down my spear, but by my oath and affirmation, know that I do not do so intending to strike at any now in this room."

Harbard walked to the front door, and removed the spear that hung above it.

It was hard to tell how it all changed, but it was different. The top of his gray head came no nearer the overhead beams, and he didn't fill the doorway any more than he already had. But somehow, as he held the worn wooden shaft, he seemed to grow, to swell until his presence if not his body filled the room almost to bursting.

A distant bass thrumming filled the air, and when Harbard set the butt of the spear against the wooden floor as he sat back down in his chair, the whole cottage shook, sending dishes dancing on the shelves, some of them falling and smashing themselves on the rough-hewn floorboards.

Ian knew that he should have felt frightened, but for the life of him, he could not disbelieve Harbard. He tried to, but he couldn't.

"You will wear my ring and carry Gungnir, as my herald," he said to Ian, his single eye unblinking. His voice was pitched low, but even so, it was painfully loud, a voice that could splinter mountains with a shout. "And you will tell the Vandestish that this war is not to be, that my peace will not be shattered, not by humans who claim the mantle of the Vanir, not by others."

He leaned the spear toward Ian, who reached out a hand to take it.

"*No.*" Hosea was on his feet, an arm outstretched. "You must not so much as touch it. Any of the Elder weapons would tear off the hand of the mortal that gripped it." His voice started to slur, and he weaved like a drunk trying to gain his balance, but he fought for stability and control.

"Unless, of course . . ."

"No." Hosea's mouth worked silently. "Ian Silverstein is brave—braver than he knows—and true of heart. But he's not Aesir."

Harbard nodded slowly. "I had considered that." He turned back to Ian. "Look down on the table before you."

They hadn't been there a moment before, but a pair of gloves lay on the table, to one side of Ian's plate. Unornamented, they were woven of fine white silk—no, not silk—it was—

Hair.

Her hair.

"She left these behind; she spun the hair into thread, twisted the thread into yarn, and knitted the gloves herself," Harbard said. "You should, perhaps, try them on."

Ian quickly slipped one on, then the other. They were, surprisingly, exactly the right size, even down to the way that the left one fit his slightly overlong ring finger perfectly. And they didn't feel like hair; they were practically a second skin, cool and comforting. And while they were soft and silky, they seemed to grip his hands like dry latex, so much so that for a moment he feared he wouldn't be able to take them off. But one nervous tug was all that it took to remove one; he quickly slipped his fingers back in.

He reached out a hand toward the shaft of the spear. It was

strangely hard to get his gloved fingers to work; his hand felt distant, remote, like it belonged to somebody else. He concentrated, and slowly, slowly his fingers closed around the shaft. The deep thrumming became a silent shout that echoed through his mind.

And then his other hand closed on the shaft, and it fell silent and still. Ian moved to set the butt of the spear against the floor. It moved slowly at first, as though it had more inertia than its weight should have permitted, then quickly, as though it was light as a straw, only to come to rest gently against the rough wood of the floor. Ian's hands tightened, then loosened, around the spear's shaft. It would be important to be careful with it; he knew that a blow from the butt of Gungnir could shatter stone.

"Yes, do treat it gingerly. It is strong, and wise, but Gungnir never has permitted itself to be abused." Harbard nodded. "When you are finished, throw it hard toward me."

Ian couldn't help smiling. "You into javelin-catching?"

Harbard didn't smile. "I have always found it blessed, not cursed."

"So," Ian said, "you want me to take your message to the Vandestish, and in return you'll heal Hosea?"

Harbard nodded.

"And what if they tell me no, to go to hell?"

"I doubt they will disbelieve you." Harbard shook his head. "And you can, if you choose, threaten them with my curse."

Ian snorted.

"My curse has . . . some value." Harbard took an apple from the apple barrel, and set it down on the table in front of him. He closed his single eye, and held out his hands, murmuring in a harsh, guttural language that Ian couldn't follow . . .

The apple writhed and shivered, split up the side, browning and rotting their eyes, leaving behind only a blackened twist of ash, a stain burned into the tabletop, and an awful stench.

"Go," Harbard said. He took the heavy metal ring from the table and placed it in Ian's palm.

Harbard's hairy fingers were probably twice as thick as Ian's, but the ring, which before had fit only Ian's thumb, now fit on Ian's ring finger snugly, without being tight, and when Ian moved it to his thumb, it fit there, too, comfortably. It didn't look any different, but . . .

"And bring my word," Harbard said.

"I shall," Ian said. "And I expect to find Hosea here, and well, when I return."

"If you return, young Silverstone, you shall." There was a twinkle in Harbard's eye. "If you return."

CHAPTER SEVEN

Margrave Erik Tyrson

The Margrave of the Eastern Hinterlands sat still while his valettes finished his midafternoon sponge bath, and then dressed him. In truth, he would have preferred to do for himself—there was something vaguely unmanly about being washed and dressed and primped by women, even if the women were young and comely.

But that was not a matter of choice, and hadn't been for many years. Since he had won his hand, he could no more properly wash and dress himself than he could plow a field. Relaxing to the inevitable was not possible for Erik Tyrson, but simulating it was by now a matter of reflex.

Much of his life was spent doing that. Too much. This day, he had spent the morning hunting. It wasn't a matter of sport for him—Erik Tyrson had been born a peasant, and then as now, members of the peasantry were far too busy with the more important matters involving scraping a living out of the soil to take valuable daylight time out to amuse themselves.

Boredom was often the peasant's lot, usually inescapable; idleness, never.

But it was a matter of appearances. His claim to the margravature of the Hinterlands was as solid as any noble-born's could have been: he had married the margravess, after all, in a ceremony witnessed and protected by the Brotherhood of the Sons

103

of Tyr—a full twelve Tyrsons had raised their metal fists and shouted their approval when the bloody wedding sheets had been displayed to the waiting crowd in the courtyard below their wedding chamber—and was the father of the margravine, his first five tries having produced but sons.

But everybody knew he had been born a peasant, and while he never would fully acquire all of the manners and mannerisms of the nobly born, it was a matter of importance that he pay due homage to the forms, at least, and do his best to imitate the manners and usages of the highborn.

The forms required that the nobles write poetry, so he spent hours in a window seat off the great room, quill in hand, writing poetry, even though the best he could manage was clumsy doggerel that he wouldn't dare to read to anyone else. The forms required that he have strong opinions about food and wine, so he worked with Cook to develop a personal style in cooking, even though he could barely have cared less what he ate, as long as there was enough to fill his belly once a day.

And while as a boy his idea of hunting had consisted of setting highly illegal traps for the deer that were properly the quarry of the nobility, the forms required that he hunt from horseback with great enthusiasm, so hunt he did, and enthusiasm he simulated.

He sat patiently on his dressing stool while the younger and more buxom of the two valettes knelt before him to lace and tie his boots. This one was perhaps the best dresser he'd ever had. She had just the right touch with her clever fingers, lacing his feet solidly into the boots without leaving them too tight. She finished with a complex knot that she sealed with a quick splash of wax from the dressing-candle, then smiled as he got to his feet, ignoring the way he clamped his left hand around the grip of his scabbard. A Tyrson's sword was a sword, yes, but mostly it and the enameled metal hand that held it were a badge of honor. One could be born nobly; one could marry into a title; but nobody could be a Tyrson without being first judged worthy of the Pain, and then surviving it.

"Your Grace," she said. "You are dressed."

"Truly. What word have you?" He was ready to face the world, or, at least, his little piece of it. Truth, he was ready to face his daughter, even.

"Your Grace," she said, "a messenger awaits in the Great Room."

He nodded as he walked toward the door. As the door was swung out in front of him, his two waiting sons sprang to attention, then fell in beside him as he walked.

Aglovain Tyrson, like his father, held his sword scabbard properly clamped in his mechanical left hand—a Son of Tyr was always to have his sword at the ready—while Burs Erikson's was belted about his waist.

Give it time, boy, give it time, he thought. His daughter was, quite properly, the margravine, the margravess-to-be, but his boys would need to marry their titles. Herris was now a town warder in an internal county—his bride's parents had abdicated in his favor—and Hralf was affianced to a border countess. Already several minor ladies of the Court had sniffed about Aglovain, and understandably so: The boy was accomplished in style, and—by Tyr!—had become a Tyrson at barely fifteen. A few more battles, some additional proof of his virtue and soundness, and he would surely be able to marry a countine at least. Count Aglovain Tyrson—that had an acceptable ring to it. Even a margravature was possible, or perhaps more for him, or for Burs?

The Great Room was cold and drafty, even in midafternoon, even with a fire roaring in the huge hearth at its head and two smaller fireplaces set into the western wall. A margrave, of course, would be seated at the head of the table, where the fire would broil his back. That was the trouble with these damn castles—they were either too hot or too cold. It was offensive

Joel Rosenberg

that a peasant's shack with its cooking hearth would be more
comfortable than the home of nobility.

A lean, homely soldier in the green and gold livery of the
Hinterlands waited patiently by the door. His name was . . .
Deibur, perhaps? That or something similar. The margrave was
bad with names.

"Greeting, Deiter," Aglovain Tyrson said, studiously not giving his father a private smile. It was Aglovain's job to protect
his father in more ways than the obvious, and he took his re-
sponsibilities as a Tyrson and as the son of Erik Tyrson seriously.

"I've ridden long and hard," Deiter started, "and report that,
as Your Grace had suspected, travelers have visited the one
called Harbard, and three of them have this morning been dispatched to the west."

"To the Hinterlands? To the Seat?" Burs broke in, excited.

"I cannot say." The soldier shook his head. "One of them
carries a spear that seems to have some strange virtue about it.
They will be watched."

"And guided," the margrave said, coldly, thoughtfully. "If
necessary."

He dismissed the messenger with a wave of his hand.

It would be good enough, perhaps, if Burs were to win his
hand in battle with the Dominion, but there were other possibilities. And if this Harbard the Ferryman were the one that the
margrave had long suspected he might be, one day his messenger would be the Promised Warrior.

Could this be the day?

Could the margrave himself have brought that on?

Oh, Tyr, father to us all, make it be so.

He turned to Aglovain. "Ask the margravine to join me at
table tonight. We'll be dining in my rooms. You will sit at the
head of the table in the Great Hall."

There were matters to discuss and plans to be made, and that

had best be done in private. Besides, with all their other re-
sponsibilities, it was all too rare that the margrave had some
time alone with Marta, and once he married her off, that would
become an even rarer delicacy.

Savoring that sort of delicacy was one of the manners of the
nobility that he had acquired with ease.

Aglovain nodded, bowed, and left.

The margrave turned to Burs. "You might spend the rest of
the afternoon sparring with the master-at-arms," he said. "I
shall write some poetry."

He turned and walked away slowly, with dignity.

The forms, after all, must be obeyed. It would be improper
to rub his hands—metal and meat—together with a shout of
triumph and a smirk of glee.

CHAPTER EIGHT

Minor Betrayals

New York to Chicago, a quick run through the tunnels at O'Hare to catch the next United 727 to Minneapolis—Maggie and Rick Foss at Ladera Travel had worked out that it would be faster to take a United flight and change at O'Hare than to wait for the next direct Northwest flight to MSP—a quick run from the far end of the gold concourse to the far end of the green (and why was the gate you had to get to always as far away as physically possible?)—and Minneapolis to Grand Forks.

Jeff Bjerke was waiting for them out in front of the terminal, his LTD with the light bar on top firmly parked in the No Parking zone, both the front and back passenger-side doors of the LTD standing open.

"Are we under arrest, Jeff?" Maggie asked, letting him take her bags and toss them into the back seat.

A thin smile crossed Jeff's broad face. "No," he said. "But things are quiet in town—"

"As per usual." Maggie made a sound halfway between a chuckle and a snicker. Torrie would have silenced her with a glare, but glaring at her didn't silence her.

"—and what the heck, your Dad said you could use a lift," Jeff finished. He motioned Maggie into the front seat and shut the door after her.

Torrie smiled. She was wearing her preferred travel outfit of a loose sweatshirt over stretch top and leggings, and if Jeff would rather glance at Maggie's legs than Torrie's on the trip home, that wouldn't hurt anybody.

"You going to run the siren?" Torrie asked, throwing his own bags in the back seat and climbing in. He leaned forward and rested his arms on the back of the front seat.

Cop cars in the city had a wire grid on the back of the front seat, presumably to keep already-handcuffed prisoners from leaping over the partition, kicking the driver unconscious, then taking the handcuff key off the keyring—with their hands still locked behind them—unlocking the handcuffs, and making an escape.

Cops in the city probably didn't have enough real problems to worry about, Torrie thought.

But, then again, making the back seat of a patrol car useless for anything except transporting a prisoner wasn't a problem for them; cops in the city didn't use their patrol cars as the family car in their off-hours.

"No, no siren," Jeff said, after a few moments. "Unless you think we need it."

"Damned if I know," Torrie said. "I don't really know what's going on."

"Your father didn't tell you on the phone?"

Torrie shook his head. "Nah. Dad . . . doesn't like talking on the phone."

"Well, okay, then let's use my nice little cop toys. You sit back and buckle yourself in," Jeff said. He reached down and gave a momentary *whoop-whoop-whoop* on the siren that caused the traffic in front of them to melt away to the right. "It's gotten a bit weird."

Part of the unofficial but entirely de facto Hardwood Town Council was well into a rump session around the Thorsens' kitchen when Torrie came downstairs, running his fingers through his damp hair.

"Feel better, Torrie?" Doc Sherve mumbled around a mouthful of lefse.

Torrie's stomach growled at the sight of it. Norwegian favorite—soft potato flatbread, rolled with butter, sugar, and cinnamon.

Ah, the comforts of home . . .

"Definitely," Torrie said, stretching. Too many hours in too-small seats had Torrie's back and legs aching, and while the best cure for that was a shower and a good workout, and a night's sleep, he had settled for the shower.

"Welcome back, Thorian," Reverend Oppegaard boomed, the voice that had never needed a sound system pitched to be merely loud, not painful. As usual, he had taken the chair in the corner, where his snowy white beard and amply cut sweater made him look like Santa Claus in mufti as he puffed on his pipe next to where the vacuum panel on the wall quietly sucked most of his smoke away. He didn't smoke his pipe indoors anywhere except here and his study at the church, and that was such a hellhole of caked-on smoke that even the notoriously stingy board of directors had unanimously voted to build him another study in the church basement so that he wouldn't have to do his ministerial counseling in the church kitchen.

Here, the pipe left only a pleasant hint of burley and perique in the air. The Nutone central vacuum system hadn't been designed to be a smoke filter, but that was before Uncle Hosea had gotten his hands on it.

"Yes, do be welcome to your own home." Minnie Hansen sniffed, whether in greeting or in feigned irritation with the minister's smoking was anybody's guess; the two of them had been genially feuding like a pair of fourth-graders for generations. She didn't look up from the needlepoint—or was it cross-stitch? The difference was important to old Minnie, but Torrie could never keep the two straight—in her lap, but during her decades teaching school, it had long been said that Minnie could see more out of the corner of her eye and the back of her head than most people could straight on, something Torrie could swear to, having been in her class.

Mom was back at the sink, after setting a fresh-brewed cup of coffee at his place at the table.

Torrie plopped down in the seat and first took a cautious sip, then a mouthful. Good, warm coffee, brewed in the frugal Norski style that let you drink it, rather than practically have to cut it with a fork, the way they made it in the city. And forget that oily, inky, bitter stuff that the French had the nerve to call coffee.

It was good to be home. He drained half the cup in one swallow, then set it down.

"Dad back?" he asked.

Doc Sherve shook his head as he drummed his fingers on the table. "No." He glanced down at the big gold Rolex on his wrist. "He's taking an extra shift out at the site. He'll be back sooner or later."

"He shouldn't have to do that," Minnie Hansen said with a deliberate sniff, never missing a stitch. "We're shorthanded with Arnie missing, and Lars out of town."

"That's true." Mom sat down next to him. "Maybe you could help out there."

"Could be." Torrie nodded. "But I think it makes more sense to see if I can catch up with Hosea and the rest." A lot more sense. Torrie had earned some credibility in the Dominions, while Ian had spent most of his by literally snatching the Brisingamen ruby out from under the nose of Branden del Branden and the rest of the House of Flame.

Ivar del Hival was another case—but Ian had taken to him too much. Understandable, really; Ian needed belonging the way only somebody brought up as isolated as Ian had been could. But Ivar del Hival was a ordinary of the House of Flame, and had been raised on conflict and conspiracy, like they were some sort of vitamins.

And Arnie? Old Arnie Selmo? Arnie was a nice old guy, but the emphasis was on *old*.

Reverend Oppegaard leaned forward. "There's been some discussion," he said, interrupting himself with a puff on his pipe, all the while eyeing Torrie from under heavy brows. "There's been some ... effort to get hold of you ... for some time now."

"Yes, Torrie," Mom said. "I think I must have called every hotel in Europe, looking for you."

His brow wrinkled. Mom knew that he and Maggie had intended to stay mostly in youth hostels. A lot cheaper—and a lot less conspicuous than spending some of the money Mom was busy turning the Dominion gold into on fancy hotels. And they had pretty much stuck to that, except for an occasional break, when he wanted the water hot and plenty, the bed soft and private, and breakfast delivered to the door.

He deliberately hadn't been staying in touch—or, mainly, in hotels. The idea was to get away, to be on vacation, to walk down an alpine trail or through the halls of the Prado without a schedule.

No books, no neighbors, no chores, no Brisingamen.

Maggie walked into the kitchen wearing a pair of pleasantly tight jeans topped by a plaid flannel shirt, tucked in but unbuttoned, revealing a skintight bodysuit or whatever they called it underneath. The jeans and shirt were the sort of thing that Mom typically wore, but the peekaboo of the bodysuit was pure Maggie.

She looked strange, somehow, and it took Torrie a moment to figure out that she had applied a bit of blush to her cheekbones and put on lipstick and had done something or other with her eyes—the sort of natural look that an ex-girlfriend of his had sworn was the most difficult kind of makeup to get right. Maggie didn't usually use makeup, and she sure as hell didn't make putting makeup on—and blow-drying her hair, too!—a priority for right after a shower.

Torrie frowned for a moment. *What's wrong with this picture?*

"Did I miss much?" Maggie asked.

"Not all that much, Maggie," Reverend Oppegaard said, eyeing her either carefully, appreciatively, or—more likely—both. "Karin was explaining that she was having some trouble getting ahold of you two until recently."

Maggie frowned at that, and then dismissed the problem with quick smile. "Well, we're here. Not for long, I take it." She laid a hand on Torrie's shoulder as she took the seat next to him, accepting a cup of coffee and a plate of cookies from Mom with a dramatically mouthed *Thank You!*

"What have you told your parents about all this?" Minnie Hansen asked.

The smile was back. "Oh, my parents and I have long had an understanding, Mrs. Hansen."

"What understanding would that be? And do call me Minnie. Thorian still calls me 'Mrs. Hansen,' but he was in my class some years ago, and both of us like it better that way. Correct, Thorian?"

"Yes, Mrs. Hansen," Torrie said, no trace of irony in his voice, he hoped. Yes, she was really just a little old lady who no more would than could do anything to harm him, but she was also his second-grade teacher looming above his desk like a displeased giant.

"Now, what understanding would that be between you and your parents?" she asked Maggie, again.

"That I'll tell them what I think they ought to know, and they'll love me and support me no matter what I do," she said. "And I don't think they would really want to know what we're doing, even if they did believe me, which ... well, my mom wouldn't, not even if she saw it all. And my dad's ..."

"A psychologist."

"A clinical psychologist," she said. "He doesn't do rats-in-mazes; he treats people. And he's used to being told things that he can't quite believe."

Minnie nodded. "As are school teachers, I can assure you. How did you reach this agreement?"

"Force of character," she said.

Torrie was trying to figure out why Mom was glaring at the two of them, and why Maggie wasn't telling the whole—

Oh. Of course. Mom was in the room. Probably not a good story for her ears.

"Force of character can be overdone," Reverend Oppegaard said. "Which is why my Emily refers to it as 'pigheadedness.' " He gave another few puffs on his pipe, then turned to Mom. "That's easy. What I—and I think Minnie, as well? Yes, Minnie? I thought as much—what I don't understand is why you're lying to them, Karin."

The room was suddenly colder.

"I don't have the foggiest idea of what you are talking about, David Oppegaard," Mom said, her lips tight. "And I do not much care to be called a liar in my home. I very *much* do not care to be called a liar in my own home."

"Then sit down and explain it to us, Karin," Minnie said, her voice soft and low. "Please sit down."

As she walked over to the table, her posture reminded Torrie of the way Dad would walk up to a fencing strip: weight on the balls of the feet, knees slightly bent, ready to defend even before the match started. At the fencing club at school, there had been a little teasing of Torrie's stance—that was how he had been taught—until after freestyle had caught on.

"What do you think there is to explain?" she asked.

"Much." Oppegaard shook his head. "It's too much. You're

one of the most competent people I know, Karin, and probably the most worldly person in Hardwood."

"Thank you so much."

"Shh," Minnie said, patting her on the leg. "Let him finish."

"—But when Hosea started getting sick," Oppegaard said. "You found yourself unable to locate Torrie, and that surprised me."

"But that was the *idea*," Torrie said. "We were just getting away from it all. It was a vacation—"

"—which was terminated only," Minnie said, cutting Torrie off like she'd thrown a switch, "when you were on your way home anyway, and only then after Ian Silverstein had been dispatched with Hosea."

"Well, Karin?" Oppegaard's heavy brows listed. "Didn't you think of calling American Express sooner?"

"No, of course not." She shook her head. "It didn't occur to me. It's not obvious, after all."

"Neither are you, after all," he said. "Obvious, that is. It's subtle, and it's very much like you, Karin, to decide when you are and aren't going to be competent."

"It is," Minnie Hansen said, "well, it is a standard tactic in a young woman's book of tricks, David. If you are attractive enough, even a slightly helpless look will get men to do whatever you want." Her smile seemed genuinely warm. "I was once almost that pretty."

"I . . . don't know what to say," Mom said. "It sounds like you're saying I endangered Hosea just to . . ."—she spread her hands—"do what?"

"Of course." Maggie thumped a hand against the table so hard that the dishes danced. "I should have figured it out by now. To keep your son safe, of course." She turned to Torrie. "That's what this has all been about. She didn't want him to take your dad with him, and she didn't want you to go, either. But Ian's expendable." She looked Mom full in the face. "You have a lot of nerve. How could you? I mean, really, how *could* you?" she said.

"Perhaps you're being too critical," Minnie said. "If you bear a child, you might feel differently. It's one thing to take a risk yourself; it's another to send a child into danger." She turned to Karin. "This isn't the first time any of us has been asked to risk a son, Karin."

"But—"

"Yes, I know. But this is *your* son. Others have sons, as well, Karin," she said, her eyes focusing on something far distant, for just a moment. When she spoke, her lips were tight. "I had a son, once."

"I don't approve, but it is slick." Oppegaard shook his head. "Ian Silverstein has no family to speak of; that's one of the things that drew him here. His mother's long dead, and his father has no use for him, since he's too old to be an emotional punching bag anymore." He puffed on his pipe again, apparently not noticing that the coal had gone out. "Which made him even more expendable, eh?"

Reverend Oppegaard broke the silence. "So: what do we do now?"

"You can't send Torrie. He's just a boy."

"Mom!"

Maggie laid a hand on Torrie's arm. "Shh, please." She turned to Mom. "He's not your little boy, not anymore, Mrs. Thorsen."

"You should be more concerned with . . . cutting your losses, Karin," Minnie Hansen said. "What do you think that Thorian's father would say if he found out?"

"He'd insist on going, as well," Karin said, flatly, staring into her coffee as though she could see something on its oily surface. "He would see it as a matter of honor. Ian . . . championed Torrie. It's Thorian's duty to protect his son. I was able to talk him out of going before, but it wouldn't occur to him that I had . . . other things on my mind than my own safety." She looked up. "We have to work something out, Minnie, David. I mean—"

No. Mom wouldn't— "You mean, Mom, that you thought that Ian and Arnie could be sent—"

"You don't talk to me like that, Thorian Thorsen," she said, a snap in her voice. "I may not be perfect, but I do the best I can."

Torrie hadn't heard that tone in Mom's voice since the time she'd caught him, at age six, trying to figure out the combination lock on one of the gun boxes, and had screamed at him before spanking his butt so long and hard that he almost shuddered from the memory.

Maggie shook her head. "You need somebody with you," she said. "I'm someone." She thought about it for a moment. "I'll need access to a typewriter or a computer and printer." She looked over at Oppegaard. "Can you get a letter postmarked from the East Coast? Safely?"

"Certainly, if necessary." He didn't seem surprised by the request. "Anywhere in particular?"

"Bangor, Maine. Or anywhere near Mount Katahdin. Torrie and I met up with another couple coming back from Europe, and decided to spend the rest of the year walking the Appalachian Trail. We're taking a break from school this year, but we'll catch up."

Oppegaard shook his head. "Two letters, if you please. One with whatever lie you want to try. Another one with the truth. If your parents come looking for you, they may well end up on my doorstep."

She shook her head. "We should only be gone a few weeks. My guess is that Ian's just fine, and that this Freya he's so clearly . . ." She paused for a moment, searching for polite word. ". . . so clearly enamored of, that's it, enamored of—she'll send them both back healthy, stuffed with apple pie so that they can barely walk."

"Then why go at all?" Karin asked. "If it's all so unimportant and safe . . ."

"If you thought it was all so unimportant and safe, Karin," Maggie said, as though she were the older, lecturing to the younger, "then you wouldn't have tried to interfere with Torrie going. And if it isn't so damn safe, then maybe a helpless-looking girl who just happens to be handier with a sword than anybody would expect can come in handy. Again."

"But you don't understand. Here, he's just my son. There, he's *his* son. Thorian the Traitor, they call him. There's nobody in the Middle Dominions who would raise a hand to protect him, and swordsmen of the House of Steel are famed and feared all over Tir Na Nog."

"As indeed we are," Dad's voice came. His blocky frame seemed to fill the doorway, and the light behind him cast his face into shadow.

"Much of it, of course," he went on, "is exaggeration; some of it, of course, is the fact that we're specialists, and very good at what we do." He shook his head, gently, as he walked over to Mom. "*Min alskling*," he said, "this is not the way I do things, as well you know." He took her chin in his hand. "I think Maggie is probably right, and your fears are largely misplaced, but what if Maggie and I are wrong?"

Torrie very much didn't like the way Dad said "Maggie and I." He was feeling more like a spare wheel all the time. Dad and Mom and Maggie had fought and killed the Sons of the Wolf themselves; Torrie might be Dad's son, but Maggie was Dad's comrade-in-arms, the relationship sealed in blood.

"Then," Dad went on, "there's the more important matter of honor. Not only do we have an obligation to Ian, but to Hosea, as well. He's been my comrade for more than twenty years now, and where I grew up, we take that seriously."

"As we do here in Hardwood," Minnie Hansen said, never missing a stitch. "As you know perfectly well."

"No offense was meant, Minnie," he said.

"Well, offense is taken, Thorian Thorsen." She looked up at him. "Winter comes around every year to remind us of that, I'll have you know. Winter has always been a cold and dangerous beast on the plains, Thorian. You need to be able to count on your neighbors to help you fight the beast, not to jockey for position to avoid being the next one eaten." She looked at Mom, and this time neither her voice nor her look were gentle. "I think, young lady, that you had best think about whether or not you wish to live in this small town of ours; your ways have become far too citified for my tastes." She sniffed pointedly. "When you start thinking of your friends as a modern convenience, to be discarded at will, you've long gone past merely not being neighborly."

Mom's face was a mask of self-control. "I have no apologies," she said. She turned to Dad. "But if you are going to go, I shall go with you."

"No, you shall not," Dad said, in that quiet, level voice, barely more than a whisper, that he used when he was past the point of arguing. "Torrie is enough of a hostage to fortune. I . . . need to protect his back, and mine, not watch out for you." If he was angry, it didn't show on his face, or in his voice. "I think Karin's worried that the return of the Sons is misguided—"

"Or a convenient way to keep you here," Maggie said.

"—but it is not impossible; I entrust my wife and home to your care, David Oppegaard," he said, formally.

Oppegaard nodded as he rose. "We'll manage. I'll call Doc and Bob Aarsted. And Jeff Bjerke," he added, clearly an afterthought.

Dad drew himself up straight, practically clicking his heels as he turned to face Maggie. "Maggie, you wish to accompany us?"

"Wish?" She shook her head. "Nah. I insist."

"You'd let her go, and not me?" Mom's lips tightened.

"*Min alskling*," Dad said, taking her hand and bringing it to his lips for just a moment, "you are my wife. I honor and respect you, and when we have had a chance to ... put this behind us, I will perhaps again trust you with matters of honor as I always have and always will in other matters.

"But you are my wife; when Maggie took sword to the Sons, she became my ... *svertbror*, my comrade-in-arms."

She didn't say anything to that.

Dad clapped his hand to Maggie's shoulder. "Well and good, then; we'll get you fitted out. A little work on some of Karin's square-dancing shirts, and you could pass as a goldstitch, and such are much prized in Vandescard." He turned to Karin. "Your skills with needle and thread are better than mine; you will follow my instructions."

Torrie had never heard Dad speak to Mom like that, and Mom clearly wasn't used to it. Her eyes held his for a long time, so long that Torrie started to say something, regretting it the moment that Maggie, Reverend Oppegaard, and Minnie Hansen all turned to glare him into silence.

Finally, Mom nodded, her eyes fixed on the floor. "Whatever you say, Thorian, whatever you say."

"Good." He turned to Torrie. "Check your rucksack, and plan on turning in directly after supper. We sleep, then we leave." He turned back to Mom, and took her hand, drawing her to her feet. "There is much you and I have to talk about, my wife."

Torrie Thorsen sat alone in the kitchen. Mom and Dad had gone off for their talk, although what they had to talk about right now escaped him. Minnie and Reverend Oppegaard had departed, as well. Maggie was down in the basement, filling a rucksack with her gear and supplies, and he knew that he ought to go help her, but he really needed to sit by himself for a few minutes.

He sipped on his weak coffee.

Please, he thought, *let it be easy this time.*

CHAPTER NINE

"The Best Fruit . . ."

T he trick, Ian had quickly found, was to keep at least one gloved hand on the spear at all times. That way, even if it happened to brush against him, nothing would happen. The best analogy he'd been able to come up with was that the glove grounded him, even though that didn't make sense. Well, it didn't have to make sense to him: it just was.

Then again, it was magic, after all, and there was no particular reason magic had to make sense. Shit, there was no particular reason that life had to make sense, and too much of the time it didn't.

What was important was that he didn't repeat what had happened the first night: he had stuck the spear into the ground, taken off Freya's gloves, and pitched his sleeping gear nearby. Sometime in the night his left arm had brushed against the spear. He had come awake, instantly, in horrible pain, a blister the size of an egg yolk already forming on his arm.

It still hurt like a sonofabitch, but he was more careful as he, Arnie, and Ivar del Hival continued down the road.

Arnie was amazing, for an old man. Ian would have expected that he would have been all-in by the end of the first day or so, but here he was, keeping up with two younger men.

"What's the matter, youngster," he said, his lined face split in a grin. "Having trouble keeping up?" Strangely enough, this whole thing seemed to be good for Arnie.

Ivar del Hival, on point, held up a hand. "If you please, there's a patrol on the road ahead, and it's about half the size it ought to be."

"Then why aren't you smiling?" Ian asked.

"Because ten lancers are enough to do all three of us in before we'd have time to more than fart, and because I don't think that the Vandestish would be sending a small patrol after us."

"Yeah." Arnie Selmo's fingers seemed to be trying to clutch something that wasn't there. He looked down as though he noticed himself doing that, and then hooked his thumbs in his pack strap. "And like Doc Sherve says, when you hear hoof-beats—and I do hear hoofbeats coming from around the bend *behind* us—think horses, not zebras."

"There's a time to fight and a time to stand easy," Ivar del Hival said. "This isn't one of those times where I'd say it was a difficult choice."

The leader of the patrol slowed his horse first to a slow walk, and then to an even slower shuffle. On horseback he towered above Ian, of course, but he seemed to be a tall man, anyway. He wore black leather, trimmed with silver thread, a thick wool cloak half-concealing the scabbarded sword held clutched in his enameled, mechanical left hand.

Ready as he and his men seemed to be, there wasn't anything to do but face them. Ian could feel the blood pounding in his ears, but the weird thing was that he couldn't help wondering what the guy did when his nose itched, what with one hand occupied with the reins and the other holding the scabbard at all times.

Somehow, though, it didn't seem like the right moment to ask.

"Greetings," Ian said, his voice just shy of a shout.

The man eyed him silently for a moment, dark eyes peering

out from under heavy brows. "I return your greetings," he said, his voice low. "Without hostility or commitment," he went on, his expression giving the lie to his words. "I am Aglovain Tyrson; by birth, brother to the Margravine of the Hinterlands; by appointment, rider-in-chief of this patrol. Declare your intentions, if you please."

"Huh?" Ian cleared his throat to cover. "I mean, er, we mean you and yours no harm. We are just bringing a message to your capital—"

"To the Seat," Ivar del Hival put in. "Just messengers, that's all we are."

One corner of Aglovain Tyrson's mouth turned up. "Of course, naturally, it's difficult for one to imagine an ordinary of the House of Flame on any sort of spying mission. Unless, of course, one had, as a little boy, met Ivar del Hival, innocent trader, at the Seat, and found out later, that he was, in fact, a Dominion spy." He turned to one of his companions, an older, barrel-chested man who reminded Ian of John Rhys Davies. "What do we do with spies these days?"

"It seems to me that we still behead them," the fat man said. His voice was nasal, and annoying. He looked them over carefully, scratching his fingers against a day's worth of stubble on his chin. "You'd have to ask the margrave about that. We also ought to see what he would want us to do about a spy's companions, come to think of it."

The hoofbeats from behind had drawn closer; Ian and his companions were pretty securely boxed in. Logic said that that wasn't a problem—they had been surrounded ever since Tyrson had split his patrol and sent the other half on a sweep to seal off their line of escape—but it wasn't logic that stood on a dusty road, surrounded by lancers, and it wasn't logic whose mouth had the metallic taste of fear in it.

It was all Ian could do to keep his hands from trembling, his voice from cracking.

Arnie Selmo's face was pale and sweat beaded on his forehead, but, strangely, he didn't look scared. He just stood there,
his thumbs hooked in the straps of his rucksack, looking puzzled, giving a glance to Ivar del Hival as if to say, *Why aren't
we dead yet?*

It was Ivar del Hival, of course, that Arnie was looking to.
Ian was just a kid. This stuff about him being in charge, about
this all being his responsibility, wasn't real to Arnie and Ivar
del Hival, and there was no good reason it should be.

In frustration, without really thinking about it, Ian banged
the butt of the spear against the ground.

Boom.

The ground trembled with a deep basso rumble that set the
horses whinnying and shook leaves from the trees. Above, the
sky was suddenly filled with dozens, perhaps hundreds, of
birds flapping their wings manically as they climbed into the
sky.

Shitshitshit. The thing only an idiot would do when surrounded by a score of armed horsemen would be to make a
sudden move that could only trigger—

Waitaminute. While most of the horsemen were busying themselves trying to regain control of their panicky mounts, Aglovain Tyrson had dropped his reins and stretched out his arm,
his hand palm out, fingers spread, in what certainly looked to
be a peaceful gesture. Sure enough, tips of lances were raised
skywards, and hands moved away from sword hilts.

Aglovain Tyrson's mouth stood wide open. He snapped it
shut, then quickly dismounted from his horse, the clenched
metal fist that held his scabbarded sword held tight against his
chest, the hilt just under his chin. It looked awkward as all hell,
but it was a position from which he clearly could not draw his
sword, and that had to at least imply peaceful intentions.

He stood upright on the dirt road, his head bowed. "I beg
your pardon, sir," he said, his voice low, but pitched so as to

carry far, "for my impertinence. Are . . . you who I think you are?"

Ian didn't have a quick answer for that. He was opening his mouth to say something, anything, probably the wrong thing, when Ivar del Hival spoke up.

"And who would you be," he said, "to think you are one who would question someone he thinks to be the Promised Warrior as though he was a merchant caught pushing his cart down a military road?"

Aglovain Tyrson didn't like that. "Now—are you saying that this is the Promised Warrior?"

"I say nothing of the sort." Ivar del Hival shrugged. "Does it matter at all what I say or don't say?" he asked. "You claim that I'm some sort of spy; why should I swear one way or the other, only to be called a liar?" He extended a hand toward Ian. "What I can say is that this is Ian Silverstein, called Ian the Silver Stone. And that the sword you see at his hip is known as Giantkiller, having drunk the blood of a fire giant, as well that of a köld."

Well, Ivar del Hival wasn't known for his understatement, and was perfectly capable of treating the truth as though it were a powerful spice that could easily be overused. But that, apparently, was the way things worked in the Houses of the Middle Dominion; they were nursed at their mothers' breasts with swordsmanship, milk, and intrigue. The truth, in this case, wasn't all that far off. While the worst Ian had done to the köld had barely frightened it away, Ian had in fact killed the Fire Giant. But that had largely been a matter of luck.

This didn't seem like a good time to bring all that up, all things considered.

"I don't know anything about this Promised Warrior of yours," Ian said, quietly. "I'm just a man carrying a message. That's all."

"Then you won't mind accompanying us to see the margrave, I suppose."

Tyrson didn't wait for an answer; he snapped his fingers, then pointed to first one horseman, then another, and another. The three men quickly dismounted and led their still-nervous mounts over, and steadied them while Ian and the others climbed up into the saddles. Ian didn't know much about saddles, but wasn't there supposed to be some sort of post—horn? Was it called the horn?—sticking up out of the middle of it?

This saddle had several brass D-rings, presumably for lashing gear, and mounted to the right stirrup was a short leather cup in which Ian could rest the spear's butt, but there just wasn't a lot to hold onto, and while Ian had been on a horse a few times before, he had never gotten used to the way the huge animals shifted as they walked, or even stood. Enough to make him seasick, probably.

Well, at least they would be riding instead of walking for a while.

"Let it never be said that the son of the margravess made even one who might be the Promised Warrior walk while ordinary soldiers rode." Aglovain Tyrson grinned a not-very-friendly grin. "I think you'll find these animals comfortable, although I wouldn't say they're quite as fast or as fresh as most of the others. You can't always get what you want."

"Yeah," he said, and thought: *but if you try sometime you just might find, you just might find, you get what you need.*

Aglovain Tyrson remounted his horse, turned it around, and started off. With horsemen in front of them and horsemen behind them, Ian couldn't see anything better to do than kicking his horse into a slow walk, so he did just that.

Through a break in the trees, the margrave's castle loomed ahead, splattered in crimson and gold by the setting sun. The elevated road twisted through the sunken rice fields, narrowing at several points to barely wide enough for two horses to ride abreast, which slowed the procession considerably, although it picked up when the road widened again, and Ian found himself almost knee-to-knee with Ivar del Hival on one side and Arnie Selmo on the other.

"Any of this look familiar?" Arnie asked, with a grunt.

"Why, yes," Ivar del Hival said, "it hasn't changed much over the years. It would be kind of hard to tell, though: they tend to do a good job plastering over any damage. Not something we have a lot of need for, not in the Cities."

That made sense. The five Cities of the Dominion had been carved into their mountains ages ago, and the stone was almost impervious to damage; this would hardly necessitate a great deal of expertise in castle building in the Cities.

Ivar gestured toward the southwest corner of the outer wall. "I know for a fact that they had a break there, a few centuries back, but you wouldn't know it to look at it. A few barrels of plaster, a couple of dozen master plasterers, a couple of hundred years of sun and rain, and it's as good, well, as good as it's ever been."

"So," Ian said, "you've been here before."

Ivar didn't answer right away. "Well . . . back before I got too old to go running all over the face of Tir Na Nog, I did a little trading here and there, hither and thither, around and about, near and far. The Crimson and Ancient Cerulean companies still have a certain amount of status, and that does give a Dominion trader a certain amount of edge in selling swords, among other things."

"Aglovain Tyrson didn't say anything about trading; he called you a spy."

"Spy is such a . . . technical term." Ivar's mouth twitched. "I always preferred to think of myself as a trader who didn't see the need to avert his eyes whenever something interesting happened to cross his path. And His Warmth—not the one you

dealt with; the grandfather of the present Fire Duke—was always interested in anything I had to say when I got back to the
Cities."

"I can see how the Vandestish might misinterpret all that,"
Arnie Selmo said, not bothering to try to keep the sarcasm out
of his voice. "You really can't blame them."

"Innocence is my only shield."

Arnie snorted.

They dismounted outside the main gate, just short of the
drawbridge, and while four of the soldiers led the horses down
a path that curved out of sight around the walls, the rest accompanied Ian, Arnie Selmo, and Ivar del Hival inside, their
boots thumping in time against the solid wood of the drawbridge.

After spending some time with Torrie and Hosea, Ian had
often found himself looking for places that a clever man might
have put an abditory, or possibly a trap, but it didn't take any
expertise to notice that the gargoyles at the juncture of wall and
ceiling were actually spouts, presumably for dumping hot oil
on invaders who had fought their way this far.

He mentioned as much to Ivar del Hival, who crooked a finger at him. "You know, young Silverstone," he said in English,
smiling sweetly, "or whatever you're going to call yourself, it's
one thing to casually notice an ... interesting feature of Vandestish construction. It's another thing to talk about it, and yet
another thing entirely to discuss it in terms of invading armies.
That's something that's guaranteed to make our fine, fine companions nervous." He gave an open-handed gesture that was
completely at odds with what he was saying.

"Eh?" Arnie shook his head. "They speak a lot of English
here?"

Ivar del Hival cocked his head to one side. "As far as I know,
none. As far as I'm eager to test the matter, they might all speak
it as fluently as you speak Bersmål." He shook his head. "The

Joel Rosenberg

gift of tongues isn't something that only Orfindel can bestow."

The main entrance—a massive gate made up of ancient timbers that had been tied together with wrist-thick rope, and then studded with jagged pieces of metal and glass—stood closed, but a tight passageway led off to the side, and it was down this dark corridor that the soldiers led Ian and the others.

"This feels familiar," Ivar del Hival said, as he handed his gear to Arnie so that he could squeeze through a particularly tight turn.

"Yeah," Arnie said. "It's like being born."

"That was," Ivar del Hival said, "an old joke when you were young, but that isn't what I meant. This entrance, it's like the ways into any of the Cities. Not as complicated, I suppose, but then I very much doubt that this castle was built by the Doomed Builder."

"That's certainly true: It was built by my mother's mother's mother's husband." Aglovain Tyrson stopped then a few feet short of the door. "Careful, now."

A score of blackened metal spikes, ranging in length from about one foot long to more than three, were mounted on the door frame. Tyrson used his scabbarded sword to push those on the left to one side, while one of his soldiers did the same thing on the right.

Ian stepped through, and into the golden light of the setting sun.

It wasn't like he had imagined the inside of a castle to be. The grounds had been carefully landscaped; trees—some of them huge—were planted everywhere except for a narrow strip along the walls. A stream wound its way around the grounds, terminating in a pond that cupped the northwest corner; a dozen swans cruised about, sometimes ducking their heads to come up with a wriggling fish in their beaks. A pack of ten, maybe twelve, children was involved in some sort of running and shouting game near the pond, and as Ian watched, a little girl in a white shift slipped on a greenish patch of what Ian assumed was swan shit. She slid feetfirst into the pond, quickly came up sputtering and laughing.

The residence, a squarish three-story building, stood at the top of a gentle slope. At least, it looked like it originally had been squarish, and the newer-looking east and west wings had been added on later.

Aglovain Tyrson stopped them on the lawn outside the main entrance.

"You'll have to leave your weapons here," he said. "The margrave doesn't permit foreigners to come armed to the margravine's presence."

Ian thought about it for a moment. He very much didn't like the idea of being separated from Giantkiller, and he had a hunch that Odin wouldn't much care for him leaving the spear here. But there were many of them, and at most three of him, and it didn't look like an occasion to try to argue the matter.

So he carefully, slowly, set Gungnir's point against the ground and pushed until the spearhead had vanished into the ground. "See that nobody touches it," he said. "It's dangerous."

He unbuckled his swordbelt and set it down on the grass touching the spear. Ivar del Hival unbuckled his, as well, and started to set it down next to the spear, but stopped himself in time; he handed it to Ian, who set it lying next to his. Their rucksacks followed, and after a quick search—more of a patting-down, really, than anything else—Aglovain Tyrson led them through the arched doorway and down a dark corridor to a thick oaken door.

It swung open silently at their approach.

The margrave's room was just about the same size as Ian's high-school gym. The floor was covered with a thick carpet the color of fresh, arterial blood, interrupted by a series of walkways of green marble that appeared to actually be set into the floor, not merely lying on top of the carpet.

The marble web concentrated itself at five nodes: in the north-west corner, a canopy bed stood covered with a fine-knit mesh screen; in the northeast corner, a table and dozen chairs pre-sided; in the southeast, a simple spinning wheel and two very plain wooden chairs stood incongruously; in the remaining cor-ner was a desk, covered with papers and odds and ends; and in what looked like the exact center of the room, an island of low couches and overstuffed chairs clustered. There the mar-grave and a young woman sat next to each other on what Ian would have probably called a love seat, although he was sure that wasn't quite the correct name. Another young man, who looked like a slightly younger version of Aglovain, sat in a chair near them.

The margrave rose at their approach. He was a slim man, tall, with a close-cropped head of black hair that was silvered slightly at the temples and, curiously, at the bangs. As with Aglovain Tyrson, he clutched a scabbarded sword in his metal-lic left hand, but it looked more like an article of clothing on him than a real weapon.

It was hard to pay much attention to him; the woman sitting next to him on the couch kept interfering with Ian's breathing.

He wasn't quite sure what it was. Yes, she was pretty enough—glossy black hair that fell to her shoulders feathered to frame her high cheekbones and exotic blue eyes above a dainty nose and full, red lips. Her black dress trimmed with silver to match the margrave's hair was a study in contrast: it came to a high, demure collar that made him itch to unlace it, and was slit up the left side almost to the hip, revealing a smooth expanse of creamy thigh down to an s-curve of open-toed sandal, displaying toenail polish the same blue as her eyes. Her hands, unadorned with jewelry or nail polish, lay folded demurely in her lap, the long, delicate fingers interlocked.

Ian forced his attention back to the margrave. *What the hell is wrong with you, asshole?* he said to himself. *You pay too much attention to the margrave's pretty young trophy wife, and you're not going to be making friends and influencing people here, or anywhere.*

The room was strangely silent, and then Ivar del Hival cleared his throat and looked pointedly at Ian.

Oops. When in Rome—

"Greetings, Margrave," Ian said. The Vandestish customs allowed for too many honorifics for the nobility, and Ian preferred to simply be seen as a little coarse in using the title, rather than try for the right title and miss it. "My name is 'Ian Silverstein,' " Ian said in Bersmål, "although I'm often called Ian Silver Stone."

"Greetings, Ian Silver Stone," the margrave said. His voice was, surprisingly, higher than Ian would have guessed; a warm, coppery tenor, not a booming baritone. "I am Erik Tyrson, Margrave of the Hinterlands," he said, not introducing either his wife or the kid. There was probably some fine point of etiquette in that; Ian resolved to ask Ivar del Hival what it was.

Later.

"And your companions would be . . . ?" There was no overt trace of menace as he turned toward Arnie and Ivar del Hival, but Ian didn't have to be tuned into whatever subtleties the margrave was playing out to remember that they were in his castle, unarmed, surrounded at the moment by a dozen armed guards, all of whom had that sort of quiet arrogance that at least promised that they knew which end of their weapon was which, even if the promise might be a lie.

"Ivar del Hival," Ivar del Hival said, "ordinary of the House of Flame, fealty-bound to the new Duke."

"I thought I recalled that face," the margrave said.

"It's a homely face," Ivar del Hival said, "but I've gotten used to it over the years."

Ian didn't know what all the playacting was for; he had no doubt that a swift runner had been dispatched with a full report for the margrave while Ian and his companions were busy disgorging themselves of anything that might in some way resemble a weapon—unless when Aglovain Tyrson had sent half of his troop to loop around Ian and his companions, he had also sent a messenger back.

"Hmm . . . and you accompany Ian Silver Stone for what reason?" The margrave raised a forestalling palm. "No, no, never mind; take a moment to think up a good story—I mean, to recall the details of the stream of life that brought you here." He turned toward Arnie. "And you?"

Arnie drew himself up straight, and actually saluted. "Arnold J. Selmo," he said, "Corporal, Seventh Cavalry, B Troop, retired." He had said it all in English, probably having trouble deciding which of two Bersmål terms best corresponded to corporal, for which Ian couldn't blame him. And he couldn't decide whether Arnie was being deathly serious or unintentionally comical; his salute was like something off a parade ground, with no trace of sarcasm or irony at all, and he held it for an awkwardly long time, until the margrave awkwardly returned it. He didn't exactly do it right—his fingers were spread and his palm faced out—but it probably wasn't a good time to mention it.

The margrave nodded slightly, as though to himself, then gestured them to seats. "Well, then, shall we be about our business?"

Nobody had introduced the girl; she simply leaned back, recrossed her legs, and sipped at a mottled mug of steaming tea, her eyes never seeming to leave Ian. "I think, honored Margrave," she said, "that there was some mention of a demand from some ferryman." Just as the margrave's voice was higher than Ian would have guessed, her voice was lower and richer than Ian would have expected; it was a musical alto, rich and sweet with just the slightest husky overtone, like an oboe. She eyed him over the rim of her mug. There was something about the way she looked at him that almost had Ian stammering.

"The margravine is, of course, correct," the margrave said. "Although I am sure he would want us to think of it as a request, rather than a demand. A demand would seem rather arrogant."

Ian couldn't imagine Harbard doing any such thing as simply making a humble request, but, then again, he hadn't taken an oath to tell the truth. "He—"

Ivar del Hival made a be-still gesture. "He would, I'm sure, be perfectly comfortable were it heeded that way," he said, carefully.

"And the nature of this request would be ...?"

Fucking inbred nobility, raised on nothing but indirection and inflection...

"He wants the war to stop before it starts," Ian said. That was the deal: pass on the information, demonstrate who sent them, then back to Harbard's Landing and a healed Hosea. Get it done, get it over with, and hope that the Vandestish didn't kill the bearer of bad news.

"War?" the margravine asked.

Is there an echo in here?

"Harbard the ferryman, well, Your Esteemed Grace, he has some concerns," Ivar del Hival said, choosing his words slowly. "He's of the opinion that the extra patrols near Harbard's Ferry, so near to the southern pass up into the Middle Dominions, well, he thinks that foreshadows a move against the Cities. He asks that it not happen."

"Ah." The margrave pursed his lips and cocked his head, all interest. "And because an ancient, decrepit ferryman wishes there to be no war, there should be no war." He nodded, twice. "That does seem simple enough, does it not?" He rose, and stood looking puzzled until Ian and the rest got to their feet. "So much for that, now, eh?"

Arnie Selmo grinned at Ian. "Didn't think it would be so easy, now did you?"

Ian cleared his throat. "With all respect, Margrave, I think you might want to take Harbard seriously."

"A ferryman."

Ian looked him straight in the eye. It wasn't what the margrave was saying; it was how he was saying it, how he was dismissing it all with a quick smile and a shrug. That was wrong; it was stupid. Even if Odin wasn't what he once was, the old god practically radiated power, and wasn't anybody to trifle with.

The margrave had to believe that. He just *had* to.

A sudden pressure made him look down. Harbard's ring pulsed on his thumb, squeezing rhythmically, like it was trying to milk his thumb. It hadn't changed, it was just a ring, motionless on his thumb, but without moving, without growing or shrinking, it was contracting and releasing in time with Ian's heartbeat.

He felt dizzy for just a moment, and took a half-step backward.

"Ian Silverstone?" The girl—the margravine—was on her feet. She took two quick steps toward him.

"Please. You really have to believe me," he said to her.

He could see in her eyes that she did. The ring on his thumb pulsed again, twice, then twice more.

The fellow sitting next to the margrave shook his head. "The margrave," he said, his voice louder than necessary, louder than it should have been, "does not have to do anything of the sort."

"Burs." The margrave's tone was of command. "You have not been introduced; you will sit quietly."

Burs Erikson seemed to ignore him. "I am Burs Erikson, son to the margrave," he said. "Now that I have introduced myself, I tell you quite properly: the margrave does not answer to foreigners; he does not answer to ferrymen. He answers to the

Table, perhaps, but any other who wants to make him answer had best try to do so by force of arms."

"*Burs*," the margrave said, his voice low but sharp, his free hand held out, fingers spread, palm up, "be still. I've chosen to hear this young man, and that means I have chosen to hear him out."

"It's important," Ian said. "I'm not sure if you know who this Harbard is, but he's not just a ferryman with delusions of grandeur; he's one of the Old Ones."

"Naturally." Burs Erikson snickered. "Of course. Every naked hermit living off nuts and bark is an Old One, bored of meat and warmth. Every decrepit derelict begging for a crust or bone is really an Old One, merely testing the mettle of the those whose door is honored with his knock. Every withered old hag, her dugs hanging down to her knees, selling horrid-smelling potions of dubious origin, is really an Old One, assuming such a form to amuse herself."

Arnie Selmo didn't look over at Ian as he murmured, "What is this idiot's problem? Think he's showing off for the girl?"

"I'll tell you one more time: Best not to make assumptions about how well locals don't speak English." Ivar del Hival's broad face displayed a grin that was in no way friendly. He gave a quick glance at the margrave, as though to say, "Watch him."

Burs Erikson wasn't done. "And, of course, any skinny peasant with a smelly leather rucksack and a gold-dipped ring is really the Promised Warrior, here to lead us toward the Winter's End. Pfah."

"Now, Burs, my beloved son," the margrave said, "that is certainly going too far."

If Ian hadn't been watching, he might have missed the even so-slight gesture that the margrave gave with his index finger It wasn't much, just a quick little back-and-forth waggle, fol lowed by a tiny beckoning gesture.

"No, Margrave, it's not." Burs Erikson's swordbelt was hung on the back of his chair. He gave his sword a shake. "Let's see just how good this . . . killer of fire giants is. I don't insist on a death-duel, or even to-the-first-scar—in truth, I'm not at all sure that I'd want to honor this . . . Ian Silverstone with my scar. But let's take out a couple of blades, and have a little first-blood match. I'll even vow to try to keep the wound small." He turned to Ian. "Come now; let's cross blades. I'll even take a dull practice blade to you, Killer of Giants."

"Just one fire giant," Ian said. "And that was largely . . . good fortune."

The temptation, of course, was to puff up his chest and act tough in front of the girl, but that wasn't only stupid, it was probably what was expected. Ian was by years of training a fencer—a foil fencer, not a duelist. And while he had been working on turning his sport into a weapon, under the sharp eyes of Thorian Thorsen and Ivar del Hival, crossing real blades with a real swordsman like this much-scarred Burs Erikson could get him killed.

But Burs Erikson was determined to take offense, no matter what he said. "Ah, so brave and talented that he can brush off killing a fire giant." He turned to the margrave. "Margrave and Father, please. Let me hurt him."

"I see no offense having been given, Burs," the margravine put in. She rested her hand on his forearm. "And I'd rather not see you treat the codes and usages of your future Order so lightly."

"Burs, my beloved son, this man is our guest—"

"No, he is our prisoner. He was brought here under arms, yes, but that was—"

"That was entirely according to my instructions." The margrave was playing his part to the hilt. It was clear that he wanted Ian to agree to some sort of duel with Burs, but it wasn't at all clear as to why.

"This problem," Ivar del Hival put in, "seems to be one that's easily solved. The honored Burs Erikson doesn't think that Ian Silverstein is necessarily worthy of a real duel, but he wants to fight one anyway." He shook his head. "I've sparred with him, Margrave, and I'll tell you, there's some demon in his right hand—he . . . he doesn't seem to know how to simply go for a quick scarring move. He doesn't seem even to see the arm, the foot, the leg as a target."

Ian didn't smile. The foot, the leg, the arms, weren't targets in foil, and it was taking him time to adjust his technique.

Ivar del Hival frowned at him, then turned back to the margrave. "You put him in what you think of as a simple little duel with Burs Erikson, and I swear to you we'll end up with a dead man on the floor, whether it's Ian Silverstein or Burs Erikson."

"I'm not afraid of that," Burs Erikson said.

"With age comes the wisdom for proper fear," Ivar del Hival said. "But I don't want to argue the point—let us just state our case, and let you deal with it as you think wise, as we depart."

"So." The margrave eyed Ivar del Hival skeptically. "There is no way to test his abilities without drawing blood? None at all?"

"None that I can think of, Margrave, and since—"

"There is another possibility," the margrave said. "We could let them . . . play with a couple of training swords."

"Training swords?" Ivar del Hival asked. "You mean a couple of those tarred sticks—"

"No, no, no," the margrave said. "That's how you do things in the Dominions, perhaps, but we train our young would-be noblemen with simpler weapons: edgeless swords, with blunt points, very flexible. As long as they're not thrust into the eyes or the hollow of the throat, one can do little damage, beyond a bruise or two."

Ian had heard of such things before. They were called fencing foils, and he had spent more hours with one in his hand than he could count.

But he didn't smile; he didn't grin; he didn't tighten or relax.

Ducks and corn, he thought, ducks and corn. Fucking ducks and goddamn corn.

Not this time, motherfucker, he thought, not this time.

CHAPTER TEN

~○~

Sparring Rules

After that scumbag of a father had kicked Ian out for failing to be a sufficiently compliant emotional and physical punching bag, Ian had supported himself mainly by tutoring in foil, augmented with the occasional odd job and college poker game.

It was amazing how good one could get at foil or poker when it mattered, when you were the one person in the gym or at the table who knew he had to win the match, had to dominate the game, to win and win and win again, and stash it away for the summer, or find yourself, once again, reduced to spending August living off corn stolen from the Ag School's experimental farms, stretched out with ducks harvested from Mirror Lake in the middle of the night, with a broomstick and a piece of wire.

Ducks and corn. To Ian, ducks and corn meant poverty and hunger. That meant fear. That could mean loss of self-control. But you didn't have to accept that loss of control as though it were a law of nature; it was just a matter of paying attention, just a matter of reminding your body, your face—and your mind!—that they belonged to you, that a moment of revealed weakness or pleasure could fuck everything up.

Ian had once allowed himself a small smile in a late-night dorm living-room game of seven-card stud when he filled a perfectly concealed baby full house that looked like a possible straight. He had only smiled for a moment, but that was too much: Phil Klein, across the table from him, paused as he was dropping his hand to the table, about to bet his flush to the hilt. Ian had watched a pot that should have kept him in rice and beans for easily two weeks fade until it was barely a Big Mac.

He had thought of that pot throughout every bitter bite of corn and duck that August.

Not again.

Total control; a poker face. Oh, sure, it would be possible to do it more cleverly, more sophisticatedly, to put on whatever expression best suited your purpose, but Ian didn't try to act it out. That way led to danger. Feigning fear, trying to display resignation or fake eagerness, all those could fail.

Nobody could see through a wall.

Ian held his face still as two vestri servants were summoned, then dispatched to get a pair of foils while Ivar del Hival and Arnie Selmo helped him get ready.

He stripped off his heavy hiking boots and exchanged them for a pair of sneakers from his rucksack, and traded the heavy cotton shirt he was wearing for a green V-necked ER shirt. Not exactly a fencer's tunic, trousers, and vest, but even if he had been silly enough to bring his fencing gear along—he had more useful things to pack his rucksack with—he wouldn't have wanted to wear them, not for this. A fencer's tunic was just fine for its intended purpose, but useless for anything else. The high-waisted trousers and crotch-strapped tunic kept the mid-section protected from the point of an opponent's foil, but any of a dozen normal movements—say, dropping into a wide-legged horse stance and then throwing a punch—would tighten the crotch strap hard enough to make the idiot doing it drop his sword and bend over, clutching himself.

He seated himself squarely on the floor and went into his stretches, ignoring the funny looks he got from the Vandestish. It didn't matter what they thought; the stretches were important. He had a little more flexibility, a little more speed when properly stretched, and he would take any edge he could get.

It also made him less likely to injure himself, and that was important, too.

But forget about injuries, forget about swords, forget about everything else.

He took his time finishing his stretches.

Ian Silverstein stood facing Burs Erikson a few yards away. The local practice sword wasn't as flexible as a fencing foil, and it was perhaps two or three inches shorter. The tip was merely blunt, not a button, and the guard was a full bell, an épée guard, not a foil guard.

But it was a foil, and by God, Ian Silverstein was still a foil player.

Burs Erikson brought himself to attention, and slashed his own foil through the air in a series of figure-eights that Ian found overelaborate for a salute.

Somewhere in the back of his mind, Ian smiled. Some things were the same everywhere. Back home, most teachers, most schools, had their own personal salute. With a bit of knowledge, you could sometimes even tell what year somebody had started. D'Arnot's salute, D'Arnot had once confessed, was the same movement that his father the orchestra conductor had used to wave his baton in 4/4 time.

Ian merely raised and dropped his own point, then dropped back to en garde, his tip up.

Out of the corner of his eye, he could see the margrave and the girl watching him from one side, while six of Burs Erikson's soldiers muttered among themselves as they kept an eye on Ivar del Hival and Arnie Selmo—

—but none of that mattered.

The marble path beneath his feet was wider than a standard fencing strip, but that was okay.

One thing at a time, boy, one thing at a time.

He dismissed the rest of the universe. It didn't matter. If you have one strength, and that strength is concentration, then you'd best learn how to use it.

Fine. There was a man with a foil opposite him. Burs Erikson was not quite as tall as Ian was, but built more solidly. Thick wrist, possibly as strong as Ian's. But he wouldn't be expecting the strength of Ian's wrist, not at first. He would want to engage, take Ian's blade, control the contact.

Timing and space would be the issues; Ian had easily three, four inches of extra reach—enough for a real advantage; Burs Erikson would be trying to work his way inside Ian's defense, quite probably by attacking his blade.

If he didn't try to end it all at the start, with a running attack.

No.

He wouldn't. The flèche was a fencer's trick, not a swordsman's. It was one thing to try a flèche, a running attack that almost guaranteed the end of the point one way or another, on a fencing strip, where the only thing at stake was a point that you could win if you did it well, and at worst maybe a touch of embarrassment if you did it too clumsily.

But only somebody crazy or desperate would do that in a real duel. Somebody who, like Thorian Thorsen of the House of Steel, wanted to live to fight another day wouldn't expose his torso so directly.

So: no flèche, but Burs Erikson would try to make it quick, to embarrass Ian.

Ian's left arm was held properly up and back, slightly cupped. Ian took every advantage, big or little: with his left arm at head-height, it added balance and stability, and by whipping the arm down and back during a lunge or ballestra, he could add a little speed, a little more balance, to an attack.

Come on, asshole, attack me, he thought.

Fencing was, much of the time, simply a battle of idiots: the first idiot to make a mistake lost. Anything could be a mistake, though—fencing was like life that way.

They moved toward each other until Burs Erikson, too eager to end it all quickly, did a strange little staggered half-step to bring him into range, then closed the distance with a bouncy ballestra, trying a quick beat against Ian's blade. A good way to fight a duel, perhaps—while you controlled your opponent's blade, he was going to have difficulty hurting you with it. But Ian was ready for it, and simply parried from sixte to quarte, then gave a quick beat against his blade, but didn't attack. It was sound strategy to spend the first few moments of a match feeling out the opposition.

Burs Erikson didn't try the obvious; a quick remise, continuing the attack, was a fine match technique, likely as it was to score before the opponent could complete his riposte, but that was a fencer's technique, not a duelist's.

In a real duel, that was far too likely to leave both duelists with swords stuck in them.

The missed beat had brought Burs Erikson's sword out of line; Ian feinted a high thrust, then lunged low, in full extension, touching Tyrson just at the belt line.

Ian recovered with a crossover retreat—a too-pretty move, perhaps, but it was handy in the arsenal of a fencer who wanted to control the distance between himself and his opponent—and had no problem in parrying Burs Erikson's next lunge, leaving their blades engaged.

Ian had decided that he wasn't going to try anything quite yet, but his muscles and nerves had another idea: he disengaged, cut over, and extended for a touch on Burs Erikson's torso, then reengaged the blades as he retreated.

Burs Erikson managed to thrust weakly toward Ian's outer arm, but Ian simply parried and continued his lunge, again scoring with a torso touch.

Ian stepped back and saluted, holding it until Burs Erikson

was shamed into mimicking the move. "Very nice, sir; you almost made the touch on the arm."

Burs Erikson repeated his complicated salute, then dropped back into a guard position. "Again."

Ian moved forward, then went into a quick false attack, which, as intended, wouldn't have quite reached Burs Erikson's chest even if he hadn't defended properly—he was just a little too far away. But it drew the expected riposte, and Ian was sure enough that it was real that he went for a full circular parry that half-threatened to turn into a disarm. He beat, lunged, touched, and recovered.

Ian shook his head. He really had wanted to go for the disarm—according to the parallel tradition both here and home, the opponent wasn't really disarmed until his sword actually touched the floor—and slap the kid a few times with his blade before Burs' sword clanged on the ground, but years of training had made him conservative.

Well, and good. Now, finally, he let a smile come to his face. He nodded at Burs Erikson. "I think we've had enough, eh?"

He deliberately glanced down toward his blade. *Next time, asshole*, he tried to shout with his mind, *I will disarm you, and if you think being beaten this badly is embarrassing, just wait until your sword's tumbling through the air and landing at the feet of your father's pretty young wife, eh?*

But that was part of what Thorian Thorsen had tried to teach him: It was best simply to beat an opponent, and not humiliate him. Victory carried with it enough benefits that it needed no supplemental ones; humiliation could be repaid later.

He tossed the sword and caught it by the hilt, upside down, then handed it over to the vestri servant before walking toward Burs Erikson. Ian briefly clapped his hands together, like a blackjack dealer showing that he was leaving the table without any palmed chips, then extended his right hand.

"Good bout," he said, smiling. Being a good winner was

something that anybody who wanted to earn some money tutoring fencing had to have down pat.

"Thank you." Burs Erikson's grip was probably firmer than it ought to have been, and his smile seemed less than completely genuine. He was probably working out that he'd been had, but probably would never figure out why, not completely.

The technical term was "decadence." Foil fencing had evolved at a time when duels were fought to the death, and a wound inside the triangle from shoulders to groin was the way somebody could be sure of delivering that kind of damage.

Épée had arisen when duels were fought to the first blood, to any wound at all, and it was unsurprising that a Vandestish swordsman would have been trained to go for the blood, the same way that duelists from the Houses did.

Ian might have given a good account of himself in a real duel, or he might not. It had taken him years to get any good with a foil, and while he had spent some time studying what he thought of as informal épée with Ivar del Hival and Thorian Thorsen, he wouldn't be a match for a really good duelist for a long time. Some of his skills would carry over, but not all of them.

But playing by Ian's rules, Burs had had virtually no chance against Ian, much less than the chance Ian would have had, had he been playing Burs' game. Ian nodded to Ivar del Hival. The big man was useful to have around, at that, and not just for carrying a stretcher.

He had won. So why did he feel like he had been playing poker with marked cards?

"Well," the margrave said, "you've proven yourself quite a swordsman, and that's been fascinating, but you've hardly given me cause to send you to the Seat and the Table with any demand."

Then what was all this for, Margrave? Ian thought, but didn't ask. That was at least an implicit promise of the bout, that if—

"Let's discuss it at table tonight," the margravine said, slipping her arm under the margrave's. "I'd like to hear more from this . . . very interesting young man."

Ian was surprised when the margrave nodded. "Very well, Marta," he said, quietly. "Ian Silverstein, you and Ivar del Hival shall join us at table, and of course you will all stay the night," he said, looking pointedly at Burs Erikson. He gestured toward Arnie. "If you want to have your servant with you, I'll have him fed in your rooms."

Ian would have protested immediately, but Arnie's eyes were twinkling in amusement at the margrave's assumption that he was a servant, and before Ian could figure out what he wanted to say about it, Arnie was on his way out of the room in the company of a couple of vestri servants, and Ivar del Hival was talking.

"That is very kind of you, of course, Margrave," Ivar del Hival said. "We are honored." He drew himself up stiffly, arms at his side, and gave a precisely measured bow, then turned to glare at Ian until Ian did the same.

"We are honored," Ian echoed. He had his mouth open to say something else, although he wasn't sure what, when he was cut off by the screams outside.

It had been a little boy, they said, although it was impossible to tell now. It was a scorched hunk of foul-smelling meat, too-white shards of bone poking through.

He had been just a little boy, and he had touched the spear and then burned up in a hot white light, too bright to look at.

Nobody had seen it, although there had been some looking.

One of them, a little girl of maybe four or five, kept crying as she rubbed at her eyes, every once in a while holding her fingers out in front of her face, as though to reassure herself that she could still see. Another, a soldier whose face was wet with tears, was already seeing well enough to walk over to Aglovain Tyrson and murmur in his ear.

Ian rubbed his fingers against the blister on his arm. "How . . ."

Ivar del Hival's thick hand was hard on his shoulder. "Not a *word*," he murmured. "Not a word, I tell you." He looked over at the margrave. "Aglovain Tyrson will tell you that Ian Silverstein warned him that nobody was to touch it," he said. "We meant no harm."

The margrave nodded slowly, his face stony and impassive as he looked from the charred mass to Ian, and then to Ivar del Hival. "Yes, yes, he's said so."

"Who . . ." Ian started, then caught himself. "Who was supposed to be guarding it?"

Aglovain Tyrson's hand was on the hilt of his sword. "That, Ian Silver Stone, is none of your concern."

"Leave it be," Ivar del Hival said. "Just leave it."

"Easy, Ian," Arnie Selmo murmured from behind him. "We're in Indian territory, and the natives aren't necessarily all that goddamn friendly."

But it was just a kid. If some adult was asshole enough to ignore the warnings, that was one thing, but you couldn't expect a kid to see the danger.

"Yeah, yeah," Arnie said, anticipating Ian's objection. "But you let the locals hand out local justice, and if it isn't exactly what you'd call justice at home, that's just kind of too bad."

"The spear," Ivar del Hival said. He swallowed heavily.

"It's called Gungnir," the margrave said, nodding. "I know of it. It can be carried with impunity only by Aesir."

"Something like that," Ian said. "Only those of the Elder Races or a few of us with . . . a special dispensation."

"Ah." The margrave jerked his head toward it. "Pull it out of the ground."

Ian nodded as he slipped his hands into the gloves. "As you please," he said.

As before, it was hard to get the first hand to close around the shaft; it was a strange feeling, as though he was a marionette under his own control, pulling the strings that controlled his own movements, as he leaned over and controlled the marionette that was himself.

But first he closed one hand around the shaft of the spear, and then another, and then, in an instant, the universe shifted, and he was himself, just ordinary Ian Silverstein, standing over the burned remains of what had been a little boy, a god's spear in his hands, tears running freely down his cheeks.

CHAPTER ELEVEN

Rumors

Torrie had been hearing the rhythmic chopping sound for an hour—he had checked his pocket watch—before they topped a hill and found Harbard's Landing spread out before them.

The weather was getting ugly, with the promise of getting downright mean before long. A storm was moving in from the west, a slate-gray mass driving fluffy puffs of cumulus ahead of it, like a massive pack of wolves scattering and then pursuing a few idle sheep.

The distant *whack* came to his ears over the dry, almost metallic rustle of the leaves in the trees. There were a few seconds of silence, and then another *whack*.

Torrie could visualize it all; the woodsman would set a piece of wood on the chopping stump, choke up on the hammer so he could set the wedge with a few taps, and then he would take one step back, bring the hammer down, back, around, and over, and—

Whack—

Then he'd take another piece of wood, set it up on the chopping stump, and—

Whack.

There it was again. Right on time, too. Whoever it was must have been in pretty good shape; he was keeping up the same pace, and had been for a while.

Or maybe there were two of them, working together, like Torrie and Dad did, one of them putting the wood on the stump and setting the wedge, the other simply swinging the hammer.

Chopping wood with Dad had always been Torrie's favorite chore. Even when he was a little kid, that was their time together—Dad would set the piece of wood on the ancient oak stump next to the barn, then steady the wedge on it so Torrie could bang on the top with the carpenter's hammer.

It had been a major rite of passage the day Dad had handed the sledgehammer to Torrie, and told him it was his turn.

Torrie smiled. "Sound familiar?"

"Very. Reminds me of home." He quickened his pace. "If we hurry, we should be there soon."

One of the hardest things for Torrie to learn about his father was that not only could he sometimes be wrong, but it wasn't just about matters of opinion that he could be mistaken, but matters of judgment, too. You grow up thinking that if Dad does make a mistake—and, hell, everybody makes mistakes—it's something that nobody could have avoided.

And then you find him about to make a tenderfoot kind of mistake like plunging ahead with a storm coming on.

"Dad?" Torrie said. "Let's take a break for a moment, eh?"

Dad's jaw twitched. "I think . . ." He let his voice trail off. "Very well, if you think it wise."

Torrie smiled.

Maggie—unflappable Maggie, who still managed to look fresh after two days on the road, just like she had through what had seemed like half the hiking trails in Europe—seconded the notion and shrugged out of her pack.

"If we can't afford a quick five, then we probably better take ten." She hung the rucksack from an outthrust piece of bark on an old elm, then gave a quick tug to test it before dropping first to a squat that gave her thigh muscles and hamstrings a good stretch, then a cross-legged sitting position on the ground.

"A few minutes' rest would probably be good," Dad said, evenly, although Torrie could tell from his tone of voice that he resented being slowed, much less stopped.

Torrie was more experienced in this, and while it wouldn't do to lecture Dad, it was nice to be better at something than he, even if the something was only hiking.

Walking quickly to try to get to shelter wasn't necessarily a bad idea, but there was also something to be said for a bit of caution.

Torrie tried to estimate the distance from the overlook down to Harbard's Landing, then factor in the speed and distance of the oncoming storm, and couldn't decide how close it was.

They might be able to make it down to the ferryman's shack before the storm hit, and they might not. If they were going to have to weather a storm outside, it would be better to do so while the forest offered some protection from the elements, and the materials to construct more.

A hastily constructed leaky lean-to under a canopy of trees was better cover than anything you could find or make on a muddy road, and even a muddy road was better than the field it ran beside.

Torrie would have said as much if the two of them were alone, but he would no more embarrass Dad in front of Maggie than he would have embarrassed her in front of him.

Maggie smiled up at him; she knew what he was up to. "Let's see if I can guess," she said, rising, swatting at the tightness of her jeans to clear off the dirt. She was dressed like Torrie and Dad: tight trousers over heavy hiking boots, belted with a silver buckle, and topped with a filigreed cowboy shirt borrowed from Torrie, which, hurriedly decorated with a few odds and ends of jewelry Mom had been shamed into contributing to the cause, was an outfit that by local usage proclaimed her to be a goldstitch.

The compound hunting bow in her hand was, granted, a bit

strange by local standards—but anybody who traveled with silver or gold would be expected to carry a weapon, as well.
Women Just Didn't Carry Swords, not in the Middle Dominions, not in Vandescard, but if the knife slung from her back
was somewhat longer and lighter than most such were, that
wouldn't be a problem. In a fight, she would try to get hold of
the spare sword Torrie had slung over his shoulder, if possible.

Maggie wasn't by any means the best fencer Torrie had ever
met, although she wasn't bad at all for somebody who had only
been doing it for a couple of years, but she was the best damn
surprise fencer that he would likely ever see. That had saved
her life, as well as Mom's and Dad's; and it wasn't likely that
the Vandestish would be anymore open-minded than the Sons
of Fenris.

She stood for a while, looking, thinking. "I think we can make
it," she said. "I could be wrong; but I think it will be at least a
couple of hours before the storm hits down there. I think."

"But?"

"But I'm not sure it's worth a try." She spread her hands.
"Win a little, or lose a lot?"

Torrie nodded. That was about the decision he had come to.
If they rushed, and if they were on the right side of the storm
front by the time they got to the cottage, and if they were made
welcome, it would all be fine.

But that chained too many ifs, and for too little reward. They
should be able to put together a decent shelter within an hour
or so, and sit out the storm in reasonable warmth and adequate
dryness. If there was anything more miserable then being wet,
cold, and outside during a storm, Torrie didn't want to find out
about it firsthand. And there was a clearing about a mile back
upslope that would do.

"Dad? It really makes more sense to do it this way. I—"

Dad silenced him with an upraised palm, which startled Torrie for a moment. He had put that on his list of things not to

do; an upraised hand was a gesture Torrie had learned not to use around Ian—it would always cause him to flinch, and would make him at least force himself not to bring up his foil— if they were working out in the *salle d'armes* or over at the gym during fencing club sessions. It had been simpler to just decide never to raise his hand that way, although it was a common gesture around the house, and Dad's usual way of conceding defeat.

"Very well, Thorian," Dad said. "Let's do it your way. What can I do to help?" he asked, then listened, smiling, as Torrie gave him the camp saw and his instructions. Dad's broad face was as familiar to Torrie as his own. Torrie would have claimed that he had seen it in every possible expression—including a lot of smiles.

But Torrie couldn't recall that particular smile before.

Lightning flashed and thunder roared overhead, and the storm's wet fingers clawed and scratched at the walls of the lean-to, but the tarps held firm.

High above the trees, a finger of lightning reached down for land, scant seconds later followed by a thunderclap that sounded like God's Own Applause. There was no point in trying to talk, with the thunder interrupting every sentence, so Torrie just sat and thought.

Dad's eyelids started to sag, again, and again he shook himself, once, twice, three times. If Torrie didn't know better, he would have thought that Dad was starting to get, well, old. But that made sense only intellectually, not emotionally. Dad was Dad like Mom was Mom and Uncle Hosea was Uncle Hosea; they were anchors of the universe, not just people.

Maggie's face was lovely by firelight; there was something about it that brought out the strength and resolve etched into her firm mouth that never grew old.

She leaned her head against his shoulder, and Torrie, far too self-consciously, kissed the top of her head, while Dad studiously looked away.

It would have been nice to have a little privacy, but you made do with what you had. It was possible to make a lean-to solely out of what you could find in the forest, and Torrie had done that in Boy Scouts, years ago, but it made more sense to use what you had available, and Torrie had been taught, by Mom, Dad, and Hosea, to substitute technology for discomfort, when it made sense. So he and Dad had quickly lashed together a pair of frames, and covered them with tarps, then anchored them in place with tent pegs and a pair of support lines that cut across one side of the clearing. Two of the mylar plastic emergency blankets had been pitched to seal off the sides of the shelter, and a third over the top of it, leaving the lean-to closed on three sides and part of the fourth.

The remaining tarp was pitched as a slanted dining fly, giving enough protection to the fire in front of the lean-to that, though it constantly sputtered and crackled and hissed, it didn't go out.

That was always the nice thing about camping in the rain: you didn't have to worry about your fire getting out of hand. The problem was feeding it constantly, slowly, giving it enough time to dry out the wood you added.

The three of them huddled together in the back of the shelter, Maggie in the middle, each wrapped in a sleeping bag.

There was something wonderful about being warm and dry in the middle of a storm.

Dinner had been the last of the hot dogs, toasted at the end of a long stick, then wrapped in flattened Wonder Bread—it still amazed Torrie how many slices of the stuff could be squeezed down into a coffee can—and washed down with Tang and a couple carefully measured belts from the brandy flask. A few squares of waxy-tasting high-temperature Swiss chocolate was dessert.

THE SILVER STONE

Not exactly a banquet, but it was filling, and it warmed his insides, and that was enough.

The fire crackled, and the storm roared.

Torrie was never sure why, but he couldn't remember enjoying a meal more.

CHAPTER TWELVE

~o~

Marta

Ian sat back in his chair and considered whether to drain the last inch of drania from his glass.

Drania. That was what they called it. What drania was, he wasn't sure. It tasted good, and sweet, with maybe an overtone of berries? He wouldn't have wanted to swear what it was made of. Some sort of juice, perhaps? A tea, sweetened with honey?

It wasn't alcoholic; just the taste of alcohol would have made Ian gag. Ian didn't drink, ever; if you didn't drink, ever, you couldn't ever beat up people you cared about while drunk—but there was something in the spiciness that was relaxing him from temples to toes—particularly around the temples.

The conversation flowed around him, and around the whole room. A Vandescardian dinner was an all-evening affair of endless courses, punctuated with breaks from the dining table by couples or groups intent on an interlude of dancing at the far end of the hall, where a six-piece band kept up a quiet rush of music.

The steps could have been either a square dance or a minuet, for all Ian could have guessed; the dancers were arranged in groups of four, two couples, who joined and broke formation, sometimes all doing the 'same thing, sometimes breaking into couples, and sometimes just the men facing off and doing something that looked more like a mime trying to escape an invisible prison than dancing.

The instruments looked vaguely familiar—two of the musicians played something that looked sort of like a guitar that had been strung by a sitar player; another bent over a lap-held harp sort of thing, ten silver fingerpicks frantically plucking at strings; another kept time with a drum that looked and sounded just like the doumbek the handlebar-mustached Hungarian across the hall used to take into the dorm stairwells and pound on at all goddamned hours of the day. The bass looked like a banjo with a glandular condition, and was played by a vestri on a precarious-looking stool, but he kept up a steady thrumming rhythm that more drove than followed the drummer.

The music sounded strange; more of a pentatonic scale than the diatonic scale, perhaps?

Ian smiled to himself. Well, if that was right, he'd finally found some use for that goddamned music appreciation course he'd had to take for distribution credit.

Up at the head of the table, framed in the huge fireplace, the margrave was lecturing Aglovain Tyrson, gesturing with an eating prong, whipping it over, around and under, as though demonstrating a *coupe-dessous*. A bit tricky—it took time to cut-over and then disengage into octave—but it could nail somebody who was expecting something else.

It was worth remembering, if he ever ended up crossing swords with the margrave. A duel really was a competition as to who would make the first mistake, and the classic mistake was to be too fond of a particular maneuver. There was no such thing as a maneuver—disengagement, riposte, parry, remise, redoublement, reprise, anything—that could not be countered, and if your opponent could maneuver you into doing even the right thing at the wrong time, he could go through your defenses like they weren't there.

Which they wouldn't be. Sixte exposed your inside, while

quarte exposed your outside, and if he was attacking in the low line, it didn't matter how you defended against a high-line attack.

The woman to the margrave's right—Ian had been presented to her, but he couldn't remember her name—watched the interplay with what was probably feigned fascination. Fine points of fencing are of interest only to those who practice it, save for the occasional weirdo who probably would find something interesting in watching paint drying.

Across the broad expanse of table from him, Ivar del Hival was holding forth on Ian's duel with the Fire Duke. Ian mostly tuned it out; he had lived through it, it had been bad enough but he had survived it, and there was no need to rehash every moment of it.

Burs Erikson had been hitting the spiced beer probably too hard for somebody of his age and mass—his face was greasy and sweaty in the firelight, and he seemed to be slurring his words. Ian tried hard not to despise him—not everybody who ever got a little tipsy went around beating up his kids, and besides, Burs Erikson was a bachelor, so the margravine had said—but failed.

Ian shook his head. He had no business looking down on Burs Erikson for drinking. Burs Erikson might bend his elbow too much, but he didn't have the blood of a little boy on his hands.

Logic said that Ian wasn't responsible for that, either.

So much the worse for logic. He drained the last of the drania, and set the glass down on the table.

While Ian had been working on the drania, Ivar del Hival had probably downed a gallon or so of the spiced beer, and other than his voice getting just a little louder than its normal boom, and his gestures becoming just a trifle broader, there was no change.

Well, each of us has his own skills, Ian thought. *Ivar del Hival can outfox a Vandestish noble, and then hold his booze and their attention. I can let little children get killed.*

"Ian Silver Stone?" the margravine asked.

"Yes?"

"Is it your custom to dine silently? Or is conversation permitted where you come from?"

Ian had assumed that the margravine would be seated at the other end of the table, opposite from the margrave, but that spot had been taken by Burs Erikson, and Ian had found the margravine as his dinner companion.

Which should have been nice, he supposed, but so far Ian had been a less than brilliant conversationalist.

"It's not only permitted, it's welcome, and I have to apologize. I've been thinking."

"You are forgiven, of course." The margravine leaned closer to him. "You seem . . . preoccupied, Ian Silver Stone. I hope it isn't the company that bores you." Her smile made the last somewhere between a joke and an invitation.

"No," Ian said, "not at all."

She was dressed similarly to the other women at the table: a simple silk shell, belted tightly at the waist, slit up past the knee on both sides. The black dress, decorated with gold stitchery in little tadpole designs that Ian would almost have called paisley, hugged her hips, and was belted tightly with a golden cord, emphasizing her slim waist. The high neck would have seemed demure—despite the scooped cutout that exposed a pear-shaped ruby that looked like it had been glued into the hollow of her throat—if the bodice had been cut more generously, instead of emphasizing her firm, high breasts.

Great. Go ahead—get turned on by your host's wife, Ian thought to himself, remembering Karin. And Freya.

Not a smart move.

"Well?" she asked, eyeing him over the rim of her own glass.

"When you're so quiet, it must be because you have some deep, deep thought to conceal. Reveal it, if you please."

He didn't know how to play along with that particular line of banter. So he just answered honestly. "I feel . . . horrible about that little boy," he said. "Just a little kid." He shook his head.

She set her glass down and laid her hand on top of his. Her fingers were longer than his, and warmer. "I guess it's a matter of how one was raised. I've been taught that guilt is a common but useless emotion; much better to simply resolve to do better next time than to flagellate oneself about mistakes, no matter how serious." Her expression grew somber, and her eyes didn't blink. Ian had never seen eyes of quite such a color before. They were a deep, rich blue, and the combination of blue eyes and black hair would have always seemed exotic, even if the blue had not been so rich and deep, and the black had not been so inky and glossy.

"But I do take your point, though. Little Dafin, Elga's son, was a delightful little child, with a lovely laugh." She pointedly looked down the table at a young woman who sat, silently, eating mechanically, her face a granite mask of grief. "But I can tell you that Elga does not blame you for the . . . accident. And I can assure you that when her man returns from the Seat, he will see to the fellow whose carelessness cost Dafin his life." She shook her head, sadly, then dismissed it all with a shrug, and seemed to give his hand a parting stroke before removing her own.

No, Ian decided, she wasn't dismissing it; she was simply acting as though she was. He reached for his glass, stopped himself when he remembered that he had emptied it, and then started when he noticed that it was full again. Vestri servants with a carafe of drania were like Denny's waitresses with coffee: they could come by and refill you without giving you time to notice.

He sipped more of the drania. "I . . . I just don't like it when little kids get hurt." His knuckles were white where he gripped the stem of the glass; he forced himself to relax his hand and set the glass down.

"Do you know anybody who does?" She tilted her head to one side. "I am the margravine here, and that does give me a certain amount of . . . influence." She made as though to rise. "Shall I ask of the company? Shall I inquire as to whether the blame ought to fall on the recklessly careless fool who was to guard the spear? Or perhaps it should be put on dear Aglovain Tyrson, who insisted that you attend the margrave unarmed? Or perhaps on the margrave himself, who issued such orders years ago? Or on you, who carried it here and warned all and sundry that it was dangerous?"

Ian couldn't help but smile. She might be a trophy wife and all, but maybe that was in part because of her obvious charm. And just maybe it was sincere.

"It's a horrible thing, Ian Silver Stone," she said. "But you're no more to blame for it than I am." Again, she laid her hand on his, and again, seemed to give it an affectionate stroke before taking it away.

It had been too long since that one-nighter with the waitress in Basseterre—Linda? No, Lindy, that was her name, Lindy— and Ian had to remind himself that the head he had better be thinking with was the one on his shoulders.

"Come," she said, making as though to rise. "Let me show you the gardens before the next course comes. I've had Cook prepare her special terrine, and it is worth working up an appetite for."

Customs differed from place to place; that was one of the few constants. Here, it was probably reasonable for a visitor to take the host's wife walking in an inner garden. At least, it must have been, because as she took Ian's arm and guided him toward the far doors, the margrave caught Ian's eye, and gave him a nod that sure as hell looked like an approving one.

* * *

The lightning and thunder had rolled past, although off to the east, there still was an occasional flash, and maybe a distant rumble that sounded more like a grumble.

But the rain hadn't stopped, and gave no sign of stopping. Its wet fingers clawed and pounded on the canopy overhead, while the wind above rushed past. The garden was fully enclosed by the walls of the castle, though, and that protected them from all but an occasional light misting spray.

Ian would have liked to have seen the garden in daytime, but even at night, even in the rain, there was something pretty about the way the cobblestone paths wove in and out among the plantings.

Marta pointed at one of the nearest flowerbeds. "That's the flower we call a Good-Morning Lily on sunny mornings; it opens up all gold and red and orange, like a sunrise."

There was something strange about the way she had phrased it. "And what do you call it on cloudy mornings?"

"Are you making fun of my country dialect?" Her smile warmed him. "Well, let me tell you that we do have a name for it on such days: we call it a Stay-Abed, because it's wise enough not to open at all."

"Ah."

She again tucked her hand under his arm, and guided him down the covered walk. "Now, right there, is my own flower bed," she said, pointing to an ordinary-looking patch of greenery. "I don't have much time for it, but I work it with my own hands," she said. "Like the proud peasant stock I come from. The best flowers grow in the humblest manure, you know, and I work it into the soil here, with my own tools."

Ian felt like he'd missed something. "Peasant?"

"Of course," she said. "I will thank you to say the word with some respect. There's no shame in being lowborn, not if you inhabit your niche with dignity, and certainly not when you rise as high as my father has. I . . . ah, I see." She raised a finger. "You're very clever, Ian Silverstein, getting me to talk about myself rather than permitting me to inquire of you." Her fingers stroked his, idly. "Since I don't dare match wits with you, let me ask you straight out: are you the Promised Warrior?"

"I'm not sure how to answer that," he said. *Other than to tell you that I don't have the vaguest idea what you're talking about, and I don't know that that'd be a smart thing to do.* "I'm just a, well, a herald right now. Harbard's asked me to, to convey a request, and has given me that which could hardly come from anybody else."

"Just a herald, eh?" she asked. "So you really aren't the Ian Silver Stone, the killer of költs and fire giants?"

"Singular, not plural," he said. "And I didn't kill the bergenisse, the köld. I just sort of wounded it." No need to mention that he had barely nicked it, and that it wouldn't have had any effect if the sword that Ian had later named Giantkiller hadn't been one of those that Hosea had tempered in his own blood. Good steel tempered in the blood of an Old One could give a köld an awful sting, and when thrust straight through the chest of a fire giant, had knocked him stone cold dead.

But it hadn't been skill or heroism, not either time. Just stubbornness.

And luck.

"And the fire giant?" She arched an eyebrow. "You didn't kill it, either? Perhaps you simply beat it to death with humility."

He shrugged. "I guess if you'd been there you wouldn't have thought it was all that heroic." It would have been easy to play the hero, to puff up the exploit, but there was something obscene about using what had happened to impress a pretty girl, and no matter if she wanted to be impressed by it. You had to decide what your standards were.

In truth, the hard part had been agreeing to face the fire giant, not the doing of it. That was like, like, trying to ski down an avalanche, maybe—there had been no choice, so you just did the best you could.

"But are you the Promised Warrior?" she asked, again. She smiled. "You can tell me." She held up a finger: "You're a stranger, from far away. You've been proven and scarred in battle. You carry that . . . that which no mortal can. You serve an Old One. And you handled Burs with embarrassing ease, and I do thank you for not making it a matter of blood, because I know you could have killed my brother as easily as you defeated him."

Her brother? Wait— "I thought Burs Erikson is the son of the margrave."

Her brow wrinkled prettily. "Well, of course he is." She touched a finger to his lips. "Now, now, you're just trying to distract me. If you're not the Promised Warrior, why won't you at least deny it?"

It was hard to look into those eyes and deny anything. But to hell with it. "As you wish: I deny it. I'm no Promised Warrior. I'm just ordinary Ian Silverstein," he said. "By your standards, a peasant, although I don't know much about farming. Now, will you answer my question? How can Burs Erikson be your brother?"

"By the usual means, I suppose. My father lay with my mother, and most of a year later, out he popped." She cocked her head to one side. "So I call him my brother because he is the son of both my father and my mother—is that called something different where you come from?"

"No, but—" He stopped himself. "The margrave isn't your husband."

"I should say not!" She drew herself up straight. "And what a horrible suggestion; it's very unmannerly." She started to turn away, then turned back, and laughed. "No, no, no—so that's why you've been so . . . shy," she said. "No, I'm not married to my father, Ian Silverstein. I'm the margravine, not the margravess," she said. "I'll be the margravess, someday, when my father dies or abdicates in the favor of my husband, who will be the margrave." She swallowed once, twice, three times. "May I speak bluntly, Ian Silverstein?"

I wish somebody would, he thought. "Please."

"We have a saying: 'The best flowers grow in the humblest manure.' There is no shame in being born of peasant stock, Ian Silverstein. My father was, and is all the more honored among his peers for the length and breadth of his rise of estate.

"It would do my family honor past imagining were we to join with the Promised Warrior, Ian Silverstein, and I think you may well be him, despite your protestations. But even were that not so, were you but Ian Silverstone, slayer of giants, were you merely as brave a man and as accomplished a swordsman as has ever sat at my father's table, were you but such a trivial thing as that," she said, her smile warming him, "still, it would do my family great honor if you were to become my husband."

He opened his mouth, closed it, opened it again.

But I'm a fraud, lady, he thought. But you hardly know me, and I hardly know you, and I have no business being involved in this.

He found himself stammering, and cursing himself silently for his awkwardness.

"Don't underestimate me," she said. She gripped his hands tightly. "Don't think me some fragile inbred flower, Ian Silver Stone, incapable of . . . vigor."

"But—"

"Please." She took a step toward him, and again put her finger to his lips. "Shh. Don't answer now. I'll beg my father to let me accompany you to the Seat and Table; he'll surely agree. Take the time to get to know me; is that too much to ask? Will you not promise to consider me, to *fully* consider me?"

He felt himself blush. "Marta—"

"Please do not make me beg. At least permit me that shred of dignity." Looking him boldly in the eye, she took his hand and held it to her breast. "Please. On the road, there will be time, opportunity. Promise me you won't waste it."

His mouth felt dry. "Of course," he said, his voice more croak than whisper.

And then she was in his arms, her mouth wet and warm on his. Her tongue tasted of orange and mint.

Arnie was waiting up when Ian staggered in.

Ian was still impressed; their "room" had turned out to be a suite at the northwest corner of the top floor of the residence tower; apparently, somebody who *might* be this Promised Warrior got first-class lodging for himself, his companion, and his manservant.

The sleeping rooms off the sitting room were small and plain, each with barely enough space for a bed, a porcelain thunder-mug, and a nightstand that looked more like a coffee table to Ian—and was at just the right height for barking his shins on; but the sitting room was easily thirty feet by fifteen, and despite the two loveseats, the scattering of low tables, and what looked for all the world like a newly recovered overstuffed armchair, just like the one in Arnie's living room in Hardwood, there would have been enough room to ride a bicycle around the softly carpeted floor, as long as you rode carefully.

Riding carefully would have been a good idea, in any case. If you didn't run the bike into the fireplace, you could end up going through the French doors—whatever they called them here—that opened on a balcony outside.

That didn't make a lot of sense, though—would whoever designed this place want to leave it so vulnerable to entry?

Well, you couldn't figure out everything, and asking about the castle's defenses might not be the dumbest thing a visitor could do, but it would have to be pretty high on the list.

Arnie looked up from his sewing. Sewing?

The question must have shown in Ian's face, because Arnie nodded. "Yes, sewing," he said. "I lost a button off my shirt somehow or other—but I just snipped off the neck button and moved it down. I also ripped the hem of my pants on the road this morning, and rather than stomping all over it, I figured to repair it a little." He bit off the end of the thread. "Particularly since the Thorsens were kind enough to put good solid curtain thread—at least, that's what Ephie used to call it—in the sewing kits."

"I'm sure you could have gotten somebody to do it for you," Ian said.

The old man chuckled, and shook his head. "Well, I could have, but it seemed to me to be a better idea to go down to the kitchen and beg a needle and thread." He picked up a small wooden box from the table, opened it to reveal a half dozen balls of thread and a red velvet pincushion stuck with so many needles that it looked like a porcupine.

"But . . ." Ian raised his hands in mock surrender as Arnie shut the box with a decided snap. "I don't get it. You have needles and thread, so you went and asked for some that you're not going to use."

Arnie's grin must have hurt his face. "Well, I'd rather use this stuff from home, sure," he said. "The thread's solid, and it's reliable, and the needle's sharp. But if I didn't go down the back stairs and wander about looking for somebody on staff to help me, I wouldn't have spent a couple hours in the kitchen, watching Cook boning a couple of geese for tomorrow's dinner, and wouldn't have had a chance to chat with her about what's going on with the noble-folk." He nodded. "It was kind of nice, really," he said. "I used to finish up the day's paperwork at the table in the kitchen while Ephie made supper." His face grew somber. It didn't take a mindreader to figure out that Arnie had just reminded himself of how much he missed his wife.

Ian didn't know what to say. "Everybody seems to be a step or three ahead of me today."

He looked over at the door to Ivar del Hival's room at the far end of the sitting room.

"No, he's not back yet. Probably found one of the castle's ladies to entertain him," Arnie said. His face wrinkled into a frown. "Ivar seems to find himself comfortable no matter where he is." He set his work aside, rose, and stretched. But it wasn't the motion of an old man, working his body to feel for what made the pain of joints and muscles less intrusive; it was just a stretch.

Ian had read once about the close correlation of retirement to death. Perhaps it was burned into the genes: when you stopped working, when you stopped providing for the next generation, maybe the biological clock started to unwind.

Well, if that was it, Arnie was at least anecdotal evidence that the reverse seemed to work. His face was no less lined than it had been, and his hair hadn't lost any of its gray, but he seemed younger, somehow.

Arnie knelt over by the fireplace, and poked at the burning logs with a trident-shaped poker for a moment, then added another log. Sparks flew, some escaping to die on the half-circle of polished stone that lay in front of fireplace. "About time to turn in, isn't it?"

Ian smiled. "I haven't needed anybody to set my bedtime for a few years now." But Arnie was right. He should go to bed.

Arnie shrugged. If Ian didn't want to go to bed, he wasn't going to nag him. "Fine. So? You have an interesting dinner?"

Ian thought about discussing Marta and her proposal with Arnie, but it was just too strange, too unlikely. It would sound like he was bragging, or something. Well, it would be bragging, come to think of it.

"It was fun."

Arnie chuckled. "Well? You engaged yet?"

Ian must have let his surprise show on his face, because Arnie laughed. "Amazing what you can learn from a talkative cook if you know when to nod and say 'tell me more.' "

Ian had been surprised enough for one day. "I'm going to bed."

"Not quite yet," Arnie said. He held up a familiar-looking square plastic packet, then tossed it to Ian, like a tiny Frisbee. "You keep a couple of these with you from now on, and that means on your person, not in your rucksack," he said, smiling at Ian's embarrassment. "Hey, really; it's okay, Ian, honest." The smile dropped away, to be replaced by a very professional-looking expression of almost judicial disinterest. "Really. You work in a pharmacy for a decade or three, you learn real quick what a young fellow having trouble asking for condoms looks like, and you eventually even learn what a young fellow who ought to be asking for condoms but doesn't quite have the presence of mind looks like."

"But—"

"But nothing," Arnie said, the professional demeanor gone, the easy smile back in place. "She's real pretty, and you're a guy, and it'll happen when she wants it to. So remember the Boy Scout motto, and be prepared."

The room was cold, but the warming-plate Arnie had—with both a heavy pair of tongs and a friendly snide comment about the duties of a manservant—taken out of the fireplace and then slipped into its soft cover would keep him warm.

By the flickering light of a gently hissing candle, Ian stripped to the buff and stretched out on the bed, pulling the thick comforter over himself.

He blew out the candle, and tried to sleep.

Maybe it all made sense. A long time ago, one of the Old Ones—some said it was Tyr, some Niord, some that it was Odin himself—had promised to send the Vandestish a warrior to lead them in conquest in all directions, starting with the Cities of the Dominion.

They had been waiting, not exactly patiently, ever since.

It couldn't be just any warrior, of course; it would be somebody special, somebody who proved himself by acts beyond what one could expect from an ordinary mortal.

Like, say, easily defeating a talented Vandestish swordsman without working up a sweat.

Like, say, killing a fire giant.

Like, say, carrying a god's weapon without it turning on him.

All of it was phony, of course; a skilled foil fencer should be able to defeat somebody like Burs, who was basically an épée player, nine times out of ten—at foil. And while Ian had killed the fire giant, that had mainly been a matter of luck, not skill. And as to him carrying Gungnir, the blister on his arm proved that it was safe only as long as he was wearing Freya's gloves.

Ian Silverstein was no Promised Warrior. He wasn't the useless loser that his father had always said he would be, but he wasn't a legendary hero, either.

But he was still a killer of a fire giant. And he still carried Gungnir, at least for a while. That made a difference here.

And if he wasn't schooled in the sometimes Byzantine politics of the Table and the Seat, that wouldn't bother a margravine who had been raised to handle not just money, the way she would have in the Middle Dominions, but politics as well. Shit, for her, it might be better if he was the brave and stupid type. All he would need to do would be to live long enough to impregnate her with a girl for an heir, and if after that he managed to get himself killed in some battle, well, Marta could rule the Hinterlands as margravess, so long as she had an heir.

And even if he didn't marry her, a child by a hero would bring a certain cachet to her house. The concept of bastardy didn't really apply in Vandescard; while men exercised the power—or, perhaps, thought they did—inheritance was through the women. The first daughter of the margravess was the margravine, and it didn't matter who the father was.

And shit, men would quite literally fight for the chance to raise a child of somebody who might have been the Promised Warrior, particularly since marrying a margravine would make one a margrave.

Ian shook his head and sighed. It would be nice to be valued for something real, instead of for having been at the wrong place at the wrong time, and being lucky enough to survive it.

But . . . no. Let the day be over; he needed his sleep.

They'd leave for the Seat in the morning, and Ian had no doubt that Marta would come with them.

His last thought, as sleep overtook him, was that it looked likely to be one hell of a second date.

CHAPTER THIRTEEN

Harbard's Landing

There is always something sweet about the smell of country air after a storm, Torrie thought. Maybe it was the ozone in the air, or maybe there was something in the trees that needed moisture to release it, but that smell was always unique, yet always the same.

Or maybe it was heading out into a sunny morning, having come through a storm safe and dry. Hell, dry socks were as much a trophy as a deerskin could be—they announced, albeit modestly, that you knew how to take care of yourself when the weather got wicked.

The stones that made up the trail had been washed clean by the rain; as long as they could keep to the trail, they wouldn't have to worry about just how much water the ground had soaked up.

And, once again, Torrie could make out the woodchopper, ahead.

Dad didn't look quite so old and tired this morning; a good night's sleep had recharged him, and by the time Torrie had walked far enough to stretch himself out and get into a decent hiking pace, Dad had done the same; there was a positive spring in his step.

Maggie's hair was pulled back, tightly, the way she always wore it when she hadn't had a chance to wash it the night before. She looked kind of overly serious that way, and Torrie's fingers itched to loosen her ponytail.

But not in front of his father.

The chopping sound continued, as it had the day before. Harbard, apparently, was laying in enough firewood for the next century or something.

Overhead, a black bird circled.

Maggie caught him looking at it.

"You think that's one of those ravens?" she asked. "Or maybe a crow?"

"Well, if it's a crow, you won't make any enemies by bringing it down." The rule that Torrie had been taught was that you were allowed to shoot a crow only when it was either damaging crops or about to damage crops. Honisted's Rule was that a crow who wasn't damaging crops was always about to damage crops. Old John Honisted used to claim that it was a matter of law, and always kept a .22 in a saddle-holster next to him on the front seat of his cop car, but Torrie never quite bought that.

But still, no farmer anywhere would complain about a traveler shooting a crow, a rat, a woodchuck, a deer, or any other crop-destroying pest. And if it happened to be Hugin or Munin, Torrie very much doubted that an ordinary arrow could bring it down, even if Maggie could reach it, which he doubted almost as much.

On the other hand . . .

Well, it really didn't matter if there was another hand, because Maggie had quickly unstrung her bow, nocked a broadheaded arrow, drawn back the bowstring until the arrowhead almost touched the bow's grip, and loosed the arrow without even a hint of a plucking sound.

For a moment the arrow seemed to accelerate as it rose into the blue sky, but the target bird spread its wings wide, putting itself into a steep bank that became a tight circle, and as the arrow paused at the height of its climb, the bird snatched it out of the sky, then folded its wings and dropped into a long stoop that ended with a vigorous beating of wings as the bird landed on the road a few yards in front of Maggie.

It was raven, not a crow. Crows don't grow to be the size of a German Shepherd.

The raven dropped the arrow to the ground and stared up at them with beady, unblinking eyes. It was a huge bird, its feathers an inky, glossy black. And it was not at all pretty.

"This is yours, I believe," the bird said. "Although I hesitate to mention that I'm not thrilled by being shot at, which was clearly your intention."

"I thought you were a crow," Maggie said.

"I am Hugin, a raven, at your service." The bird ducked its head in what could have been a nod of agreement with itself, or a bow. "Although both Thought and Memory have been known to make mortals nervous." It ruffled its feathers, and twisted its neck until it could reach a spot just under the wing with its beak. "Thorian del Thorian," it said, turning to Dad, and then to Torrie, "and Thorian del Thorian, again, I greet you. I'd suggest we hurry, for I believe I know someone who is eager to meet you."

Hugin leaped into the air, his broad wings flapping maniacally, and with a harsh cry of "Follow me . . ." flapped off toward Harbard's Landing.

The chopping sound stopped as they walked around the cottage.

For a moment, Torrie almost didn't recognize the man who stood there, wearing only hiking boots and blousy drawstring pants, his dark torso slick with sweat, glistening in the sun. He looked sort of like a pale, skinny John Henry—

It was! "Uncle Hosea!" Torrie said, rushing up and hugging him. "You're okay."

Uncle Hosea's hug was stronger, firmer than Torrie could

remember it being. It made him feel like he was six again. "Yes, Thorian, I'm quite well." He stepped back and held Torrie at arm's length, looking him up and down. "And it appears you're doing well, also. Am I wrong or have you actually gotten taller over the past few months?"

"I doubt that," Torrie said with a smile. "Maybe you've shrunk a little."

"That would seem unlikely," Hosea said. "All things considered."

Maggie took a step forward and clasped hands with him. "It's so good to see you again, Hosea," she said.

"That it is." Dad nodded. "There was some concern, old friend. But it seems as though the air and soil of Tir Na Nog have treated you gently."

Hosea's smile wasn't quite as wide as Torrie was used to, but it still warmed him inside. "That they have, Thorian. I've missed that." He set the sledgehammer down on the chopping-stump and mopped at his sweaty chest with a soiled rag. "Come inside; I have a pot of soup simmering, and some of yesterday's bread to mop it up with."

Dad's forehead wrinkled. "Is . . . *he* about?"

"No." Hosea shook his head. "He is off somewhere, for at least a few days, I'm sure. Come; we have much to discuss."

They ate dinner in the flickering light of the fireplace. It would have been possible to light any of the lamps, but Dad had argued against it; best not to use up what appeared to be Harbard's small supply of lamp oil.

It was good to spend a night out of the cold, and with plenty of hot food to fill the belly and warm him in ways more than physical. That was one of the funny things about camping out, whether it was in Vandescard or over in Minnesota in the BWCA—when you finally got to eat a hot meal with a solid roof over your head, it somehow felt as good as it tasted.

Torrie used his last piece of bread to mop up the last of what Hosea had called soup but what he would have called a thick stew. There had been plenty of it, and it was rich with chunks of meat, hunks of onion, and slices of slippery tree ear, but it wasn't up to Hosea's usual standards. It was kind of bland before Torrie had added some of the peppers—white, red, and black—from the spicer in his kit.

Then again, Torrie figured that Hosea deserved to be cut some slack. Even though he looked good, he had been through a lot, and was working in a kitchen that not only was primitive, but was somebody else's.

Maggie toyed with the spicer before opening one compartment—Torrie couldn't see which, but he would have guessed the cayenne—and sprinkling some powder over the last of her soup.

Dad had long since finished. He seemed to have three modes for eating. On Thanksgiving, or Christmas, or Midsummer, when the Thorsen house was usually filled with guests for a celebratory meal, he would take hours at the table, pacing himself so that he would always have room for the next course, no matter how many there were, enjoying each dish slowly, carefully, decidedly, whether it was something as simple as boiled potatoes or as complicated as that boned-turkey-stuffed-with-a-boned-duck-stuffed-with-a-boned chicken thing that made Ingrid Orjasaeter, who had found it in some Cajun cookbook, Hardwood's favorite invitee for a potluck supper.

For family suppers, he would only nibble at appetizers, and later at dessert, filling up with neither haste nor leisure on the main course and whatever green vegetable was put in front of him, as though he was eating for two patient people. Which, since he tended to expend enough energy for three, left him in awfully good shape for a man of his many years—Dad would be fifty pretty soon, hard as that was to believe.

For informal, catch-as-catch-can meals, a third mode came

into play: he would simply wolf down whatever he could get his hands on until he was full, and then he would get back to whatever he was doing. When Dad was busy with a project of any sort, food was just a distraction.

For whatever reason, this meal seemed to have fallen into that third category; Dad had mechanically gobbled down his bowl of stew or soup along with a hunk of bread, then washed it down with about a quart of water before excusing himself from the table to unpack, sort, and repack their rucksacks.

Torrie could have told him that everything was okay—the rubberized canvas bags that had protected the rucksacks during the storm would have kept them dry at the bottom of a lake—but there was no point in arguing with Dad once he set his mind to something. Stubbornness ran on both sides of the family.

"So," Hosea said, as he stacked the dirty dishes carefully, "you were not happy with your mother's behavior in all of this."

"Understatement, Uncle Hosea," Torrie said, "is the least clever kind of humor, somebody once told me."

"Oh?"

"I believe it was you."

"So it might have been, at that." Uncle Hosea picked up the stack of dishes and carried it to the fireplace. Two cast-iron pots were already bubbling as they hung from their pivots over the fire. Hosea simply swung the arm out, carefully slipped the dirty dishes into one pot, and swung it back. Torrie looked for the tongs that he would need in order to move the dishes from their first bath to their second, but couldn't find it—perhaps Harbard used the wood tongs for that.

"But Ian, and Arnie, and Ivar del Hival—"

"Will be well, I'm sure," Uncle Hosea said. "Harbard hardly sent them empty-handed on their errand. I'm sure they will simply deliver his message to . . . whoever runs things in Vandescard these days, and come right back." He spread his hands. "You could go after them, I suppose, but I see little need."

Maggie's mouth twitched. "I think we know Ian a little better than you do, Hosea. He can get into trouble drinking a beer in a bar."

Torrie shook his head. "Maggie, that's not—"

"That's not your opinion," she said, a definite snap in her voice. "It's mine. I'm entitled to it."

"Yes, you are, Maggie," Uncle Hosea said. "And it's certainly true. But I think that this is not a time when you should worry."

"But—"

Maggie's hand gripped Torrie's thigh hard enough to hurt, cutting him off.

But it wasn't fair. For one thing, Ian didn't drink, at all. For another, he wasn't the getting-into-trouble type. That probably went with the territory—Ian had been self-supporting so long that he weighed any expense of effort in the light of what reward it might bring, and picking a fight or even responding to somebody else trying to make trouble didn't pay—

—Outside of the *salle d'armes.*

Well, there, of course, it was different. If you wanted to make your food and rent money tutoring novice and intermediate foil players—and Ian pretty much had to; the days when somebody could put himself through school on some sort of minimum-wage job had vanished probably about the time that disco died—you not only had to be a good and patient teacher, but you had to be able to beat anybody short of a master fencer, just for the advertising benefit, and it definitely paid to be aggressive not only on the fencing strip, but in getting there. Not mean, not hostile, not cruel—but it paid to show a presence.

"Still, though," Uncle Hosea said, "while I can assure you Ian and his companions are safe, there is something you might want to do. It's just in a different direction; that's all."

"Oh?"

"I think your grandfather, Thorian del Orvald, would like to know that . . . Harbard is trying to keep the peace. He is, so it's said, very much in the confidence of the Scion, and his counsel might help keep the Scion from being . . . precipitous, perhaps, in his concern about developments along the border." He looked over at Dad. "I am concerned that the Crimson and Ancient Cerulean companies could be assembled, and that would be threatening. Even if they might not be what they once were, they might give a decent account of themselves in battle."

"A decent account?" Dad lifted his head from his work. "They might do that, or more than that. Perhaps much more. It would be a mistake to underestimate the Crimson and Ancient Cerulean companies, I think."

"Indeed." Uncle Hosea smiled. "I guess one who once trained many of them in the rudiments of swordsmanship would know better than I."

Dad smiled. "Yes, he would, at that." He picked up a first-aid kit from the pile of unchecked equipment, both looked and felt inside, then snapped it closed, adding it to the second pile. "But it is more than that, as you should know. We folk of Middle Dominions are perhaps not what we once were, but there is something of the old spirit in us, at times." His eyes seemed focused on something far away. "Men have underestimated that in the past, and some may well do so in the future."

Hosea nodded soberly. "Yes, there is truth in that. So you agree that it would be better to leave for the Cities than to follow Ian and his friends."

Dad was starting to nod, when Maggie leaned forward. "No," she said. "You can't ask Mr. Thorsen to do that." She laid a hand on Dad's arm. "Hosea is an old friend of yours. There's no need to take offense."

Dad raised an eyebrow. "Oh?"

"Yes," she said, gesturing at Hosea. "He meant no harm. But Ian left so hurriedly, so precipitously," she said, turning back to Uncle Hosea, "because your wife pressured him." She raised a hand to forestall Hosea's objection. "I know; I know. You were in horrible shape when Ian and Arnie took you through. But Torrie would have been home if his mother had tried to get in touch with us." She placed both of her palms on the table and rose. "It's a matter of honor: If Ian gets hurt, even by accident, it would be Mr. Thorsen's shame—he and Torrie should have been the ones to go."

Torrie nodded. Looking at it that way, Maggie was right. As a matter of honor, it was incumbent upon them to see to Ian. He didn't mind that. It was just that she had made it sound like it was, well, Ian's fault for getting into trouble, and it wasn't.

Dad was frowning. "I see your point, Maggie." He turned back to Uncle Hosea. "You wouldn't want me to leave such a matter to your judgment, would you?"

Uncle Hosea nodded, accepting it with good grace. "Your point is well taken." He stood, and gestured at the four leather-and-wood bedframes stacked by the side of the room. "I'll take mattress bags out and gather straw. Let me offer you the shelter of Harbard's home for the night. You'll leave in the morning, I take it?"

"We shall all leave in the morning," Dad said, firmly.

"No." Hosea shook his head. "I am better than I was, old friend. But I need more days of hard work, much food, and deep sleep, rather than of tramping along the road." He raised a hand, palm out, to forestall an objection. "And there is some danger here, for me. Not all would believe that I am . . . not what I used to be. It would be best if I remain here." He looked at the door. "I am under his protection here, and that means quite a lot, here and now, even if it's not what it should have been."

Dad and Uncle Hosea locked eyes for a long moment, but then Dad shrugged. "As you wish, Orfindel. As you wish."

"It is not as I wish, but as it must be. Soon, soon, I'll be well enough to leave." He rose. "But for now, you have eaten, and now you should sleep."

Maggie gestured at the floor by the fireplace. "Torrie and I will just use the floor there, if that's okay," she said. "I don't think it's necessary we pretend to sleep alone, do you?"

Torrie hoped the flickering firelight kept Dad and Uncle Hosea from seeing him blush.

Closing the door behind her upon her return from the outhouse, Maggie dropped the bar over the single door, then quickly stripped down to a tight T-shirt and panties, and then slipped under the blankets next to Torrie.

Torrie was already half-asleep, but when she slipped her arms around him and put her mouth next to his ear, he woke up, one hand sliding down her back until it cupped her bottom.

"Not now," she whispered. "Don't start something we're not going to finish, not with your father and your uncle sleeping in the same room."

"Then what—"

"Take your pick," she whispered again, her breath warm in his ear. "Do you want first watch or second?"

Now that was paranoid. "If Uncle Hosea or Dad thought we needed—"

"Shh. First or second?"

He could argue with Maggie. Hell, he could refuse to play; he could just tell her that he was going to get some sleep, and that she could do what she wanted. But Maggie was mule-stubborn, and she would, sure as anything, keep herself awake all night, and be oh-so-incredibly pleasant about it in the morning.

"I'll take first watch," he said. "You next, then—"

"No," she whispered again. "Me next, then you. Just the two of us."

"Okay," he whispered back. "But . . ."

She had already closed her eyes and relaxed in his arms. Either she was sleeping or pretending to sleep.

What the hell was going on?

Torrie stroked her hair gently. He could fall asleep now, but he had already had one lesson for the day on a matter of honor.

He sighed. Women. Can't live with them, and can't outsmart them.

CHAPTER FOURTEEN

To the Seat

I t was too easy so far; there had to be a catch, Ian thought, as the coach rattled along.

Ian sat facing backwards, Gungnir's butt-end wedged in at the juncture of the seat and wall of the coach, its point projecting a couple of feet out the starboard window. That way, Ian could keep both gloved hands on it, making sure he never let it go.

It was crowded in the coach—he was almost knee to knee with Marta—but it wasn't really uncomfortable, particularly when you compared it to horseback.

He wasn't sure what the tires were made of, but they were definitely inflated, and soft, and took most of the bounce out of the road. Much better than riding a horse, his still-aching butt bouncing against a hard saddle with every step of the animal, holding Gungnir with its butt-end in the little cup attached to the right stirrup, all the while worrying about what would happen if his gloved right hand were to let go, even for just a moment.

He had spent part of one summer helping D'Arnot rewire D'Arnot's uncle's house—for not enough money; but D'Arnot was Ian's meal ticket—with the constant fear that he would sometime grab hold of a live wire and spend the very short rest of his life frozen to it while electricity coursed through his body.

This was like that, but much worse. One slip, one moment of carelessness, one goddamn sneeze and Gungnir would have been tumbling through the air to maim, to kill.

This way, at least if he screwed up, he endangered only himself. What with Gungnir wedged in tightly, it would be Ian that suffered, and not the folks riding alongside, and not Arnie Selmo and Marta, sitting across from him.

"You appear to be thinking deep thoughts, Ian Silverstone," Marta said.

She was dressed for the road in what Ian would have called culottes—although that probably wasn't the name; they were brown trousers, but cut very full, so that the effect was more like an ankle-length skirt—topped by an almost glaringly white blouse with a biblike bodice sewed on. The sleeves were large and blousy, cuffed tightly at the wrists; and a cummerbund-like belt emphasized her trim waist. A perfectly reasonable outfit for riding—and for Ian to drool over.

"Hardly deep, Marta," Ian said.

"Yeah," Arnie Selmo muttered, his voice low, "my guess is you're thinking about what the goo they served us for breakfast was. Is. Whatever. Jellied eel? Chicken-flavored Jell-o? Give me plain shredded wheat any time."

Arnie had skipped his morning shave, and he looked like a derelict, albeit a very well-dressed one—his jeans and plaid shirt had been laundered and pressed while he slept, and the plain white buttons on his shirt had been replaced by slightly larger, oval ones that looked to be carved from bone.

Marta gave an empty smile at that. Which didn't—

Ah. Arnie had spoken in English. Which was a secret language, as far as most local people were concerned, sort of like the way Ian's Zayda Saul and Baba Rivka used to chatter in Yiddish, knowing full well that neither Ian nor his father could follow.

Ian nodded, as though agreeing with both of them. "I'm more

concerned about how easy this is going, so far," he said, in English to Arnie, then shook his head as he turned to Marta and switched back to Bersmål. "Not at all, Marta. Just thinking about the . . . weighty responsibility that carrying this is." He made sure his gloved left hand gripped Gungnir tightly before patting it with his equally gloved right. He had to let a hand go every now and then, or his fingers would start to cramp up.

"Yeah," Arnie said. "It's been easier than I thought it would. It's about like *he* said it would be."

"And you don't trust him."

Arnie snorted. "You could say that."

Marta cocked her head to one side, her smile fading a trifle. "Might one ask what you two are discussing?"

Ian forced a smile. "I was telling Arnie that I hope things go well."

"I'm sure it will, when you appear in front of the Table. Given who I think you are." She dismissed his coming objection with a smile and a toss of her head that flicked her hair with an almost audible snap. "Yes, yes, I know you deny it, and I would be the last to call you forsworn. But there's nothing in any prophecy I know of that swears that the Promised Warrior will proclaim himself, or will even know what he is."

Outside, the twisting forest roads had given way to a straight highway across flat land, several feet above the fields to either side. It would have reminded Ian of North Dakota, except that the far-off horizon was covered by a mountain range that vanished into the clouds.

Ivar del Hival's broad face was suddenly bobbing at the window. "Enjoying the ride as much as I am?"

Apparently, riding a horse was yet another one of the big man's talents; he seemed to honestly be enjoying himself, despite the fact that he was leaning off to the side of a horse in a way Ian wouldn't even have considered, anchored only by his feet in the stirrups and his one hand that not only held the reins, but gripped the reinforced loop on the front of the saddle where Ian would have expected a saddlehorn to be.

"Our noble leader has suggested we stop for a midday meal at the village ahead," he said, his voice its usual boom, "and hopes that that will meet with the agreement of both the margravine and the herald."

"Sure." Ian nodded. "Fine with me."

"If that pleases Ian Silver Stone," Marta said, "it could hardly fail to delight me." Her forehead wrinkled prettily. "I've not taken this route to the Table since I was a little girl, but I do recall a local specialty we've had at table every now and then." She leaned forward, as though about to confide a great secret. "It's a fish the locals call a firemouth—they breed them, grow them in ponds, then season the filets with some secret combination of herbs; they then smoke them until they're barely cooked through. The herbs and the timing are apparently a matter of some great art; when Cook attempted to get the recipe some years ago, she was told that it would take a direct command from my father." She dismissed that idea with a flick of the fingers. "Who is, of course, much too wise to put himself in the position of depriving people of something in which they put so much pride."

That sounded sensible, come to think of it, although it wasn't the way Ian would have done things, if he was in charge. Then again, ruling villages, or a margravature, or, well, anything, wasn't something he had ever given a lot of attention to.

He sighed. It didn't really matter. Whatever he was, it wasn't this Promised Warrior, and it didn't much matter what he would do if he was, because he wasn't.

He wished he could convince Marta of that. It would be one thing for his exaggerated real history to eventually bring her to his bed—hell, in the final analysis, he had killed the fire giant, after all, and if one of the benefits that came with that was Marta naked in his arms, well, he could live with that.

But Ian had never been the type to use "I love you" as a seduction line, and "I'm the Promised Warrior" seemed every bit as dishonest. He could lie by omission, he supposed, but— No. You are what you do.

He leaned forward, his hands clenched on the spear. "Listen, please. I'm not any Promised Warrior. I've done what I've done, and if that makes you think me special, somehow" —she smiled at that— "that doesn't bother me at all." There was something about looking into her eyes that made it difficult to breathe. He swallowed, hard, then forced himself to continue. "But I'm *not* what you people think I am," he said, surprised by the fire in his own voice. "I don't mind what your father or your brothers think, but you have to believe me. *You* have to."

The ring on his thumb pulsed, as it had before. Once, twice, three times, in time with his heart. And then again.

For a moment, her eyes seemed to fog over, and then she nodded.

"I believe you," she said, laying her hand over his.

But it doesn't matter, her eyes said.

Lunch was eaten on two benches, one on either side of a narrow weather-beaten table outside of a long wattle-and-daub building Ian supposed was a tavern, although nobody had specifically called it that.

The contrast of the tables, which looked to Ian more like picnic tables than anything else, and the fancy clothes, made him smile. Ian associated picnics with shorts, jeans, t-shirts, and sneakers; with awkward plastic eating-ware and leaky paper plates, not with fine spun-glass plates, handblown glasses, and silver eating-prongs all gleaming in the sun, a tight-woven linen tablecloth fluttering like a butterfly in a light breeze.

Vandescardian meals were, at least among the nobility, a formal affair: Marta had changed into a filmy white dress that wouldn't have looked out of place at a prom, while all twenty of their soldier-bodyguards had changed from their road leathers into silken robes and blousy pantaloons that Ian would have been more likely to wear to bed than to table.

But each to his own. If anybody noticed that Ian hadn't dressed for lunch, no comment was made. Nor was any comment made about the way that a small corral outside the tavern had been cleared of horses so that Ian could plant Gungnir, point down, in the center of it, with a watching soldier, in leathers and livery, on each of its four sides.

As road food went, the meal wasn't bad. Hell, as good restaurant cooking went, it was pretty good. The local specialty had sounded more like lox than anything else, but it turned out to be some white-fleshed fish that looked like a miniature flounder, and tasted richer and meatier than any fish Ian had ever had. The thick green sauce that went with it was served in little mussel shells, and was hot and pungent, with a delayed kick that cleared the sinuses and made the eyes water.

The talk was of politics, mainly. There seemed to be endless jockeying for position among the nobles who had seats at the Seat, so to speak, and who were collectively known as the Table. It was hard to keep them straight, as the majority of them were Tyrsons, and were referred to as such, always. Ian thought he'd figured out that there were three different Erik Tyrsons—the margrave he had met, and two others, one called a count and another a count-wanting, until Marta explained that there actually were *four* at the Table.

Ivar del Hival held court down at the far end of the table, drinking seemingly endless glasses of wine while encouraging his soldier-audience to try to keep up with him. Ian couldn't help feeling disgusted by their boozy laughter, but he tried to write that off as just a matter of his own prejudice against drunks.

"I have to wonder what you're so angry about," Marta said, leaning toward him. Her hair smelled of roses and lemon. She had chosen to sit on Ian's right—or, more accurately, she had beckoned Ian to sit on her left, putting him at the left end of the bench.

"Nothing," he said, with a sigh. "Nothing much." He fingered the silver clamp that held the corner of the tablecloth tightly to the table.

"Of course it's nothing much," she said. "You merely glared at your friend Ivar del Hival as though you wished him dead, then shook your head as though to reprove yourself for doing so." Her smile mocked him, but the twinkle in her eyes took any sting out of it.

Remind me never to play poker with you, Ian thought. "It was nothing much."

"Yes," she said. "I know. Were it anything serious, you would have called for him to take up a sword."

Ian would have sworn that Ivar del Hival couldn't have heard her low-pitched voice down at the other end of the table, but the big man had lurched to his feet, and beckoned to one of the soldiers, a blocky man with the sort of V-shaped physique that Ian associated with those idiot bodybuilders who spent hours on hours in the gym trying to make already bulky muscles bulge just a little bit more.

Practice swords were produced, and Ivar del Hival and his opponent squared off, saluted, and dropped into en garde.

It was fun to watch Ivar del Hival fence, particularly if you'd seen him in action before. As Ian had expected, he spent a few moments fiddling around in between teaching his opponent his beat-and-feint-to-the-open-line routine, then followed it up with a beat-feint-and-lunge that scored squarely in the middle of the chest. A better fencer would have ignored Ivar del Hival's attempt to dominate the match and played his own game, but on the next point, the blockhead tried to turn Ivar del Hival's act against him, and Ivar waited for the real attack, and then, moving faster than somebody would have credited him as capable of, took one step backward to parry, forcing the other's blade down, out and up, then took a quick bouncy step forward, completing the touch.

Ian had to chuckle. Ivar del Hival had been learning foil fencing from Ian at the same time Ian had been learning swordfighting from Ivar. And for somebody who had had as much to drink as Ivar had, he was moving awfully well.

"He's quite good," Marta said, as Ivar tossed his sword to one of the waiting servants, then returned to the table, a thick arm thrown around his former opponent's shoulder.

Ian nodded. "That he is."

"But you are better." Her smile was vaguely challenging, as though she didn't quite believe what she was saying.

"Is that so?" Ivar del Hival's voice boomed down the length of the table. He was back on his feet. "I hear that you think you can still beat me, even on a glorious day like today."

Ian shrugged. He did pretty well against Ivar, even when they sparred by épée or freestyle rules, which much more closely mimicked a real duel. It had taken some work—Ian had had to put aside a lot of his foil repertoire—but his slightly greater reach and his much greater speed gave him a natural advantage against Ivar del Hival's greater strength. Yes, all things being equal, any advantage could be telling, but all things weren't equal, and swordfighting wasn't arm wrestling.

"Could be," he said, rising.

"Let's see," Ivar del Hival said, beckoning for the return of the practice swords.

Ian held up a finger. "Just give me a minute to stretch out." Well, even though local practice didn't include the protective equipment that Ian wouldn't have considered stepping on a fencing strip without, Ian was still more worried about pulling a muscle or straining a tendon through lack of a proper warmup than he was about a bruise from a practice sword tip.

Of course, he probably was in more danger of losing an eye, but . . .

"No," Ivar del Hival said, placing himself so his back was to the people at the table. "Let's just fence, shall we?"

One eye closed in a slow, deliberate wink.

Ian kept his face impassive as he squared off against Ivar del Hival. But he was disgusted with Ivar del Hival for setting this up, and with himself for playing along. He could do whatever he wanted; Ivar del Hival would be fencing to lose, not to win. This wasn't a practice match; it was all about playing up Ian's image, his reputation. Ivar del Hival probably hadn't been drinking as much as he had seemed to, and had been simply planning this all along.

The right thing to do, the moral thing to do, would be to drop the practice sword and return to the table without a word.

Instead, Ian saluted, closed in, and responded to Ivar del Hival's just-barely-telegraphed lunge with a circular parry that left Ivar's practice sword tumbling end over end through the air, Ivar del Hival returning to the table shaking his head in feigned amazement at how easily he had been defeated, and Ian with a victory that tasted like ashes in his mouth.

A sliver of a moon hung high above the lake, a gentle if cold wind rippling its dark, satiny surface, rustling the leaves in the gnarled trees that stood at the edge of the campground like ancient giants, frozen on watch.

The Vandestish nobility treated themselves well, even when it came to camping out. This camping site by the side of a small lake had been improved over the generations to the point where flattened mounds rose a foot or so above the ground to be sure that the tents pitched on them would not be flooded in case of rain. Fire pits had been dug and lined with rock, and cords of wood waited, seasoning, serving for a time as a fence around the campground. One of the creeks that fed the lake had been diverted into a rock-lined channel that snaked through the campground, not only making it possible to catch fresh trout for dinner or scoop up some drinking or washing water, but tinkling and burbling so pleasantly that Ian suspected it had somehow been tuned.

And a marble bench had been erected, so that anybody camping here could sit and admire the night, listen to the creek, and inhale the woodsy smell of banked campfires, and watch a sliver of moon hang in the sky above the lake.

He had been hoping that Marta might join him. He could hardly walk over to her tent and expect to brush past her guards, but it would have been nice to have her company. He could still smell her hair, almost.

Well, there would surely be time to themselves, somewhere between here and the Seat. Just not in a campground with both of her brothers and a troop of soldiers a few yards and fewer thicknesses of cloth away.

The trouble was, there was nobody to talk to. He wasn't comfortable around Marta's brothers—he felt guilty, still, about the way Ivar del Hival had set up Burs Erikson, and Aglovain Tyrson was an older brother who didn't like the way his sister had taken to this stranger, possible Promised Warrior or not. Arnie had turned in, and Ivar del Hival was off swapping lies with some of his new friends.

He should have just felt a little bit lonely, maybe. But why did he feel like such an asshole? The whole point of this had been to get Hosea well, and Ian didn't doubt for a moment that Harbard was as good as his word on that point. And if stopping a war was the price to be paid for that, that wasn't exactly a big moral problem. It wasn't like Ian had been asked to *start* a war. So a few hundred or thousand or hundred thousand innocents who would otherwise have died in battle or as a consequence of it would now likely lead longer lives.

Was this a bad thing? No.

Arnie had a theory that it was going too well, but Ian didn't buy that, not really. Things going well didn't bother Ian, or he couldn't have settled in to Hardwood so well.

A brush fence had been thrown up around the spot at the edge of the campground where Ian had secured Gungnir, and a guard posted, so he didn't have to worry about that.

But he still felt like shit.

Ivar del Hival plopped himself down on the bench next to him.

"Art thou greatly wroth?" he asked.

"Eh?"

"It's from your Bible, Ian. God to Jonah."

"You've read the Bible."

Ivar shrugged. "I've been around. You read a little of this, a little of that. Learn a language or three." He patted at his ample belly. "Back when I was younger and had less of this to haul around, His Warmth used to send me on some errands, here and there." He shook his head and sighed. "Getting too old for this, perhaps, but some of the old skills, the old talents, they stick with you."

"Like faking a disarm."

Ivar del Hival chuckled. "You have a strange faith, Ian. I have heard you claim that this fencing thing was merely a shovel, simply a way to make a living after your father kicked you out."

"Well, it was." Ian had taken it up mainly as yet another regular activity that kept him out of the house, and by the time Benjamin Silverstein had made it clear that he despised this activity just as much as he despised everything else his useless son did, Ian had been hooked. At first, of course, he had expected to become Errol Flynn overnight, but it hadn't taken more than a dozen lessons for him to learn that that wasn't what fencing was all about. There was something beautiful and elegant about fencing, about foil fencing in particular, that suited him.

But then, when he found himself standing outside what no longer was his home, a duffel bag in one hand, his gear bag in his other, a bruise on his left cheekbone matching the one on the knuckles of his right hand, he had had in his pocket $87.50 and the key D'Arnot had given him to what almost everybody else called the fencing studio, but which D'Arnot insisted was a *salle d'armes*. He slept in the supply room that night, his duffel bag for a pillow, and had woken that morning looking at his gear bag, realizing it contained his only salvation. Ian had had no living relatives—and certainly no close friends—it was hard to make friends when you didn't dare bring them home and were too ashamed to ever explain why.

But he could tutor beginning fencers, and that and odd jobs here and there could keep him fed, and get him through the last couple of months of high school, and put him through college.

If he was good enough.

And he was good enough. He had to be.

But in doing that, in making sure he dominated the fencing strips, in being certain that he could regularly defeat any of D'Arnot's other students, in carrying himself with the sureness verging on arrogance that made others willing to spend money for his time and tutoring, the joy had gone out of it. A foil was a tool, that was all.

He patted the hilt of Giantkiller. Until the moment that he had faced the fire giant, with nothing but a blade tempered in the blood of an Old One in his hand, knowing that what it would take would be him, Ian Silverstein—not D'Arnot, not Torrie Thorsen, not anybody else—to save them all, and that he had to do it as a foil fencer, because nothing else would serve, until then the joy had gone out of it.

That had brought it back, until today.

Ivar del Hival was watching him. "Then why do you look like you've bitten into a steak and found half a maggot? Is there something we need to talk about?"

"Nah. It's just me being silly, and glum." Ian shook his head. "It's nothing much, I guess, not really. I've just been a bit . . . spoiled lately. Give me a night to sleep it off and I'll be back to my usual cheery self."

Ivar del Hival clapped a hard hand to his shoulder. "Then go to bed, go to sleep, and let me ruin a whole new day for you tomorrow."

Ian's tent was like the nobles': A-framed, pegged down at all four corners, supported at both fore and aft of the peak by guy ropes that looped over one of the several cables that criss-crossed the campground a dozen feet above his head—they ran between trees on the edge of the campground. It meant that he didn't have to sleep around a tent pole, and he didn't have to worry about tripping over ground-planted tent guys in the dark.

Inside, his gear had been neatly stacked in a back corner of the tent, and sleeping blankets laid out on top of a canvas groundcloth that had been waterproofed with wax.

He quickly stripped and slid under the blankets, unsurprised to find that his bed was already warm. The nobles did well by themselves in this, too; vestri servants had dug up little divots of grass, and placed hot stones from the fireplace inches beneath the surface before replacing the divots.

The social pyramid here came to too sharp a point for Ian's comfort. But it did mean that he would sleep warm.

Ian was never sure if he'd been sleeping, or if she simply slipped into his tent while he was yawning.

But it was her. Even if her outline hadn't been framed in the door of the tent as she dropped the blanket she had wrapped around her, the sliver of moon high in the sky behind her, Ian would have known it was Marta. She smelled of flowers and sunshine, with just a trace of musk.

God, she was lovely in the moonlight.

She turned, and tied the door of the tent shut.

"I thought," she whispered, "you were going to stay up talking to that loud friend of yours all night."

"But—" But what? But her brothers? But her guards?

But what? If it was something that she thought she couldn't handle, she wouldn't be here.

"Shh. I slipped out the back of my tent, and even if somebody saw me, they wouldn't have seen me." She knelt down beside him, then slipped under the blankets. "Still, we must be quiet. Should I make too much noise, Ian, you may silence me as you wish."

And then she was in his arms. Her skin was cold from the night, but only for moments.

When he woke in the golden light of dawn, she was gone.

He didn't think even for a moment that it had been a dream. A dream wouldn't have left a bite mark on the palm of his left hand and on his right earlobe, or scratches on his back.

But he wasn't quite alone. A flower, that on cloudy days would have been called a Stay-Abed, lay, all red and gold and glorious, on the blankets beside him.

CHAPTER FIFTEEN

Storna's Stele

arket day in the village of Storna's Stele was a medley of sights and sounds and, particularly, smells. And tastes.

At the entry to the market a side of something that looked too large to be a cow roasted slowly over an open fire pit. The sweaty proprietor, a magnificently fat man, naked from the waist up, reached out with his tools—a carving knife and a two-tined fork, each tied to the end of what looked to Torrie like four-foot-long chopsticks—and sliced off sizzling hunks, conveying each with a practiced flick to the rough-hewn surface of the serving table. The fat proprietor's assistant—wife? sister? partner?—a lathe-thin woman in a dingy gray dress, quickly sprinkled each slice of meat with a practiced pinch of seasonings from a wooden bowl, then wrapped it along with a few strips of green and red vegetable in what looked like an overlarge pancake, then rolled the whole thing between her palms before exchanging it for a small copper coin from the next person in line, occasionally dipping her fingers into the pockets of her apron to produce change.

Torrie had quenched his thirst at the spring just outside the town gate, but it had been a long time since breakfast at Harbard's Landing. "I could use a quick bite," he said.

Dad nodded. "Wait here." After a quick, appraising look at

the crowd, Dad walked slowly to the front of the line—the crowd parted around him like he was Moses at the Red Sea—and held up three fingers, accepting three of the sandwiches in exchange for a coin from his pouch. He returned to where Torrie stood trying not to gape openmouthed, and handed one of the rolls to Maggie before giving one to Torrie.

They walked on, past a stall where dozens of plump chickens of some unfamiliar breed waited in their wooden cages, while a bald man in a badly bloodstained tunic, his head sunburned and peeling, stroked a sharpening rod up and down an oversized cleaver.

"Dad—"

"Hold for a moment," Dad said. "I haven't seen this for twenty, thirty years."

"You haven't seen a chicken sold?"

"Be still."

A thickset woman in a shapeless peasant's dress, her wicker basket brimming over with bundles of carrots and long, thumb-thick loaves of bread, stopped in front of the chicken seller to argue for a moment, her fingers flashing to and fro as though she was speaking in sign language, although Torrie had no trouble hearing her coarse voice berate the man for his ungenerosity, greed, dishonesty, uncleanliness, and other sins.

Finally, though, the two came to terms with a quick palm-slap of coins, and the seller took a chicken out of its cage and set it on the cutting board. Torrie had seen chickens killed, of course; back home, Sandy Hansen's fried chicken recipe required that the meal had been walking around the coop until very late in the afternoon.

But the chicken seller didn't give its neck the quick practiced wring that Torrie had seen dozens of times before. Instead, he set it down gently on the chopping block in front of him, gave it a quick, affectionate pat—pulling his fingers back to avoid a bite from its attacking beak—then picked up a chunk of chalk and quickly, smoothly drew a straight line on the surface of the chopping block from the chicken to himself.

The bird stood, stock-still, as though it had frozen in place.

But not for long; the chicken seller made a quick movement with the cleaver and a syncopated pat with his free hand, and the chicken fell over, the stump where its head had been briefly gushing blood, while the head arced up into the air, to land on a pile of offal a few feet away.

Dad smiled. "See?"

Torrie shook his head. "Magic?"

"No. It works back home, too. There is something about an absolutely straight-drawn line that seems to hypnotize a chicken." Dad shrugged. "I once tried to teach Sandy how to do it, but she wasn't interested."

The chicken seller produced a short, sharp knife and made a couple of practiced slashes on the body of the chicken. Torrie turned away; he had seen a chicken dressed-out before.

Dad led them through the markets, past a stall piled high with bundles of fresh-picked onions that made Torrie's eyes sting; past a skinny, balding, red-faced potter, his long fringe of hair pulled back into a braid, who smashed a plate against his own knee, shouting that it made more sense to make plates simply to enjoy the sound of them breaking rather than to sell them for the pittance his erstwhile customer had offered; past a leather-aproned cobbler trimming the excess off a fresh sole for a lady's boot; past a skeletally thin little man pushing his two-wheeled wheelbarrow piled high with all-too-ripe horse manure through the parting crowd, his broad, gap-toothed smile in sharp counterpoint to the awful smell . . .

Until they reached what Dad had, apparently, been looking for: a vestri stonemason, busily patching a section of the waist-high stone wall that encircled the market. The vestri was so busy working that it took him a while to notice them, his huge wooden mallet tapping the chisel with quick, precise, measured strokes.

The vestri was a short, thick man, his arms disproportionately long, his forehead strongly sloped; virtually chinless. If it wasn't for the peasant's loose shirt and trousers, the neatly trimmed beard rimming his face, and the finely braided queue of hair that hung down his back, he would have looked exactly like a Neanderthal out of some museum exhibit, although he was smaller than Torrie had thought of Neanderthals as being; erect, even standing straight, the top of his head would have barely reached the middle of Torrie's chest.

Finally, he noticed them, and turned expressionlessly, setting his tools down before touching both index fingers to his brow. "Can I be of some help, Honored Ones?" he said, just a trace of the lisp that was common among his kind.

"I do seek thy help, Son of Vestri," Dad said, in the guttural Vestri language.

Perhaps Dad had learned vestri when he had lived in the Middle Dominions, but more likely his fluency in it, like Torrie's, was yet another example of Uncle Hosea's gift.

The vestri's eyes widened. The vestri, whose status ranged from slaves to serfs to lowborn freemen, depending on where in Tir Na Nog you found yourself, weren't used to humans knowing their language, much less addressing them formally in it.

"Of course, Honored One, of course," he answered in slow, careful Bersmål, "this one will do all he can to be of assistance, but . . ." he spread his hands and gestured at the wall, "the day grows no younger and my work goes no faster while I talk with you. May I?"

"Of course." Dad gave a quick gesture of permission. "Please."

"Son of Man," the vestri said in his own language, as he resumed his work with hammer and chisel, "why doest thou

202

ask of me? I am but Valin, a stonecutter by trade, and surely I know nothing that would be of interest to important ones such as thyselves."

Dad squatted beside him and lowered his voice. "I have no time for this, Valin, Son of Vestri. I need knowledge, and I may well need assistance. Look at me," he said, his voice low, but with a ring to it that Torrie couldn't remember having heard before. "I am Thorian, Thorian's Son, known to some as Thorian the Traitor, but that is not how I am known to the Folk."

The hammer fell from Valin's fingers. "You are ... ? But— it's said that he has long been dead."

Dad just looked at him, his face impassive.

The vestri weren't, by and large, the cleverest folk that ever were, although certainly some were reasonably bright. It took Valin a few moments to decide that such an admission out in public was an awful risk even for somebody who really was Thorian del Thorian, and unlikely to be false. Then again, perhaps Dad really *was* a phony who wanted something, perfectly safe in pleading his innocence if Valin were to raise cry.

The stonecutter's eyes narrowed.

Dad leaned forward and whispered something in Valin's thick ear.

It was as though he had thrown a switch: the vestri immediately gathered all of his tools together, and quickly, neatly, stowed them away in a large canvas bag that he slung, Santa-like, over his shoulder. "Please, Friends of the Father of Vestri, Father of the Folk, do thou come with me," he said, immediately taking off in a quick stride that Torrie had difficulty matching.

The vestri led the three of them down winding streets, past the wall that separated the village proper from the surrounding unchartered settlement, where the cobbled streets were replaced by dirt, and the carefully inset gutters by, well, nothing. Where houses in the village proper were usually wattle and daub set on chest-high stone walls that gave them a solid foundation and kept the base of the walls free from rot, here the houses were only of wattle-and-daubed-over timber frames that tended to rot from the ground up.

At the end of a long row of such houses, Valin stopped, knocked twice on the door, and beckoned them all inside.

Torrie leading, they pushed through a series of damp musty curtains, into an almost total darkness that smelled of old sweat and worse. Maggie gasped, and her slim but strong fingers gripped his hand tightly.

He didn't blame her. At first, all he saw were dozens of eyes, seeming to glow red, glaring unblinkingly.

It took Torrie a few moments for his eyes to adjust; when they did, he saw that they were in a small room, illuminated only by an inch-wide hole in the wall, filled with easily a dozen vestri men lying in stacked hammocks supported by the house's beams. In one corner of the room, a small hearth held an even smaller fire, where two unbathed vestri were stirring a pot of some burbling liquid, and eyeing Torrie, Maggie, and Dad with barely concealed hostility.

It was, Torrie decided, a vestri flophouse.

Dozens of eyes were trained on the three humans, but for a long time, nobody said a word.

Valin dropped his bag to the floor. "I am Valin Stoneworker, son of Burin the Broken, himself the son of Valin One-Ear," he said.

"Yes, yes, yes," an old, gray-bearded vestri said, peering out from under his thin blanket. "You are of sure lineage, and we are but filthy vestri bastards, ones who should count ourselves lucky to know our mothers' names, fortunate beyond wishing if we could so much as guess at our fathers'." A thick hand made a come-on gesture. "And you have some reason to wave rank under our noses, no doubt—" He raised his hand, stopping himself. "No. I forget myself; I do humbly beg *thy* pardon.

Please forgive this one, and remember me as saying: and *thou* has some reason to wave *thy* rank under our humble noses, no doubt . . . and perhaps that has something to do with these Honored Ones," his tone made the polite term a curse, "standing here looking at us as though we were a bunch of ill-washed vestri mongrels." He chuckled thinly. "Which we are, of course."

He gave a push against the wall, setting his hammock rocking, and tumbled clumsily out of it, nevertheless managing to land squarely on his thick, hairy feet.

He spat a huge, disgusting gobbet onto the liver-spotted back of his hand, then wiped it on his blanket. His face was lined with age, and his beard was a dirty gray. He was old, and probably not going to live much longer; vestri didn't tend to show their age until near the end.

"I am called Durin of the Dung," the dwarf said, "of no known lineage or skills; I make my living, such as it is, emptying the chamberpots and excavating the outhouses of the rich and poor alike, conveying their precious contents to dungheaps outside of the village walls." He made a broad bow. "And I am, of course, at thy service, Honored Ones."

"Be still, Durin," another one said. "Valin brought them here for a purpose; would you not care to hear it?"

"I, for one," yet another said, "have labored long and hard until but a few moments ago, and I shall get some sleep." He rolled over in his hammock, gathering his ragged blanket about him, and immediately began to snore quietly.

Valin drew himself up almost straight. "I say to all of you that this Honored One is a friend—"

"Yesyesyes, we all know how friendly the Honored Ones are," Durin said. "Daily, they do me the great favor of permitting me the privilege of carrying away their—"

"—a friend of the Father of Vestri!" Valin shouted.

Nobody spoke for a moment. It was so quiet that Torrie could hear the bubbling of the pot of stew.

"Well," Durin said, "that would be a different matter, would it not." He shuffled over to Dad and eyed him up and down. "There is a story that some years ago, the Father of Vestri was locked in a tiny room, his mind and body tortured once again for knowledge only he holds."

"Yes," Dad nodded. "That he was. Bound with the guts of a god."

"Hmmm . . . and it's also said that a friend of his freed him, and they escaped together." He cocked his head to one side. "Surely, surely he would have given such a close friend, one he cared to reward, some way of proving himself, should the occasion arise."

As he'd done at the market, Dad once again bent over and whispered momentarily into the vestri's ear.

Durin immediately straightened. "Well then," he said, his voice sober and level, all trace of sarcasm gone from his voice, "what would thou have of me, friend of the Father of Vestri? Shall I cut open my belly so that my guts might warm thy tired feet?"

Dad chuckled. "That won't be necessary." He shrugged out of his rucksack and opened it, rummaging for a moment before pulling out a package of freeze-dried beef. He gestured with it toward the burbling kettle. "I ask that we eat together, while you tell me of the ones who have recently passed through. I need to know everything—when did they come through? Where are they? Who have they talked to?"

"Ah." Durin nodded. "Ian the Silver Stone, the one who some say is the Promised Warrior. He and his companions passed through the village in company with a troop led by a One-Hand. There is some little news and, as always, much rumor."

"I need to hear it all."

Durin clapped his hands together four times. "Wake up, all you sluggards. Wake up. Valin, help me wake these lazy ones." He reached out and shook first one hammock, then another, cuffing the dwarf hard with the back of his hand when he didn't immediately wake.

"Wake, I say," Durin said, shaking yet another. "A friend of the Father is here, and he and his companions will honor us by sharing our kettle, and our knowledge." He drew himself up straight, and for just a moment, the slope-headed, smelly little man seemed to radiate dignity. "Even dung has its place. Mongrels we may be, carriers of wood and water and dung we are, but we are still Sons of Vestri."

Between eating and talking—the stew turned out to be quite good, and with the addition of some freeze-dried beef, carrots, and some of the seasonings from their packs, even better—it took some time to get it all told, and more time to get it translated for Maggie's benefit. She had been around Hosea long enough to learn Bersmål, but not Vestri. Hosea's bestowal of his gift of tongues took time.

Finally, Torrie held up a hand. "Let me see if I can get this straight. Ian is going to the Seat and Table, where he's going to tell them that Vandescard isn't to wage a war on the Dominions. There's some rumor that he's this legendary Promised Warrior, who will do just the opposite, and lead the Vandestish in battle with not only the Dominion, but with everybody else, too."

There were grunts of assent from around the table. "So far, so good." He spread his hands. "Since they're not going to kill him for being the bearer of bad news, I guess Uncle Hosea was right; we can just leave the three of them to it." He turned to Dad. "Ian's my friend, but it doesn't sound like he needs any rescuing. Why go looking for trouble?" Particularly given who Dad was. Thorian the Traitor wasn't wanted in Vandescard—

it wasn't Vandescard that he'd betrayed, after all, by releasing Uncle Hosea.

But that didn't mean it would necessarily be wise—or safe—to try to involve themselves in local politics.

Maggie shook her head. "There are two problems with that. How do you think they'll test him for being this Promised Warrior?"

"I don't think they'll test him at all," Torrie said, confused.

Dad looked as puzzled as Torrie felt. "I don't understand."

"That's because you haven't been listening," she said. "Think about it. What is this test they have for membership in this warrior society of theirs, Durin?"

The dwarf shrugged. "I know not. It's called the Pain, and it leaves them one-handed, as Tyr was after he put his hand in the mouth of Fenris-wolf, as hostage." The few of his blunt teeth that remained made a loud clacking sound.

"You think they won't make him try it? That's what they do for their elite warrior society, but they won't test their so-called Promised Warrior that way?"

Valin shook his head. "I think it is thou who doesn't understand, perhaps," he said in Vestri, then switched back to Bersmål when Durin hit him on the forearm in an unsubtle reminder that Maggie didn't speak Vestri. "The girl is right. It is you who doesn't understand. Of course he would be so tested; it is a great honor for an Honored One to become a Tyrson. How could he refuse?"

Dad shook his head. "I strongly doubt that Ian would be interested." He smiled. "I think he would likely decline with thanks, and while that would cause him to lose some . . . status here, I'm certain he could live with that."

"No," Maggie said. "It can't be that way."

Torrie shook his head, realized that he was making the exact same gesture that Dad had just made, and stopped himself. "Why can't it? Just because that would make things too easy?"

She nodded. "Precisely. Why, if it's all so easy, are there, even now, rumors flying about three travelers, two men and a woman, who are up to some evil in Vandescard?"

Durin spread his hands. "I have listened and spoken with care and attention, Honored One, but I've heard no such rumor here."

"The day's not over yet. There will be rumors like that flying around, before nightfall," she said. "We'll maybe be, oh, Dominion spies, or perhaps assassins, seeking to kill the Promised Warrior before he can demonstrate who he is. But there will be rumors, and everyone and anyone will be on the lookout for us, and anyone loyal to the Table and the Seat who believes those rumors will try to stop us, and the rest will try to stop us for the chance of a reward."

Dad shook his head. "I think—"

"No, you don't think," she said, her voice low but intense. "That's the trouble with you. You're a strong man, Mr. Thorsen, and you're brave, and I wouldn't have asked for better . . ." her fingers fluttered as she looked for the right word, ". . . a better companion the day we fought the Fenrir. On your worst day you're probably a better fencer than I'll ever hope to be. And like your son, you're a good man.

"But when either of you turns his goddamn brain off, either because you're thinking with that little head on the end of your penis or because you're too damn comfortable with the people around you, you're easy to fool.

"Your wife did it without working up a sweat. Not because she was all that clever about it. And neither of you would have looked past that, not if Dave Oppegaard and Doc and Minnie and the rest of them hadn't been watching out for you. You're wary around strangers, but any friend could pick your pocket, and if you found his hand in your pants, you'd just assume he was warming his fucking fingers."

Torrie was even more confused. Why all the heat and anger? And why the swearing? Maggie almost never swore.

So he spoke slowly and quietly, but not too slowly or quietly.

"Maggie, please," he said. "What makes you so sure? Why can't it be easy?"

"Because if it was all so easy," she said, her brittle voice holding not a trace of hysteria, "if there was no reason in the world for us to go, why would that asshole pretending to be Hosea have tried to stop us?"

CHAPTER SIXTEEN

↩o↪

The River

Jottendal turned out to be a walled city, the count's castle set on an outcropping high over the Jut. Where the fast-moving Gilfi ran like a swift gray snake through the land, the wide, slow Jut meandered around long, wide bends. But the bends were deep cuts in the land; Castle Jottendal stood on a bank easily a couple of hundred feet above the murky brown surface of the river below. In some things, time and patience could serve as well as youth and vigor.

"You're being quiet again, Ian," Marta said, from her usual seat opposite him in the coach, knee to knee. "And you look sad."

"No, not sad." He shook his head. "I was just thinking about rivers."

"Now, there's a deep subject," Ivar del Hival said. "And a wide and wet one, as well."

Ivar del Hival had taken Arnie's usual spot in the coach with them, while Arnie took a turn in the servant wagon, where he seemed more comfortable. Ian didn't think it was the issue of status, but it was that the servants, both human and vestri, talked more, and Arnie was, above all, a good listener.

Marta arched an eyebrow. "So? What were your thoughts about rivers?"

"Nothing important," he said idly, watching a small barge,

piled high with boxes and bags, making its way downriver, staying toward the center of it, apparently without any effort.

"Oh," she said, her voice cool. "Well, perhaps you will have something important to say to me at some point, perhaps."

When he looked again, the barge was gone.

Local guards, none—as far as Ian could tell—a Tyrson, went through a brief, clearly pro forma conversation with Aglovain Tyrson. It concluded with a handshake and a nod, and then the simple pole blocking the already lowered drawbridge was withdrawn, after which the party was permitted to enter the castle grounds. By the time that the carriage wheels had ground to a noisy halt—the road to the stables was made of flat stones covered with a thin layer of sand, a loud combination—and the passengers disembarked, a welcoming party was already assembled.

The group was led by a broad-shouldered man in crimson tunic and leggings, a short yellow cape thrown across his left shoulder with what looked like practiced casualness.

His smile—white teeth in a salt-and-pepper beard that was barely a finger's width around his broad jaw—was proper, but not overly friendly, until he turned from Aglovain Tyrson to Marta.

"Marta, my dear," he said, stepping forward and taking both her hands in his, "how good to see you again. Not since the Seat; really, you should favor us with your elegance and your smile more often."

He gave Ian a dismissive glance, then turned back. "And you must be this good fellow who claims to be the Promised Warrior." His smile wasn't insulting, not really, but the way he held up his hands, palms out, was a bit much. "News travels quickly, even more quickly than your fleet horses and swift carriage—please, please do not strike me with that spear, as it is not the act of a welcome guest, and welcome guest you surely are, even though it is but for a brief time."

"Pel," Marta said, her words light but with a serious undertone, "I have the honor of presenting Ian Silver Stone, a warrior of some great accomplishment, and the herald of an Old One known as Harbard."

"Ah, yes, Harbard the ferryman, yes, yes, yes, the fellow who is kind enough to watch over a no-doubt-busy crossing over the noisy, nasty Gilfi river," he said. "But you are quite right, my dear, I forget my manners." He turned and faced Ian, all playfulness gone from his manner as he drew his heels together, rested his near hand on the jeweled pommel of his sword, and made a quick, proper bow. "I am Count Pel Pelson," he said, "your grateful, albeit momentary, host. You honor my home, Ian Silver Stone."

Ian bowed, careful not to lose his grip on Gungnir. It was easy to imagine the spear falling among a crowd, each touch a burning, each spastic movement in response kicking the spear over to another, until—

Stop it. It had become an obsession with him, and one that did him no good.

"You'll pardon the countess for not greeting you, I hope," the count said. "She is due any day, and the glum little vestri midwife has ordered her to her bed."

"I'm sorry to hear that," Marta said, concern in her voice. "Do we have enough time for me to at least pay a quick visit to her bed?"

"How kind of you." The count smiled. "Well, of course we do. Your goods can quickly be loaded aboard your barge, but not quite instantly. She'll be happy to receive you, I'm sure."

He beckoned to two of the young women in his entourage. They were dressed in identical short plaid skirts topped by white blouses. The outfits were something like that of a Catholic school uniform—save for the minor detail that the blouses had the sort of sewn-on bib thingee that Ian still couldn't think of a name for.

But their legs were clearly shaved, and bare to sandals, and each had her hair swept up in a complex sort of bun secured by jeweled prongs.

No, definitely not Catholic schoolgirls.

"Please, my dears, take the margravine up to see your mother—and quickly, quickly, if you please. She must not be delayed." He watched them go, then turned back to Ian, his hands spread and his head tilted in a clear request for permission, although Ian didn't have the slightest idea what he was asking permission for.

An awkward silence hung in the air for a moment until Ivar del Hival gave Ian a slight shove from behind, which the count clearly took as a sign that it would be safe to take Ian's arm, which he did.

Using Gungnir as a walking stick in his free hand, Ian walked with the count across the paved assembly yard, toward a stone path that led around the residence, rather than toward it, the rest of both Ian's and his own entourages following in their wake.

"Your barge waits below," the count said. "I hope you will understand that I would very much enjoy your company this evening, but more . . . vigorous ones than I have sent word that it would be unwise were I to slow your progress to the Table and the Seat."

"Thank you." Ian nodded. "I'm grateful anyway."

"Oh? You are? How nice." The count nodded, as though pleasantly surprised. "I would accompany you to the Seat, but it would be awkward." The count released Ian's arm for a moment, and tapped his right hand against his left hand. "Those of us who can still fold our hands together generally don't take our chairs at the Table on matters of war and peace. The large band of Tyrson brothers seems to resent it, and I can tell you in truth that I'd not want to irritate many of them."

The index finger of his right hand looked like it was more weighted down by than wearing a large gold ring featuring an inset dark-green flat-cut stone. The ring reminded Ian of the high-school class ring that he had wanted, and that he had been fool enough to mention to his father that he was thinking of getting—with his own money, of course.

Frippery, Benjamin Silverstein had said, nothing but frippery, knocking his own Harvard Law School ring against the supper table with each syllable. It was a heavy ring, deeply engraved, the smooth red stone centered on it inscribed with a golden scales of justice.

That symbol had always made Ian want to puke.

A high school ring? Benjamin Silverstein had sneered. *What the fuck is that? You work hard on getting one of these instead of spending your time with that Errol Flynn swordfighting shit, and then you'll have something. You get one of these, and then you're somebody.*

"Ah. You notice my new ring?" the count asked, slipping it off. "I'm rather pleased with it, all in all." He held it out, pulling on Ian's left arm, and placing the ring in Ian's gloved palm. "Do you like it?"

Even through the sheer glove, it felt warm, and was even heavier than Ian had expected. "It's very . . . nice," Ian said.

That was a polite thing say, even though it wasn't all that nice. The engraving was not particularly fine; in fact, it was really kind of coarse, with lots of little scratches that probably should have been polished away. Ian was so busy deprecating it to himself, that it took him a moment to see that on either side of the stone, the engraving showed a hand reaching out, fingers spread, as though supporting the round green stone.

"One might say it suggests that it's those of us with two hands, be we noble or peasant, who support the world," the count said, quietly, all trace of the overbred ninny he had been playing gone from his voice.

215

"No, no, no, please don't give it back," he said, as Ian tried to return the ring. The count's hand fluttered like a panicky bird; and his normal foppish tone was firmly back in place. "Would you be so kind as to keep it, please? It might amuse you to look on it, from time to time, and it would surely do me good to think that I had given it to you." He took the ring from Ian's fingers, but only momentarily, only to place it in Ian's palm and close his fingers tightly around it. "I would take that as a favor, Ian Silverstein," he said, his voice again quiet.

Ian nodded slowly. "I'll keep it with me, Count Pelson," he said. "And look upon it often."

"Really." The count smiled vaguely. "That would be so very nice."

I'm not entirely sure what the message is, Count, but it's been delivered, Ian thought.

And there's another one been delivered, too—that I'm an asshole who can write somebody off as an effete dandy at first sight and be proven wrong inside of five minutes.

There is such thing, Ian discovered, as a mystery with a simple solution: the barge, like all barges riding downriver on the Jut, was controlled by bargemen with their long poles. Once out in midriver, keeping it aligned properly was simply a matter of the two steersmen at the back corners of the barge occasionally dragging their poles against the river bottom. By far the most exercise that the burly six-man crew got was in the launching, where they poled hard to move the barge out of the quiet shore waters where upriver-bound craft were pulled by mule teams that plodded along the riverside road.

After that, it was fairly simple to trail a pole off the stern— *storn*, in Bersmål; it was almost the same word—and scrape it along the bottom to make sure that the barge didn't skew about.

For Ian, the first problem had been to see to securing Gungnir in the center of the barge, anchored by several muslin bags and guarded by unsmiling Hinterland soldiers—with yet another silent prayer that he'd be done with this damn spear soon, and be rid of the responsibility and danger that went with it.

He had checked it yet again, and again, and again, and finally decided that it was safe enough to leave, so he tucked his gloves in his belt and found a quiet place by the railing to lean and think.

Riding downriver was a peaceful, if slow, process, as the Jut wound its way in the dark, floating past outcroppings where occasional sparks in the night sky spoke of some habitation nearby; past dark docks, unlit and vacant in the night.

Aglovain Tyrson and half the soldier detachment lay in their blankets near the stern, sleeping, while Arnie and Ivar del Hival had joined a discussion among the off-duty soldiers over near the prow.

A quartet of vestri servants had taken musical instruments out of their bags and started an impromptu concert, a duet between a wooden flute and what looked like a set of bagpipes with a glandular condition. It took three vestri to play it: two to huff and puff to keep the bags inflated, a third to play one chanter with each hand, occasionally dropping the smaller one for just a moment to give a quick twist to a drone or two, either shutting it off or turning it on.

Ian had always liked the sound of a bagpipe. There was something straightforward about it, something insistent, and while the scale wasn't the one he was used to, the skirling sound was still contagious.

He stood by the railing, away from the others, listening. It was good to have a little time to himself.

A pair of soldiers set their armor and accouterments to one side, and broke into what Ian would have called a jig, although he was sure that wasn't the correct term back home, and didn't know what they called that here.

"I don't know about you, but I like the pipes." Arnie Selmo

was leaning up against the rail near him. Ian hadn't seen him walk up.

Ian nodded. "Yeah. Me, too."

"Well," Arnie said, "they tell me we should pull into the Seat tomorrow." He rubbed the back of his hand against his chin; it sounded like sandpaper. "You ready to face these folks?"

Ian shrugged. "I don't know."

"Really?" Arnie smiled. "Seems to your, er, humble and obedient servant you've done pretty well for yourself, so far. And not just here."

"About that servant thing . . ."

Arnie laughed as he raised a palm. "You're finally going to get around to apologizing for that?" He laughed as he shook his head. "Shit, boy, I know what I am." He clapped a hand to Ian's shoulder. "I'm your landlord, once we get back home."

"It doesn't bother you."

"Not for a second." Arnie smiled. "You got to know what you are. I know what I am." His face fell. "What I was." His eyes were large and round, and Ian would always know what sadness was, remembering. "I was Ephie's Arnie, and that, boy, that was enough for me. More than enough.

"And before that, I was something else." Arnie's laugh sounded forced, but Ian didn't call him on it. "There was this guy I knew. Different outfit—he was a tanker, I was in the Seventh Cavalry, which was really infantry, even though we were technically an armor outfit—but shit, it was always the same war, and shit, boy, killing is killing, whether you do it with a tank or with a Garand." He leaned against the rail and considered the water. "And it's a world of shit, boy. Frozen shit, in a Korean winter.

"But I lived through it, and he lived through it, and I went home and went to pharmacy school, and Adams, well, he stayed in, and made master sergeant, I think, before he got out and did something else.

"It was sometime in the mid-sixties that he was living in Alexandria and spending half his time with his old model 1911A1 down at the pistol range, because, shit, after you carry a piece of metal around and it saves your life even once, you kind of grow attached to it." He looked down at the way that Ian's free hand was resting on Giantkiller's hilt. "Yeah. So you know that part of it. Well, he wasn't supposed to still have it, but, hell, a lot of those things got combat-lossed. Guys didn't want to turn them in.

"So one day, he's come home in the middle of a Saturday afternoon from the range, and locks himself in the bathroom to clean it—that way the cats won't bug him, and if he drips some gun oil on the floor, well, it's easy to clean up with some toilet paper and then flush.

"After a while he sees a shadow pass across the floor, you know, at the bottom of the door?

"Doesn't look to him like it's the shadow of a cat, and besides, you don't hear a cat's footsteps.

"So, Adams, he does the most natural thing in the world: he puts the pistol back together—shit, after you get used to the thing, you really can do it blindfolded, although you want to be careful to keep control of the spring, or it's going to go flying away—thumbs some rounds into a mag, slips the mag in, cycles the slide to put a round into the chamber, and cocks-and-locks it.

"Now, cocked-and-locked is a pretty goddamn silly way to keep a gun, unless you're thinking you're going to be using it right away, but Adams thinks he's got an intruder in the house, and the hairs on the back of his neck are standing straight up and down, and he's not just a guy who used to wear a uniform to work, not now.

"He comes out of the bathroom, moving quick, and comes face to face with a guy coming out of his bedroom, with his TV under one arm, his typewriter under another arm, and a bunch of his suits thrown over his shoulder.

"Well, this guy lets out a yelp, and drops everything, and makes a run for the door, Adams running after him, shouting all sorts of things, no doubt—did I mention that Adams is an old Southern redneck, and the burglar's what he used to call 'a colored boy'?

"At the door, Adams points the piece at the guy and tells him to freeze. I wouldn't be surprised if he adds a few ruffles and flourishes.

"I don't think Adams really wanted to kill him. If he did, the burglar would never have had the chance to try and jump at him, but the guy does just that, and before he can put a hand on Adams, Adams has wiped the safety off with his thumb and shot him at least two or three times. He pumped all seven rounds into him, at just about punching distance.

"You can guess that the burglar didn't make it, what with looking like a roadkill and all by the time the cops got there.

"Now, remember, this was at a time when the whole civil rights thing was pretty hot. Didn't make much of any difference to us in Hardwood, but politicians all over the country were doing all sorts of smart and stupid things, and this local prosecutor decided to haul Adams in front of a grand jury, see if he could get him indicted. Damn stupid thing to do, but the times were like that.

"So, eventually, Adams gets up on the stand, and tells his story.

"Now, I'm not sure where the prosecutor worked before he took the job—Adams used to claim he knew, but I don't think there's really an En Double-A Cee Pee El You—but, in any case, all this white liberal prosecutor sees is a dead Negro kid and a live redneck who has shot him seven times, and never mind that this dead kid has a history of burglary and robbery going back to about the time he was weaned. Adams figured the prosecutor was going to run for something, and wanted to be sure to keep the black community on his side. Me, I don't know.

"So, he puts Adams on the stand in front of the grand jury and asks why Adams shot him so many times, why he emptied the piece, and Adams, trying to be polite, and honest, he says, 'Sir, that was the way I was trained.'

" 'Ah,' the guy says, 'you were trained to shoot an 18-year-old boy seven times in the chest. And where did you get this training?'

" 'In the United States Army.'

" 'The Army, eh?'

" 'Yes, sir,' Adams says.

" 'Oh, then,' the lawyer asks—and remember that there's this war in Vietnam going on, 'are you one of LBJ's hired killers?' I think the lawyer just saw his slim chance for an indictment flying out the window. I mean, a Virginia grand jury indicting an ex-soldier for shooting an asshole who was burglarizing his apartment?'

"Adams draws himself up real straight. 'No, *sir*,' he says. 'Sir, *I* am one of Harry S. Truman's hired killers.' " Arnie raised his head. "See my point?"

"I'm not sure." Ian smiled, and tried for a light answer. "Shoot the burglar seven times?"

The look on Arnie's face said that Ian had flunked a test. He started to turn away.

"Arnie—stop, please. I'm sorry."

Arnie turned back, with a tired smile. "It's okay. I guess I preach too much. Comes from living for too many years." He dismissed it with a wave of the hand. "Old men talk too much, and do too little of anything else."

He walked away, looking more his age than he had in a long time.

* * *

221

Marta approached Ian as he stood alone, her brother Burs on her arm. Burs had barely exchanged a dozen words with Ian on the trip; despite Ian's resolve not to embarrass him, it seemed that he had.

She had exchanged her travel clothes for something less practical, a dress that seemed to consist of a single sheer strip of white silk perhaps a foot wide, looped over one shoulder, leaving the other shoulder bare, then wrapped and rewrapped up and down her torso from under the shoulder to just above the knees. There were enough layers to leave it opaque where it clung to her breasts, but only a single layer covered her smooth, flat belly. It was held in place by a simple brooch at her hip, and perhaps it was an accident that as she stood there, the brooch came within inches of his fingers, as though daring him to remove it.

"My brother Burs," she said, her voice so smooth and silky he just knew that she was trying to tell him that there was deception in the air, "has a favor to ask."

"So let him ask," Ian said.

Burs nodded, his near hand on the pommel of his sword. Like an open hand, that originally meant peaceful intent—there was no way one could quickly draw a sword from the scabbard with the near hand—although Ian had no doubt that there were people who practiced using the near hand to support the scabbard more firmly for a quick draw.

But Ian wasn't worried, not particularly. The kid's manner didn't suggest hostility.

Burs Erikson drew himself up straight. "My—the margravine has said that she thinks you might consider me as one of your companions when you face the Pain."

The Pain. Ian frowned. That was the ceremony by which warriors considered worthy enough lost their left hand and gained the status of Tyrson.

What he really wanted was Ivar del Hival at his side to run

interference, but the fat asshole was all the way across the barge.

Well, best to take the bull by the teeth, or between the horns, or whatever the goddamn metaphor was. And best to be who and what you were. "And what if I told you that I don't intend to face 'The Pain'?" Ian asked. "What would you ask of me then, Burs Erikson?"

"If?" The boy's nostrils flared. "If you were to say such a thing, I'd ask if you are a coward, I suppose, or if you know your niche in life to be a lowly one, not worthy of the metal hand of a Son of Tyr."

"Ah." Ian smiled. "Do you know how Tyr lost his hand, Burs Erikson?"

"Every child hears the tale," he said. "The gods were binding Fenris-wolf, claiming it to be but a game, although in earnest they wanted the dog tied until the end of time. But he burst through every bond they could try. Then, finally, they . . . created something that even such as he could not break, and asked to try that.

"But Fenris-wolf, son of the Trickster himself, grew suspicious, and demanded a hostage. Great Tyr placed his hand in the wolf's mouth as that surety, and when Fenris-wolf found itself bound beyond escape, it bit his hand off. From that day on, Tyr wore that stump as a sign of his courage."

Ian nodded. "I was once told, by someone who should have known, that he lost it through accident, through clumsiness in striving with Fenris-wolf, and later claimed it to have been through bravery and heroism."

" 'By someone who should have known'?"

"Friend of mine. You haven't met him." Ian still remembered the moment when Hosea had said that. It felt like eons ago that he had sat at the table in Harbard's cottage with Hosea, and Harbard, and *her*. Harbard had frowned at the story, but Freya had merely nodded.

Ian had no doubt about the truth. "Do you know what we in Hardwood call somebody who puts his hand in a wolf's mouth to no purpose, Burs Erikson?"

Burs shook his head. "No, and I'll play questioner to your jester, Ian Silver Stone. What do you call such a person?"

"We call him 'an asshole,' " Ian said, the last two words in English. "But yes, if I ever chose to face such a thing, I would be proud to add you to my companions," he said, carefully, "although of course Arnie Selmo and Ivar del Hival and others you don't know have prior claim. But yes, I'll add you to the list." He raised his right hand and made a sign that he hoped looked mystic and meaningful, although all it was, was the salute D'Arnot had taught him, and spoke in English again.

"Do not," he intoned, carefully, "call us, for we shall call you."

Burs Erikson didn't quite know how to take it, but after an awkward moment he decided that a bow and a quick exit was the best choice.

Marta leaned up against the rail, watching her brother go. "Oh? So you don't intend to face the Pain? Not even for me?" She turned back to him, standing close, her face upraised.

"Ah. You want me to be one-handed?" he asked. He let his left hand rest on her arm against the rail, and then let it drop to her hip. "I've some use for both my hands, as you may recall," he said, surprised at how easily the words came without stammering.

Her eyes locked on his. "So, again, Ian Silver Stone, you insist on having it your own way." She took one step toward him, as though daring him to reach out and touch her. "Is this the way it is always to be with you?"

"Perhaps," he said.

"We'll see," she said, her face upturned, her mouth twisted ever so slightly. Her eyes caught the twinkle of the stars overhead, and somehow made the cold distant light close and hot.

Her arms wound around his neck. "We make landfall at the Seat late tomorrow," she said, her breath warm in his ear. "You'd better get some sleep."

She stepped back, turned, and walked away, her slim hips swaying from side to side perhaps a trifle more than was strictly necessary.

Still, every eye on the barge seemed to be on him, rather than her. So, moving as slowly as he could, he raised his hand to his brow in a brief salute at her vanishing figure, then turned about, rested his forearms on the railing, and considered the night.

CHAPTER SEVENTEEN

The Seat

If Torrie's backside didn't hurt with every plodding step the pony took, if his lower back hadn't settled into a permanent ache, if his shoulders didn't hurt when he slumped—and hurt when he didn't slump—if it didn't feel like glowing coals had taken up residence under his kneecaps, if he wasn't always hungry but too gut-tired to eat, if his eyes didn't feel hot and scratchy, then Torrie might have enjoyed the view.

It was, in theory, magnificent. The road twisted back and forth down the rich green hills like a piece of ribbon candy. The Seat lay below, spread across the fork where the slow, gentle Jut joined the faster-flowing Gilfi, to become the Great Gilfi.

They moved their ponies to the side of the road to make room for a carriage and its accompanying horsemen. The last of the riders, a tall, bearded man on a high-stepping gray gelding, turned in the saddle as they passed.

Torrie hunched forward more in the saddle, pulling himself deeper into the hood of the dwarven cloak. Dignity had long since been thrown to the wind; there was nothing dignified about riding a broad-shouldered dwarf pony, particularly not when you had to keep the stirrups short and pull up your legs and hunch down into the cloak anytime somebody might be watching.

It had been done before, Dad had said, and it would probably be done again: Humans expected to see dwarves riding the dull, placid little ponies, and if their attention wasn't drawn to the three outsized riders scattered throughout the dozen, they wouldn't be noticing them.

It was all very logical, if painful.

Just as painful, just as relentlessly logical as Maggie had been, back in Storna's Stele.

I was suspicious from the first, she had said. *It seemed strange.*

Hosea chopping wood? Why? His . . . his talent has always been cleverness with his hands. Delicacy, not brute force. I wouldn't have been surprised to find him reworking the plumbing, or carving a secret hiding place in the main overhead beam. If we had found him making a pin-and-tumbler lock out of wood, well, sure, that would have made sense.

But taking a wedge and sledgehammer to turn sections of a log into chunks of firewood?

No. That's not Hosea. That's somebody else. Think about it, dammit.

At first, I wrote it off. Okay, I said to myself, Harbard healed him up, and it's been so long since he's had such a use of his hands that he's felt like doing something as simple, as primal, as uncomplicated as turning logs into firewood.

But there was too much wrong. I notice things. I don't feel like I have to tell everybody everything I notice, but I notice things. Back in Paris, Torrie, I noticed how some kind soul decided that I didn't need to know that my brand new black French beret had been made in the Philippines, and removed the tag.

And here, well, maybe it's a girl-thing and not a boy-thing, but didn't you notice that he seemed too, well, comfortable in Harbard's cottage? Men are so . . . territorial, so much of the time, even when you're not quite peeing against walls to mark your territory. When you're in somebody else's home, you think before taking something down from a shelf, you look like you're about to ask permission before you sit in a chair—you act like, well, like you're not at home.

I saw it from the first. When he moved around, it wasn't as though it was somebody else's house that he was staying in; it was like it was his.

Okay, write that off, too. I'm just a paranoid girl, you're thinking. Fine. If you start talking about time of the month, we're going to have a problem, but if you just want to think that I'm too suspicious for my own good, okay, fine, no problem. I can live with that.

But then there was the cooking. It was edible, but that was all. I've eaten Hosea's cooking before, you've both eaten his cooking for years, and he's better than that. I mean, come on, the two of you had to spice it up yourselves, and not only didn't he make a comment at that, he didn't even look surprised, or hurt.

That's not enough. Okay. Fine.

Well, by then I knew that it wasn't him, so I laid a trap: I talked about Ian getting into trouble having a drink in a bar. I've seen Ian smoke dope a time or two, but I don't think anybody has ever seen him take a drink. Ever.

Come on, Torrie, you've been counting on him to be the designated driver for three years that I know of.

And getting into trouble? Come on. Ian?

No. Ian doesn't drink, Ian doesn't look for trouble, and Hosea knows that. But this so-called Hosea didn't.

So: that wasn't Hosea.

My best guess is that was Harbard, or Odin, or whatever he wants to call himself these days. We know all the Old Ones are shapeshifters to some extent—remember the fire giant? And read your Eddas, dammit, Torrie. Read the Lay of Harbard. It's clearly Odin, in disguise, taunting Thor—who, like the two of you, was too blind to catch on.

I don't know what happened to the real Hosea, but I didn't think that the time to find out was in front of this character, not with you two so well taken in.

Now, I know we can't always tell what these Old Ones are up to, but some of it is obvious. He didn't want us going after Ian, and he went to some trouble to try to misdirect us. That means that if we do, he thinks we can screw up whatever he's got planned.

So, we've got to make him right.

Let me try a bit of speculation. Once he wasn't able to fool us, he could have tried some other way to stop us. But my guess is that with that empty rack over the doorway indicating that his spear is gone, he didn't particularly want to face the two of you, each of you armed with a sword that Hosea tempered in his own blood. He, himself, killed a bergenisse with Ian's sword, if you'll remember; he knows what it's capable of, and I don't think he's going to think that the real Hosea equipped either of you with an inferior weapon.

No. It wasn't worth the risk, not to him.

It just occurred to me: maybe he has Hosea secured somewhere, and just maybe he doesn't want to irritate Hosea by killing us, or at least the two of you. We'll find out, but not now. Right now we have to deal with the problem in front of us.

So: what do we have? We have him not wanting us to come this way; we have him sure that the three of us are able to screw up whatever he has in mind, if we do get to the Seat in time; and we have a certainty that we're not going to be able to just walk right into the Seat, sit ourselves down and say no.

So that means we have to get there as quickly as possible, and the three of us can't do it by ourselves, or even as ourselves.

I think that means we need horses, and cloaks, and we need some way of concealing that it's the three of us. I think we need to get lost in a crowd. These vestri are a crowd.

And I think we need to get going, well, now.

She had folded her arms across her chest.

Well?

Which is how he found himself clinging to the almost bare back of a vestri pony. Vestri weren't terribly comfortable on horseback to begin with, and favored broad, high-peaked saddles with fore-and-aft bellybands that held the saddle firmly to the back of the animal, where they could feel that they could ride the saddle more than the pony. Substitute a smaller Vandescardian saddle, and Torrie could ride a little lower, his cloak concealing the saddle as well as the way his legs were drawn up under him.

It had been a hard ride, and an almost constant one, day and night starting to blur together.

Money, at least, had been no problem. It was amazing how far even a single golden Middle Dominion mark went—vestri had a legendary and almost insatiable appetite for gold, and while there were only four vestri ponies for sale at any price in Storna's Stele, that had been a start. Durin, who turned out to have an unexpected talent for haggling, had managed to increase their herd first at a vestri burrow and then in two villages, until all twelve of them had spare mounts, plus an additional four dray horses, split into two pairs that alternated pulling the supply wagon.

Money couldn't solve all problems, but it could keep the three humans and nine dwarves horsed and fed.

What it couldn't do was take the road weariness out of Torrie, Maggie, or even Dad. Plodding almost continually, save for a few hours' rest mainly for the horses rather than the riders, had left him barely able to focus on the city spread out at the river junction ahead of him.

The stone walls of the old city came to a point at the V of the fork, although it was hard to tell whether the walls were originally intended as dikes or as fortification. Probably both—the ramparts circling the walls seemed designed for defense.

But the inner city lay open, at least at the moment: seven bridges spanned the rivers, and the outer city had grown up around the roads leading into it.

A few feet above river level, a pair of large open holes belched a constant stream of dirty water into the roiling waters below. Within the walls, spires and windowed towers rose, a jagged outline against the blue sky. Smokestacks left a haze that disfigured the city without disguising it. Even from this far away, it still had the stench of a city about it.

Tiny figures of people and wagons clogged the streets below, as though they were brown and gray corpuscles, bringing in food and oxygen and removing waste.

Durin called a halt. "Well, friends," he said, his voice still the same even rasp it had been in Storna's Stele, as though the days of riding hadn't made a mark on his body or mind, "we could rush in and arrive all tired, in the dark, and stumble around for a place to stay until we recover, meanwhile trying to figure out if and how to deal with the problem of the three Friends of the Father, or we could pull the cart off the road onto that little grassy sward over there, and catch some much-needed sleep."

Torrie tried to keep his face from showing his weariness. Even a little force of personality, a smidgen of character, could go far. "Which do you think we should do, Durin?" he asked, trying to keep his expression serious.

Durin smiled. "Sleep."

The docking at the Seat was simpler and easier than Ian had expected.

Shirtless, poling in unison while they seemed to sweat in unison under the hot noon sun, the polemen had worked the barge into the slower waters near the shore. As they rounded the final bend, a watcher at the docks dispatched a six-man oar-propelled craft that looked like a racing shell, from which trailed a long thin line.

The crew drew the thin line through a solidly mounted brass doughnut at the front of the barge. The thin line pulled a wrist-thick rope. Once the rope had been made fast to the docking doughnut, the whole barge was slowly reeled in from shore and made fast to a floating dock between another, smaller barge and a high-drafted sloop.

While the Hinterlanders prepared to debark, the crew busied itself securing the barge to the dock—apparently, if it wasn't tied down in twenty-'leven separate places, it would leap away and slide downriver, and be gone.

Ian slipped on his gloves and retrieved Gungnir. It was still the same: as he reached for the spear, it was as though he was becoming more and more distant from himself, pulling the strings that manipulated himself, a puppeteer whose own body was the marionette.

But he adjusted, and just closed his hand around the spear's shaft.

And then he was himself, again.

A troop of soldiers already waited for them by the dock.

At least, they lined up like a troop. They looked more like a crowd: no two of them sported the same livery. If Ian hadn't known better, he wouldn't have thought they were in uniform, but had just chosen a variety of colored tunics and accouterments; colors ranged from the now-familiar green-and-gold of the Hinterlands to flashy crimson and glossy black, to muddy black and brown.

One fellow wore a blousy white shirt and tight leather trousers, with no insignia or decoration, except for his left hand.

The only badge of rank among them all that Ian could detect was that hand, which was a silvery version of the Tyrsons' enameled mechanical hands. It clutched a scabbard, in the tradition of the Tyrson—shit, they probably slept with their swords.

The silver-handed man placed his right hand on the railing and lithely vaulted over it and down onto the barge, his boots thunking against the wood with a clunk that was louder than Ian had expected.

With a quick glance more through than at Aglovain Tyrson

and Burs Erikson, he walked up to where Ian stood holding Gungnir, stopping with his face perhaps only two, two-and-a-half feet away.

He came to a stiff brace, slamming his right boot down next to his left.

Ian hadn't been expecting it, but he didn't let it startle him. It was an old fencer's trick, a quick stamp of the foot to draw attention. It had probably been old hat around the time bronze swords were replaced by steel. It might have worked once or twice since, but Ian had never fallen for it. You had to learn to concentrate.

The face and shoulders of the man staring into Ian's eyes were large, and square, and his jaw clenched tightly. Perhaps he had rushed himself, preparing himself for this: there was a small cut on his cheek, right near the jawline, that spoke of a hurried shave.

"Greetings," Ian said, quietly.

"I am," the other said, his clear, deep voice one decibel short of a shout, "the Argenten Horcel Tyrson. You are Ian Silver Stone, who claims to be one sent with a message for the Table, are you not?" He made it sound like an accusation.

"I am," Ian said, pitching his voice at the same volume. "And I ask to be taken to your Table."

"What proof have you that you are to be taken seriously?" the argenten asked. "What proof have you to offer that you are, as I hear you have claimed, the Promised Warrior of myth and legend?"

After all this time holding Gungnir carefully, it was almost a relief for Ian to lift its butt a scant quarter-inch from where it rested on the deck of the barge.

He brought it down firmly—not as firmly as he could have, not as firmly has he had back in the Hinterlands.

Wham.

233

The barge rocked, once, hard, and thrummed with a deep, rich note that filled the air and sent the bargemen leaping for a rail or a line, while the soldiers clapped hands to the hilts of their swords.

"You don't want to see full proof of who and what I am," Ian said, letting some of his pent-up anger and frustration reach his voice. He didn't want to be here, and he didn't want to be facing this asshole and trying to talk him into or out of anything. Fuck them all.

No; that was wrong. He had to persuade Horcel Tyrson, and he couldn't let his anger rule him. It was important that he be believed.

Once again, Harbard's ring pulsed against Ian's thumb, this time so hard it hurt.

"My name," he went on, "is Ian Silverstein. I have been sent by one who calls himself Harbard the ferryman. I make no outrageous claims, but I am *exactly* who I say that I am." He met the argenten's gaze unblinkingly. "And I expect to be believed that I am who I say I am," he said, knowing that the argenten would not be able to look him in the eye and deny it.

Their eyes locked for a long moment, and then the other nodded.

"I do not say that I doubt you, Ian Silver Stone," he said, quietly, leaning forward close enough that Ian could feel warmth of the argenten's breath. "I am not at all sure who or what you are," he said. "I do know that we've received word of assassins trailing you, trying to prevent you from reaching the Table. But I'm no child, new to intrigues around the Seat." He brought up his silver hand until the scabbard that it clutched came between the two of them. "I am well aware that such rumors might have been started by anyone, in an attempt to lend credibility to your claim." He stepped back and raised his voice. "The Table will meet tomorrow night, to see you and hear you, and perhaps more. In the Hour of the Long Candles, in the Hall of the Wolf."

His lips tightened. "And then all, perhaps, shall see exactly who and what you might be."

CHAPTER EIGHTEEN

~o~

Introductions

D urin was the last of the nine to return to the dingy room at the end of Dung Street. Valin had staggered in, looking more like he was dying than just tired, but a few minutes before; the vestri had been trickling in for hours.

Torrie had taken to whittling—it gave him something to do with his hands—while Dad slept. They had probably each had about four, five hours of sleep before gathering themselves together by lantern light, to make their way down the twisting road. They had entered the Seat through what the locals called the Dung Gate—it was the only gate that would admit civilian horses and horsedrawn carts.

It had taken maybe another hour for Valin to find a place to stable the animals, and a nearby room to rent—it probably could have been done more quickly, if Durin hadn't cautioned him against being too quick to flash gold and silver—and, as well as Torrie could remember, about thirty seconds to unroll his blankets, unbelt his sword, stretch out, and fall asleep. Waking as morning sunlight oozed in through the greased-paper windows, Torrie had been itching to get going, to do something.

But the two vestri who remained with them—either on guard or baby-sitting, depending on how you looked at it—had prevailed upon him to wait until the rest came back with some information. Maggie had given him a skeptical glare, and he'd done just that.

Meanwhile, Dad slept. He had woken twice, each time coming awake instantly to ask quickly if there was anything he was needed for, then stumbling off to the privy for an amazingly lengthy piss into the thundermug, followed by a huge draught from a water bottle. And then, both times, he had staggered back to where his blankets lay up next to the wall, lain down, and instantly fallen back asleep.

It was amazing how much Dad could sleep when he was behind, just as it was amazing how long he could go without sleep when necessary. It was like with food and water—and Torrie didn't want to think about how it was with sex; there were some things a guy just Didn't Want To Know about his mom and dad.

Maggie just chatted, mainly with Valin, Vindur, and a broken-nosed vestri with a name that contained a glottal click, whom Maggie had decided to call Fred.

So Torrie had taken out his drop-pointed hunting knife, given it a few quick sharpening strokes with the stone from his kit, and spent the rest of his time trying to turn their firewood into sawdust.

It helped to have something to do.

"He and his friends are here," Valin said. "Their barge docked yesterday; they are appearing in front of the Table late this evening."

"But where are they?" Torrie demanded. "I've got to get to them."

"I do not see how that is possible." Valin shook his head. "They don't use vestri servants in the Seat itself, so we can't call on the Folk. There's a large number of guards on duty at all times. Almost all of the nobles keep their own guards around them, rather than trusting to a soldier fealty-bound to somebody else to keep him safe. We'll not get within the gates of

Joel Rosenberg

the Keep, not without a pass, and there will be no pass simply for the asking."

Durin's bloodshot eyes stared out of dark sunken hollows. His face had an unhealthy grayish tinge to it. "I contemplated bribery. I think you would have to bribe at least a dozen or so in order to get into the Seat, but . . ." He spread his hands and shook his head.

Maggie shook her hand in a syncopation that, despite everything, made Torrie chuckle. She silenced him with a glare and a short chopping motion. "But," she said, "if just one of them won't be bought, or won't *stay* bought, we find ourselves surrounded by a bunch of drawn swords and nocked arrows." She pursed her lips for a moment. "Is there any way we could get a note smuggled in to them?"

Vurden, a vestri who had the nauseating habit of constantly picking his many-times-broken nose, grunted. "Of course you could, if you would risk it being intercepted."

Durin's mouth twitched. "And if it were intercepted, if it were seized, then they would not be in communication with their friend. Which is as it is now."

Torrie shook his head. "No, we'd be worse off. If it's intercepted and read, that is. I mean, I'd have to specify a meeting place or something."

"You *are* wearing out," Maggie said, her facing lighting up with a smile. "I think we can figure out a way around that."

The dwarves looked puzzled.

So did Torrie until he realized that she had been speaking in English, and not Bersmål.

Oh. That made sense, but— "No." There were people in Tir Na Nog who spoke English. He opened his mouth to remind her of that, but Maggie was one step ahead of him.

"Omeboyhay," she said, "ouyay eckonray atthay a antsfulpay ofway emthay ouldcay uzzlepay oughthray a ombocay of igpay atinlay andway angslay?" She had been opening her

238

rucksack as she spoke, and dug through it, pulling out a note-book and a pen. "We need a place and a time to meet."

While a pair of soldiers at each end of the balustrade kept watch, Ian made yet another touch on Burs Erikson's left arm, while over by the railing, his audience of Ivar del Hival and Marta watched carefully, Ivar del Hival barely concealing a knowing smile, Marta clapping vigorously at her brother's latest embarrassment.

Well, at least that part of the audience was nice. But it was getting a little irritating being watched all the time they were out of their rooms. Shit, for all he knew, they were watched *in* their rooms.

Ian understood—he wouldn't have wanted to let three for-eigners run around unaccompanied if he was running the cas-tle—but he didn't have to like it.

Of course, it cut both ways. There were these rumors about a team of assassins out to kill the Promised Warrior, and the argenten had assured him that he was safe here in the Seat.

Yeah, sure.

Well, it was just as well Ian wasn't this Promised Warrior person, and the sooner he could meet with this Table and tell them that, the sooner this was done.

Still, the surroundings were pleasant, even if you didn't in-clude Marta.

The Vandestish went in for simple names here, which Ian found pleasant, if sometimes confusing. The city itself was the Seat; the triangular section of the city that sat between the two rivers was the Seat; the keep itself was the Seat; and the large residence that sat high on the northeastern corner of the inner ward was also the Seat—when somebody talked about the Seat, you had to infer from the context which one was meant.

Even with the Seat within the Seat within the Seat—the Keep—the names were simple. There was the Seat, of course, and the Hall, where the Table met. Or was. Or met and was. The Hall, diagonally across the lawn, was a long, square building whose only walls appeared to be the close-packed columns that would have reminded him more of pictures of the Parthenon if these columns had been less slender and hadn't been covered with an interlace of stone vines and lush greenery.

The Residency was the other big building in the Keep; it was where Ian and company had been put up, along with some other visiting nobles who didn't have the rank to claim a seat at the Table.

Unsurprisingly, the rulers of Vandescard did well by themselves.

The inner ward of the Seat had been landscaped and planted over the years, until it was more sculpted garden than lawn. Ancient hedges, dense clumps of green, had been carved to allow flowers to grow in their centers, as though the hedges themselves were huge vases. A single stream from one fountain arced high into the air, constantly splashing into another fountain, while the spray kept the leaves beneath glistening and sparkling in the golden late afternoon sunlight.

All in all, the long veranda that ran across the width of the Residency wasn't a bad place to spend a sunny afternoon, in the shade of the veranda's roof, a nice breeze cooling him, doing something Ian was starting to enjoy again: fencing.

There were times when this sparring was just too easy.

It was the converse of one of the basics of swordfighting that Ivar del Hival and Thorian Thorsen had taught Ian, a variation on an old truism in épée, that the wrist of the sword arm was the fulcrum around which a duel could easily spin.

Years of perfectly good training for dueling and war had also taught Burs Erikson that the key was the wrist of the sword hand. With real weapons, a touch to the hip or thigh or to the shoulder of the free hand would slow you down, but it would take deep penetration to even threaten to end things right away.

A wound to either leg—particularly the kneecap, but anywhere from toe to thigh could do very nicely—would slow you down.

But any injury to the wrist would end things right away, and an injury to anywhere else on the sword arm would leave the wrist vulnerable.

The wrist wasn't just the most important target, it was the most exposed. Any lunge, any thrust, by its very nature, brought your wrist forward, making it the closest possible target to your opponent's blade.

That made space important. Control the distance between you and your opponent, and any time that you could get him to extend himself, that exposed his sword arm, at least to some extent.

So, Burs Erikson, like most duelists most of the time, set most of his strategy around the wrist, both his and Ian's. His favorite deception was to bring his blade just a trifle out of line, thereby almost offering his wrist, trying to draw an expected attack for his riposte. Once he had committed to that, there were any of a number of ways for Ian to score his touch, the simplest of which was simply to counter-riposte.

But if Burs Erikson was ready for that ... well, that would give Ian a chance to use some of the options he was considering.

So Ian varied his game, first with a carefully timed stop-thrust that caught Burs Erikson on the attack, moving to an engagement and cut-over, and finishing with an ugly-looking boar's-head squat-and-lunge that would certainly have got him kicked in the face and then skewered like a marshmallow in a real fight, but this time allowed him to get the touch on Burs Erikson.

Burs Erikson was ready for another point—and the smile on his face said that he was at least learning to take defeat with good grace—but Ian held up a hand.

"Enough, please," he said. "Be so good as to have some pity on an older man."

He flopped down on the stone bench next to the railing, and gratefully accepted the tall mug of cold water that Marta handed him without being asked. It was amazing how quickly fencing could leave you winded. It wasn't just the physical—although the bouncing back and forth got tiring, very quickly—it was the need to be focused, concentrating at every moment. One break in concentration, one instant of wandering attention, and it was all over.

Accompanied by two guards, Arnie Selmo walked out of the Hall, through the darkened archway, blinking in the sun. The two guards dropped out of step and took up positions on either side of the arch.

"Just spent a couple of your silver marks," he said, his voice low.

"Buy anything interesting?"

Arnie nodded, as he dipped two fingers into his shirt pocket and brought out a folded square of paper. "I think so," he said.

Ian's hand shook as he accepted it. This wasn't local paper. Paper hereabouts didn't have that distinctive ripped-loop edge that you got only by tearing it out of a spiral-bound notebook.

Printed in bold letters, the outside read:

For Ian Silverstein, omfray ishay oomieray

Ishay? Pig Latin. Ian grinned. Looked like Torrie had come after him, after all.

Eetmay atway ethay ornercay ungday and oncoursecay undownsay, it said.

Ivar del Hival was at his elbow, trying to see what he had.

He passed it over to him, and watched the big man's forehead wrinkle.

Well, for once he didn't know everything.

"You think there's any chance I can get out into the city?"

Ivar del Hival pursed his lips. "I don't know for sure what orders the guards at the front gate have about letting you out of the keep, but . . ." He shook his head. "You probably ought to check with the argenten—"

"Or I can assume that it's easier to get forgiven than to get permission." Ian stripped off the sweat-stained shirt and mopped at his chest and underarms. A fresh white tunic lay folded on the chair next to Giantkiller in its scabbard. He slipped it over his head, shrugged into it, and belted Giantkiller around his waist. "Let's see."

He beckoned to Marta, who rose and walked to him.

"Let's take a walk in the gardens," he said, taking her arm, and waving at the others to stay put. Arnie picked up the cue quickly, and engaged Ian's guards in a discussion, while Ivar del Hival did the same with Burs Erikson. That would keep them distracted for a while at least; their job was more to prevent Ian from getting into the Residency, really, than to shadow his every step.

Ian and Marta walked down a twisting, narrow path, dampened slightly by the spray from the fountain. "Marta," he said. "I need some directions. And I need to get out into the city. Will you help me?"

Marta stopped for a moment, then let out a quick hiss of surprise. "Well, that is awfully direct, isn't it?" A thin smile crept across her face. "Yes, my Ian, I will help you in this. Just nod and agree with everything I say. And then, when I tell you to say something, you will make them believe you."

The gate that led out of the keep was covered with a lowered portcullis. It had a door in it, which seemed strange to Ian until he noticed that another portcullis hung high above in the arch over the entranceway. That made sense; it let the guards control who got in or out easily, but allowed them to lock up the keep by dropping the outer portcullis instantly, should the need arise.

"Margravine Marta Eriksdottir," said a fat, bearded guard who looked more like Louisiana chef Paul Prudhomme than a soldier. "Surely you don't intend to go out into the Seat unaccompanied."

"Ah, Halberdier-Senior Escoben," Marta said, "I most certainly do not." She gestured at Ian. "I don't believe you have met my betrothed, Ian Silver Stone."

The guard looked Ian up and down. "I've had reports, every now and then. I hadn't been informed of the betrothal."

"Really." The temperature of her smile dropped a full ten degrees in an instant. "You think he would turn down my proposal?"

"Not for a moment, Margravine. No man in his right mind would." He gave a flick of his flipperlike hand towards the Residency, or at least toward the garden that blocked the Residency from view. "I hear he's been giving sword lessons to the margravine's brother, the Honored Burs Erikson."

Marta laughed, a sound like silver bells. "You might say that, Halberdier-Senior, and it would be true. You might also say that he has been beating my brother, an accomplished swordsman, with embarrassing ease. And that would be true, as well." The smile dropped from her face. "Perhaps you might wish to take a lesson from him at some time; I know that he's always interested in a new sparring partner." She looked at Ian. "Tell the Halberdier-Senior that you can protect me, if you please."

Ian looked the fat guard in the face. "I will see to her safety," he said.

"I have no doubt you will do your best," he said, beckoning to another soldier." Damn. It wasn't going to work. The guard didn't believe him, and looked away. "Heran, be so kind—"

"No," Ian said, putting some snap into his voice. "You look me in the eye when I talk to you," he said.

Again, Harbard's ring pulsed against his thumb. What made it do that? It wasn't just emotional intensity—it hadn't done any such thing while he was in bed with Marta, or challenging Burs Erikson—but it was something else. It was damned frustrating to have this thing squeezing his thumb while he was trying to persuade the guard to let him and Marta through the gate.

"I said," Ian said, trying to keep a sudden rush of anger out of his voice, "that I will protect her, and that she will be safe with me."

Marta laid a hand on Escoben's arm. "Surely," she said, "surely you're not saying that the streets of the Seat are unsafe these days."

Escoben's eyes never left Ian's. "No, Margravine Marta, no I am not; and yes, I do believe that this young man will keep you safe. Have I your word that you will protect her, with your sword and life, if necessary?"

Ian nodded. "Of course."

He turned to the soldier he had been speaking with before. "Open the door, if you please."

"But—"

"But nothing. The margravine wishes to see the city, and she will be safe." He bowed them through. "I await your return."

Ian waited until they had gotten past the far pair of barbicans, to where the road into and out of the Seat dumped out on a row of merchants' stalls. Fine bolts of cloth, leather, and metal worked into shapes familiar and strange, and fresh meat and vegetables crowded the stalls.

Eager voices called out to them.

"If it please you, good sir, please run your fingers through my fine woolen cloth. Virgin wool it is; there's not a fiber of shoddy in it. A fine coat it will make for you—"

"Please, Honored Lady, sample my balms and lotions, guaranteed to make your already soft skin even softer and smoother—'

"Honored ones! Taste of my relishes, if you please!"

Ian gave a vague smile and walked on. "Everything for the nobility, eh?"

Marta tucked her arm under his. "Oh, not quite everything, but much. Now, where are we going?"

"Not we. Me." Ian frowned. "I need directions. You need to get back into the Keep. Just tell them I decided to see more of the city, and that you found nothing of interest in the markets—"

"Surely," she said, the sweep of her arm taking in the marketplace, "surely you aren't going to abandon me here? After you've sworn to protect me? You would leave me in such danger *here*?"

Here was a market filled with people who appeared to make their living off selling to the nobility of the Seat. *Here* was a matter of her just walking a couple of hundred yards to the gate and back into the Seat. *Here* was within a shout of any succor needed, although it wouldn't be. Marta would be perfectly safe *here*, and hell, Ian could watch until she was back inside the gate.

"I won't have you forsworn, Ian," she said, her lips pressing primly together. "Shall we walk on?"

"Marta—"

"Ian." There was steel in her silky voice, and her hand tightened on his arm. "A wife obeys her husband, although a wise husband compels obedience only rarely. A daughter obeys her father, when she has to, or her eldest brother, should her father die. But you are neither my father, nor my brother, nor are you yet my husband, and you have promised to take me for a walk through the city, and that you shall."

Ian shrugged. "Well . . ."

Her grip loosened, and she ended the moment of tension with a giggle that made her sound about five. "So, where are we going?"

In for a penny, in for a pound . . . "Where's the corner of Dung Street and the Concourse?"

She pointed down the cobblestone street with her chin. "That way. May one ask who we're meeting?"

"A good friend of mine. Probably a few of them."

"Well and good," she said. "I've always said that you can tell much about how good a husband a man will make by taking the measure of his friends."

"Oh." Ian laughed. "I thought you wanted to marry me anyway."

"Oh, I do," she said. "But if you turn out to be a *good* husband, I probably won't have to poison you or knife you while you sleep." She kissed him gently on the shoulder. "Shall we go?"

The Concourse turned out to be a long, wide, gently sloping street lined with houses, two cobblestone pathways separated by a grassy median. Stately elms spread their branches high and wide, giving the road a green, leafy canopy that felt cool and minty in the golden light of the setting sun. The houses were large and extended, built of whitewashed stone, with what looked like honest-to-God driveways, which Marta told him in fact were driveways leading to carriage houses in the back.

They walked down the grassy median, drawing an occasional look from a passerby, but no surprises. Marta's blouse and culottes were perfectly ordinary clothes for the daughter of a rich merchant, and the idea of such going for a stroll with a swordsman escort or companion was hardly unique; Ian counted at least four similar couples before he stopped counting and worrying.

That helped to explain what Marta was up to. At least in part.

"I wish," she said, "that I could tell what you're thinking about when you're so quiet."

As the street sloped down, the houses began to become less luxurious, bit by bit. Large became less large; bright whitewashing that must have been done that year became older paint, showing stains. Broad driveways narrowed, and neatly trimmed hedges interlaced with rosebushes turned into simple bushy barriers.

It wasn't a slum, by any means, but it wasn't what it had been further up the hill.

"There's a saying in the Seat," Marta said, "about how hard it is to move uphill and how easy to go down." She gestured at a smaller house, less fancy than one would have seen at the top of the Concourse, but still well maintained, its hedges square, its walls gleaming. "I have forgotten the name, but they are a family in the barge business. They used to live further uphill, and had their eyes on a large manse near the crest, but then, during a storm, one of their barges smashed into one owned by a competitor. The Table decided that the competitor had the right of way." She pursed her lips. "But give them a generation or two, and they'll be back uphill."

"You take the long view."

"Men would be wise to do so." She patted his hand. "Women must."

The Concourse terminated in a park a few hundred feet from the riverwall, where a walkway overlooked the water flowing through the open aqueduct below, vanishing into a hole in the riverwall.

Dung Street lay to their right, rising in front of them. The buildings here were wattle and daub—a framework of timbers filled in with a kind of stucco made of clay and interleaved sticks and twigs, sort of like a woven basket covered with mud. It was cheaper to build with—but that was about its only virtue.

Broad gutters on each side of the street carried a vile green sludge down to a couple of what looked like manholes, each of which was supervised by a pair of filthy men in knee-length work tunics that probably had been washed sometime, but not within human memory. The sewer workers wielded long shovels to push sludge down the holes, making sure that the flow didn't create little dams of some vile offal that might let the sludge overflow.

A team of lamplighters worked its way down the street in a boxy horse-drawn wagon, the driver expertly stopping the cart at just the right point for his partner, from his post high atop the wagon, to open the cage on top of the lamppost and quickly exchange a fresh lamp for the dead one there. He then lit the fresh lamp with a quick motion of a stick he touched to his firepot, then extinguished the stick with a practiced flick, set the used lamp down on a rack, and clapped his hands together to signal his partner to start the horse towards the next pole.

But there was no sign of Torrie or Maggie or anybody familiar.

Ian shook his head. "No sign of them."

Marta's forehead was wrinkled, and her mouth pursed prettily. "It's certainly sunset." She thought for a moment. "Shall we walk up the street, then?"

Ian nodded. "At least a short way." He didn't like any of this, and he particularly didn't like having Marta here right now. "If you'll promise me something."

"Yes?"

"If there's trouble, and I tell you to run, you'll run. Without a hesitation. Without an argument. And particularly without waiting for me. Run, scream, shout, get attention, get help."

"Yes, Ian," she said.

"No argument? No discussion?"

"No, Ian," she said, her eyes fixed on his, her lips slightly parted. "It will be as you say."

"Let's go." He started walking, Marta taking up a position a full two steps behind him.

He didn't remember unfastening his swordbelt, but he had, and Giantkiller's scabbard was clutched in his left hand in perhaps open imitation of the way the Tyrsons always carried their weapons. His right hand settled comfortably on the hilt that always felt like it gripped his fingers back, and he pulled an inch or so of blade free. It would take just one quick pull to free the sword.

He walked past the sewermen, and up the street.

It was quiet in the oncoming dark. Windows had been shuttered for the night, and the smell of cooking fires filled the air. Up ahead of him, a face peeked out of a doorway, then ducked back in when it saw him.

That didn't necessarily mean anything.

Ian walked on, looking carefully into each darkened doorway as he passed.

It was the eighth or ninth doorway—Ian wasn't keeping count. As he passed it, he felt more than heard a door swing open behind him.

He spun about, tossing his scabbard to one side, bringing Giantkiller up.

Something, somebody moved out of the shadows—

And Torrie Thorsen, his face more tired and weary than Ian remembered seeing it, his clothes ragged and torn, definitely looking somewhat the worse for wear, stepped out into the twilight, his hands empty, held waist-high. A broad grin was spread across his face.

He raised his hands, slowly. "Yeah, I'm sure you've got a lot to be pissed about, Ian, but can we talk about it before you run me through?"

CHAPTER NINETEEN

Decisions

Ian Silverstein the Promised Warrior? No. Torrie shook his head. If there was a Promised Warrior in the room, it was Torrie.

The idea made his stomach feel like he had swallowed a cup of cold steel.

Maggie eyed Ian and his girlfriend over the rim of her cup, a thin smile on her face. "I think I'll accept Chosen People," she said. "But I'm not sure about this Promised Warrior thing."

The lantern light picked up red and gold highlights in her hair, and reflected flickers of flame danced in her eyes.

Maggie had, for some reason Torrie couldn't fathom, run a comb through her hair and used his shaving mirror to put on some makeup. Hell, until a few minutes ago, he hadn't even known that she had tucked a makeup kit into her rucksack when they were packing back in Hardwood, and would have tried to talk her out of it if he had known.

He wouldn't have been able to, more than likely.

There were eight of them sitting in a circle around the fire—Dad, Torrie, Maggie, Ian, Ian's girlfriend, Durin, and Fred. The rest of the vestri stood around them, some shifting from foot to foot, others pacing.

And of them all, Ian looked the most tired. The weight of all this had been bearing down hard on him.

"Half of me," Torrie said, conscious that this Marta couldn't speak English, "says that we should just fold our tents and sneak out of the city, and go back and confront this Harbard." He patted the hilt of his sword.

"No." Ian shook his head. "That would leave me forsworn," he said in Bersmål. "And then," he added, in English, "we'd have to figure out some unlikely way of getting Arnie and Ivar del Hival out of the Seat, as well. Surely they'd be in trouble."

Dad grunted. "They would, perhaps, but that was not what Thorian was saying. You and he don't have to both either steal away into the night, or face the Table together. One could go one way, while the other goes the other."

No. That was where Dad was wrong. If there was a test to be taken, a challenge to be met, it would be Torrie who would have to meet it. It was what Dad and Uncle Hosea and Mom had been training him for for his whole life.

Besides, it was the only thing that made sense. Harbard had tried to prevent Torrie from even coming here. He wouldn't have done that unless he knew that it was Torrie who was the key to it all. He wanted Ian to make them end the war, to carry his word. Torrie had no trouble at all believing that Harbard would stop or start a war to bring Freya back to his house and his bed, and if he could at the same time endanger or rid himself of the one who had given the Brisingamen ruby to her, why that would be all the better. Harbard, or Odin, was no gentle Old One like Uncle Hosea. Maggie was right about that. He was a cruel and manipulative old trickster, who would never do something honestly if there was a dishonest way to do it, one who would kill an otter just because it had caught a fish he wanted, or taunt Thor from the safety of his ferry, or walk through a battlefield, relishing the sights and sounds and smells as he picked his favorites from the dead warriors.

Dad was looking at him. It was hard to read Dad's face sometimes, impossible at others. Did he know what Torrie was thinking?

And if he did, what would he do? Dad had been raised with and in the Byzantine politics of the Cities of the Dominions, where endless posturing and preparatory positioning might suddenly resolve itself with a formal duel or a less formal clash of blades.

Dad would try to stop him, of course.

But it was Torrie's call, not Dad's, and not Ian's.

If it was simple, if it was safe, if it was just a matter of explaining things, then Odin would not have tried so hard to stop Torrie from coming here. That wasn't what Torrie had been studying the sword for almost since he could toddle.

No. Whatever was going to happen would be brutal, and it would be something Ian couldn't handle.

Whatever it is, it will be up to me, he thought. *So be it, by God.* He was Thorian Thorsen, son of Thorian del Thorian and Karin Roelke Thorsen, and while he could—and did—fault Mother for her methods, he couldn't blame her for doing her duty as she saw it.

And he couldn't help but do the same.

He looked Dad straight in the eye, opened his mouth, then shut it. How could he put it? What could he say?

He didn't have to. Dad just nodded, as he leaned toward Torrie. "Do what you must, Thorian," he said, quietly. "As will I."

"Torrie?" Maggie was leaning over toward him. "What's going on?"

"I don't know," he said. "But think it out—why are we here? Why are all of us here? What, and how, can we stop things?" Torrie held up a hand. The vestri stopped talking, but Ian was still muttering something to this Marta of his.

Ian would understand, but he might not agree.

But there was another reason to lay in front of all of them.

253

"We all go," Torrie said, rising. "Dad will—I mean, Dad and I will need Ian at our sides if we're going to face Harbard. Two swords tempered in Uncle Hosea's blood was enough to give him pause and make him try to trick us; three swords, plus Gungnir in Ian's hand, will be enough if anything will."

He tried to put the worst possibility out of his mind. What if Harbard had killed Uncle Hosea? Yes, yes, they would kill Harbard, but that wouldn't bring Uncle Hosea back. Then again, he thought to himself, neither would anything else.

Best to concentrate on what could be done.

"So we all go to face this Table," Torrie finished. Maggie's hand was warm in his. She gave it a squeeze and gave him a puzzled look. Her mouth worked, whispering without sound: *What is it?*

Later, he mouthed back. *It's not important*. If there was a later for them, it wouldn't be important. If he passed whatever test this was, it would be easy to explain. And if he failed, well, then, he wouldn't have to.

She gave his hand a final squeeze before releasing it.

Torrie helped Durin to his feet, the vestri's callused hand gripping his assisting one strongly, although with a tremor that the old dwarf could not quite suppress.

Dad was on his feet, facing the vestri, his stance rigid and formal. "Here is where we part, my friends," he said in Vestri, his deep voice letting the gutturals rumble like distant thunder. "I thank thee for thy help, and thy loyalty," he said, his voice formal, almost singsong. "And I hope we meet again, some day, in better circumstances than these." He gestured at the dingy room.

"I hope so as well, Friend of the Father of Vestri, himself the father of us all." Durin bowed deeply, then straightened again. "I would—" He broke off into a fit of coughing, which ordinarily would have spoiled the effect, but the slope-headed little dwarf had wrapped a strange dignity about him as tightly as the tattered cloak he held closed with one bony hand. "I would . . . I would accompany thou, if it is permitted."

"Me, as well." Valin took a step forward. "We've come this far, Friend of the Father. I am a stoneworker, and used to finishing what I start."

"And I," the vestri they called Fred said.

"I, as well—"

"I—"

"No," Dad said, quietly, but firmly. "It is not permitted, because it would do no good. What will be here, will be. You all have lives to get back to. Some of you have families." He produced a small leather bag, which clinked with the sound of metal-on-metal as he threw it to Valin. "You will see to the distribution of it."

Valin opened it. The gold inside picked up the light of the overhead lantern and reflected a buttery sheen on his face. He tied it closed and tossed it back to Dad. "Does thou think so little of the Children of Vestri that thou would buy our honor? Even with thine gold?" His expression could have been carved out of granite.

"No," Dad said, quietly. "The honor of you Sons of Vestri is not in question. Were there any dishonor among you, I would have been sold to my enemies for gold long ago, long before I had a son of my own." He held up the leather bag again, and again clinked the coins inside. "But honorable ones can take gold, as well as dishonorable, and children will need to eat."

One of the other vestri reached a hand out toward the bag, but Valin slapped it away, a heavy, meaty sound. "No. We do not take money for this."

"Shh. Be still." Durin held out a hand, and accepted the bag.

Joel Rosenberg

He weighed it carefully in his palm. "It is for hungry children, Valin; there is no shame in feeding children."

Ian beat on the knocking post with the butt of Giantkiller. "Open the gate," he said, his voice loud, demanding. "We would speak with the Table."

CHAPTER TWENTY

The Table

High above the gardens of the Seat, a crier—more of a singer, really—marched about the ramparts on the wall, his firm baritone cutting through the rustle of the wind in the bushes.

> *"The dusk is fully ended,*
> *"And remnants of twilight have fled.*
> *"Horses have been settled in their stables,*
> *"And children put to bed.*
> *"But before the day ends,*
> *"And before the day dies,*
> *"The Hour of Long Candles comes,*
> *"The Hour of Long Candles arrives,*
> *"The Hour of Long Candles appears,*
> *"The Hour of Long Candles arrives."*

Well, Arnie Selmo decided, the locals had a taste for theater. Flaming torches thrust out from hidden sockets in each pillar, hissing and spitting as they cast flickering shadows all around the garden. The Hall had been impressive in the daytime, when the cool green of the vines wrapped around the tall columns, but at night, its white marble peeked through its clothing of vines like the bones of a long-dead giant.

The six of them walked across the broad marble expanse toward the Table, their bootheels clicking against the stone like loud drumbeats.

Ivar del Hival, Maggie Christensen, Torrie Thorsen, Ian Silverstein, and Thorian Thorsen walked in a single line, abreast; Arnie Selmo followed a careful couple of paces behind Ian, the way a good squire would.

Playing at being the squire hadn't bothered Arnie. You had to get along, and if that meant ignoring some things other folks would have thought of as slights, that was fine with Arnie.

No point in taking offense, particularly when you could take advantage. While Ian and Ivar were eating at formal tables, having to worry about which fork—well, eating-prong—to use, Arnie was in the kitchen, his wooden or chipped or everyday plate piled high with tasty bits of this and that, his ears filled with shop talk and laughter.

Not a bad trade. Useful, even.

And besides, sometimes it put him in just the right position. He had known that that Eriksdottir girl was going to propose to Ian hours before Ian did, and why a child by Ian would be a safe bet for her even if Ian didn't turn out to be this Promised Warrior. Giving out condoms to young men who were too shy to ask for them or too preoccupied to think of it was something Arnie had been doing before Ian had been born, and it had felt kind of nice to have to do it again.

Sometimes, like now, it put him in another good position, as he kept pace behind Ian. Ian held that spear out in front of him, almost in port position, while the rest of them took up a formal stride, each with a free hand on the hilt of a sword.

There were advantages to letting others go first, after all.

Thorian del Thorian's first and last lesson from his own father had been in self-control, and while he had, for some reasons he could explain at least to himself, abandoned many of the good and wise lessons he had learned at the feet and sword of Thorian del Orvald, that one had stayed with him. It served him well, as he paced across the marble floor in pace with his . . . his companions.

Self-control. That was the key. It didn't matter how many times you had faced it, and had survived—the very idea of going to die was frightening. But while he had let his tongue admit it, he would never let his face or body betray it. That was different.

That would shame him, among his svertbren. And worse. And yes, there was worse than to be shamed among his svertbren, his comrades-in-arms.

Still, it was a strange thing, to think of Maggie Albertsdottir as a comrade-in-arms. The Bersmål word *svertbror* was best translated as weapon-brother, or sword-brother; it was a masculine term, like brother or husband or warrior.

But in the Hidden Ways, with a sword and knife in her hand, she had shown that being a svertbror did not require a siitinrod, and from Harbard's cottage to the Seat, she had reminded him of something that he had already known, and had no business forgetting, even for a moment: battle was first joined with the mind and the spirit, not the arm and the sword. She had parried Harbard—and on his own ground, by the Ghosts of the Old Ones!—with a smile and a whisper and a shake of her pretty head, and had even kept that victory to herself until she had decided to share it.

A svertbror, indeed, that one. He had been raised to think of money and commerce as women's work, while men handled matters of governance and battle and honor, and had been silently aghast at the way women in the Newer World did not see their place—although as a guest in their world, it was not something he would have commented upon, awkward as it made them look.

But things were different with this one.

He forced himself not to sigh. He hoped such unwomanly ways had not shriveled her womb beyond use. It would have been nice to at least know that he would be a grandfather before he stepped into the final blackness.

But so be it. Young Thorian had seen a test ahead, and had steeled himself for it, even though he feared it. No other could have read his concern and his decision—young Thorian del Thorian had learned his lessons well—but his father could see it.

Thorian del Thorian would not . . . what was the phrase? He would not rant and rail and whine against the slings and arrows of misfortune, be they outrageous or justified. That was not his way. It could be that whatever test, whatever danger, faced them would leave his son dead on the ground. That possibility always existed; the world was filled with danger. So be it.

But it would not happen easily, and it would not happen without Torrie's father going first.

It had been many years since Thorian del Thorian and Orfindel had helped Robert Sherve pull Torrie, all wet and bloody, from his mother's womb, but that had changed everything, that one moment. From that instant on, as long as there was life and breath in Thorian del Thorian, no sword would so much as prick his son's little finger without passing through his own heart first.

He didn't give a sideways glance. That might be read. A duelist from the House of Steel never signaled a move in advance, and Thorian del Thorian had been born a duelist of the House of Steel.

And if today he would die, he would die a duelist of the House of Steel.

Karin, min alskling . . .

She would understand. She understood him all too well, perhaps.

So be it.

*   *   *

Ivar del Hival tried to keep calm as he walked in step with the others. It only seemed fair that the Middle Dominions should have a representative here in front of the Table and Seat, and while Ivar del Hival was hardly what the Scion or His Warmth would have chosen as an emissary, that didn't much matter to him.

Taking on responsibility came naturally. That was, after all, what life was all about. It was the same in dueling, or in politics, or in draughts. You moved the little wooden disks across the checkered board, and positioned them as bloodlessly as possible, waiting for the moment when a small offering could be turned into an opponent's bloodbath. A move here, a thrust there, a hint of an intention to move here or thrust there, and it would all come together.

It was starting to come together, and he even had a feel for who the other players were.

He was not surprised to see the Margrave of the Hinterlands sitting at the Table with the rest. The purpose—well, at least one purpose—of the trip to the Seat was for Ian to get to know Marta, and for her to gauge the chances of a union with her family. It would have been just fine with the margrave if she had managed to get with child by him—Promised Warrior or not, he was still Ian Silver Stone, the killer of fire giants—but if she could ensnare him with more than that it would be all the better. Whether Ian survived facing the Table or not mattered much less to the margrave.

As it did to Ivar del Hival. Survival was one thing; success was another. Ian must succeed, and in that Ivar del Hival had common cause with Harbard, although Ivar del Hival had long dismissed as trivially unlikely the idea that preventing a war was Harbard's only objective in all this, or even his primary one.

Gods, like men, lie.

A time would come when the Crimson and Ancient Cerulean companies would again be assembled to ride south out of the Cities, but now was not that time. The Cities were not what they once were, and they were not what they someday could be.

So let the pieces march into their place, Ivar del Hival thought.

And if he was to be one of the pieces pushed toward the center of the board, well, what of that? This would hardly be the first time.

Let the game begin.

Ian stopped a few feet away from the Table, as though answering a silent command. He more felt than heard the others do the same.

Somehow, he had been expecting something grander and more impressive, but the Table was, well, a table, stretching most of the way across the width of the Hall. It had a leg at each corner, each looking like a slice out of the much longer columns that supported the Hall's roof.

There was something impressive, certainly, in that it was a single expanse of white stone that apparently needed no support along its length—for there certainly was none. The long, smooth surface held only the empty scabbards and naked swords of the men who sat behind it. The flames of the rows of candles lining their approach danced in the mirror surfaces of the brightly burnished blades.

Ian had never seen any of the Tyrsons without his scabbard clasped in his hand until now. He'd had silly visions of the Margrave of the Hinterlands having sex while clinging onto his, but somehow the vision wasn't amusing right at the moment.

Not a lot was amusing right at the moment.

The Margrave of the Hinterlands set the palms of both his hands, metal and flesh, against the surface of the Table and pushed himself to his feet. There was nothing effete or vague in his expression as he looked at Ian and his companions with eyes that looked like they ought to have shutters behind them.

"My fellows of the Table," he said, his tenor voice more penetrating, less silky than Ian remembered, "I present you with Ian Silver Stone and his . . . companions. They bring with them the spear Gungnir as testimony that they come from one known as Harbard the ferryman, Harbard of many names. He and they carry with him and them a request for the Table, and I invite my fellows of the Table to consider, each and all, whether the Table shall hear this request." He sat down, neither quickly nor slowly.

Several seats down, another man pushed himself to his feet, just as the margrave had. "I did not hear my fellow the Margrave of the Hinterlands make a request," he said, his voice thin and reedy with age. He coughed into his hand to clear his throat before continuing. "I understand that he neither vouches for this Ian Silver Stone nor accuses him of wrongdoing," he said and unceremoniously dropped back into his chair.

The margrave nodded, and a whisper passed up and down the line of seated men.

The square-jawed Argenten Horcel Tyrson was the next to rise; he, like the margrave, set his hands on the Table and used it to push himself to his feet. "I join my fellow the Duke of the Highland Reaches in noting that my fellow the margrave only notifies, and does not request." He lowered his voice. "I am, unlike my fellows of the Table, not of the nobility, nor do I seek to be. I have always felt," he said, raising his right hand, his silver hand, "that the weight of the honor of the silver hand of an argenten was sufficient burden for me to carry through life.

"I say this neither claiming nor denying virtue in that. Elsewhere we are argenten, and ordinary son, margrave and count and duke and commoner. Here, though, we are fellows of the

Table, and perhaps my . . . commonness gives me another view of the matter.

"I would see some proof of the virtue, of the steadfastness, of the soundness of this Ian Silverstein, or Ian Silver Stone, or whatever he chooses to call himself." His eyes were fixed on Ian's. "He is, by his own claim and admission, a killer of fire giants and kölds. Surely he has the courage to put his hand in the mouth of the Wolf, as have all who sit here tonight, a night, an Hour of the Long Candles, where the Table meets on a matter of honor and war." He folded his arms across his chest, but did not sit down for a moment. Instead, he stood, his eyes locked on Ian's.

Ian didn't hesitate to meet that gaze. He held it, until a throat-clearing from another of the seated men drew Horcel Tyrson's glare.

Horcel Tyrson nodded and gestured a quick apology, and flopped back down into his seat.

Another man, tall, all in black save for the copper color of his artificial hand, which was matched by a double row of coppery buttons down the front of his tunic, was next to set his hands on the table and rise. Apparently, the rule—at least for the folks behind the Table—was that you had to be standing to speak, and that only one could stand at a time.

"My fellow the Argenten Horcel Tyrson," he boomed, "is correct. If we are to give any serious weight at all to the words of this messenger, this herald, than he must stand the test.

"But what if he were to fail the test? And what if he were to fail the test not because of some failure in his message, but of some failure in himself?" He looked up and down the table, as though expecting an answer, although if Ian had the rules figured out correctly, the question was entirely rhetorical. "What if he is a flawed messenger—no Promised Warrior, no Tyrson-to-be, just an ordinary herald—with a true message?" He gestured at Ian with his flesh-and-blood hand. "Should we then deny ourselves the hearing of the message?" He spread his hands theatrically. "I await the wisdom of my fellows on this."

Another rose. "My fellow the Margrave of the Gilfi's Mouth speaks with words that puzzle me. What message could be borne by one so flawed that we should trouble our ears with it?" He extended a hand toward Ian, but Ian had no inclination whatsoever to step forward and shake it. "We have all heard the rumors of a team of assassins dispatched to prevent his words from reaching the Table, but there have been no such assassins run to ground, and look! Here he stands. Could it be that someone, for some reason, decided to buy him credibility by starting such a rumor? Could it be that even as we sit here at the Table, the Crimson and Ancient Cerulean companies of the Middle Dominions ride forth, to sweep through the Hinterlands and inward, gutting Vandescard like a cook with a sharp knife coring an apple?" He glared at Ian as he sat down.

Marta's father rose again. "My fellow the Duke of Bight's Bay perhaps speaks less wisely than is his usual custom. I have long since established watch posts on the approaches to the Hinterlands. I'm sure that the other margraves have done so as well, and perhaps some of the counts and dukes. Were riders pouring down from the Dominions, like ants out of an anthill, swift messenger birds would have long since been dispatched, and we would know of that." Grumbles of agreement moved up and down the table. "And while perhaps things are different on the shores of Bight's Bay, I can assure my fellow that should the Hinterlands be called to battle, my troops will give a good account of themselves in my absence, and miss this hand and this sword only a little." He allowed himself a small chuckle. "No. We of the Table must decide on many things, but the absence of the swords of a few dozen old men . . . no, that will not decide the issue one way or another." He sat down.

Another rose. "Yes, that is not the issue. I say that my fellow the Margrave of the Hinterlands is right; I say we should hear

the message, and then proceed to the testing of worthiness."
He gestured to the broad curtain behind him. "We can decide
how seriously the message is to be taken after that. These ears
do not come virgin to this table; they have heard lies and eva-
sions before."

Yet another: "I agree with my fellow the Count of the Pine
Barrens."

And another: "As do I."

Marta's father rose yet again, and faced Ian. "So, Ian Silver
Stone, you claim to be the herald of one Harbard the ferryman,
with information for the Table." He made a come-on gesture.
"Declare yourself, if you please." He sat back down and folded
his hands in his lap.

Ian's shoulders were aching from holding Gungnir at port
arms. He brought it down, to set the butt against the floor,
gently. "Well—"

Whoom.

The floor vibrated, a gong of an infinitely deep bass.

All of the men behind the table were on their feet, most
shouting, their faces contorted with anger. It took a moment for
Argenten Horcel Tyrson to quiet them, by forming his silver
hand into a fist, and pounding it on the table, like a built-in
gavel.

It felt like a long time until the argenten spoke again. "It will
not be necessary to threaten us with the spear Gungnir, nor will
that win you a vote from the Table that is to your liking." He
looked up and down the Table. "I see no dissent here on that,
Ian Silver Stone."

"But . . ." Ian was going to say that he hadn't intended to do
anything with the spear. He had been able to set it down without making everything shake before, and that was all—

But an explanation would seem like an excuse, and this
wasn't an audience that would tolerate excuses. He squatted,
slowly, and carefully, gently, set Gungnir down on the marble

floor, willing it to do nothing, to shake up nothing, willing it so hard that, again, Harbard's ring pulsed on his thumb.

The spear lay there, a foot in front of him. He looked from side to side, among his companions. "Whatever you do," he said, "don't touch the spear, not even with the toe of your boot."

He pulled off his gloves and tucked them into the back of his belt. "I apologize," he said, quietly, "for the disturbance. It was unintentional."

"As it was at the dock?" Argenten Horcel Tyrson asked. "Did you not mean it there, either?"

Ian didn't like Horcel Tyrson, but that didn't mean he could ignore him. And it didn't mean that the guy didn't have a point, after all. "Oh, I meant it there," he said. "I wanted to make the point to you that I'm not just a guy with a stick." He raised his voice as he addressed the rest of the Table. "I am not this Promised Warrior of yours. But I'm not somebody to be ignored, either. Not here and now. What I am is the herald of one who calls himself Harbard the ferryman. He believes that a war is about to start between Vandescard and the Middle Dominions, a war that threatens to shatter a peace that he finds to his liking. He has gone to some trouble to send me here to stop that."

Horcel Tyrson was still on his feet. "And what if we do not want to heed the words of this . . . ferryman?"

"He said I was to threaten you with Odin's Curse," Ian said. He extended his hand toward Horcel Tyrson with the curious cupping gesture Odin had made. "He set an apple on the table, and murmured something, willing it to . . ."

At first, Ian thought that Horcel Tyrson was simply sitting back down.

But then he made a sound that was halfway between a gasp and a scream, and pitched forward from his seat, the spastic motion smashing his face down on the Table itself so hard that Ian couldn't help groaning in sympathy.

But it didn't slow him; Horcel Tyrson fell to the floor, his body contracting and relaxing like a frog's leg touched by an electric wire.

Ian took a step forward, stopped, then leaped across the spear and onto the surface of the table, and then to the other side, unsurprised to find Thorian Thorsen at one side of the twitching man, Torrie at the other. Arnie Selmo was only a few moments behind; he slid under the table and came out on the other side of Horcel Tyrson.

The argenten was still in seizure, and Ian grabbed onto his tunic to prevent his bloody face from being smashed against the table again. Arnie Selmo kicked the chair out of the way, and the two of them bore Horcel Tyrson to the ground, Ian following what felt like centuries-old direction from Doc Sherve on how to handle an epileptic.

There was the quick clickety-click-click of steel on steel, and Ian looked up to see Thorian Thorsen standing between Ian and a dozen drawn swords, while Torrie protected him on the other side. Both Thorsens had drawn their swords, and the sounds of clashing swords had announced that they had engaged, but Ian could see no blood on either of their weapons.

Moving slowly, deliberately, Thorian Thorsen dropped the point of his sword. "There is no need for a fight," he said.

"Don't be foolish," Ivar del Hival said, his voice loud and booming. "They seek only to stop the argenten from hurting himself further."

Maggie's voice cut through the babble of voices. "Leave them be!" she shouted. "They do no harm."

Well, they weren't doing a whole lot of good, but they weren't doing any harm, either. That was the idea when you were dealing with somebody having a grand mal seizure. Don't interfere with his movements; just try to keep him from hurting himself.

The twitching slowed, then stopped, and Horcel Tyrson

sagged back onto the floor. It was slick and wet with blood from his nose.

Arnie was mopping at Horcel Tyrson's face with a blue bandanna, now mostly dark with his blood. "It's okay," he said, turning Horcel Tyrson's head to the side. "Don't need to inhale any vomitus, eh, Argenten?" he asked the unconscious man. "Just rest," Arnie said, patting him gently on the shoulder. "You have had what you would call a fit, but we call a 'seizure' where I come from." He was supposedly talking to Horcel Tyrson, but his voice was pitched loud, to carry throughout the hall. "You'll be just fine in a little while," he said. He raised his head and looked Ian in the eye. "A seizure. Brought on by Odin's Curse. You're thinking what I'm thinking."

Yes, he was. Perhaps it was no wonder that Hosea had been having seizures, and that they seemed to stop when Hosea had reached Tir Na Nog, heading for Harbard's Landing.

Odin, you cheat, he thought.

Odin had lived up to his reputation for trickery and deception when he had tried to keep Maggie and the Thorsens from coming after them. It was entirely possible that Odin's Curse had been what had started all of this, that his scheming had been intended, from the first, to bring Hosea to Tir Na Nog, accompanied by some sucker who would carry his spear—and his curse—to the Seat.

And if all that ended up neatly disposing of that merely human nuisance Ian Silverstein . . . well, that wouldn't bother the old god at all, now would it?

Arnie laid a couple of fingers against the side of Horcel Tyrson's neck, and held up his free hand for silence. "He looks bad, but he's okay," he said, his mouth twitching. "I just happen to have some medicines for epilepsy back in our rooms, but I think we'd best not use them. I don't think we'll need to."

"Yeah." Ian nodded. There was a serious question about how effective Newer World medicines would be in Tir Na Nog. And there was, at least in Ian's mind, some real question as to whether or not Harbard would have found occasion to tamper with them while they were at his cottage.

He looked over at Torrie and at Thorian. If they hadn't been here, Arnie would be dead right now, a sword of a Fellow of the Table stuck through him. Or, at best, if they hadn't vaulted the table and tried to help Ian, they all would have been hauled away to the local dungeon.

And the two Thorsens wouldn't have been here at all if Maggie hadn't come along with them.

Ian caught Maggie smiling at him. He raised a finger to his forehead, in a casual salute.

Nicely done, he thought.

CHAPTER TWENTY-ONE

The Mouth of the Wolf

It took some time to quiet the Table. By then, soldiers in the many uniforms of the Seat Guard arrived, and had borne off the now sleeping Horcel Tyrson on an improvised blanket stretcher.

When the nobles of the Table resumed their seats, it was a different atmosphere, less formal but even less friendly.

The Duke of Bight's Bay stood up, and the murmuring ceased. "I assume that you didn't intend to harm Horcel Tyrson."

Ian shook his head. "*I* didn't harm him, at all. That was Odin's Curse, not mine." He spread his hands. "I . . . don't have those kinds of powers," he said. "I'm not an Old One, after all. I'm just a . . . just a man."

"But you hold the spear of a god, and it doesn't harm you. And you . . . seem to have cast Odin's Curse on Horcel Tyrson."

Ian shook his head. "I . . . if I did, and I don't think I did, I don't know how." He spread his hands. "I just don't know."

His mind raced. It was obvious that Odin could cast his curse from some great distance. Was it the ring? No; that didn't seem likely. The only thing the ring had done was to pulse on his thumb every now and then. If it had simply been Ian extending his arm . . .

Not the right time to test it. But it should have felt different, or it at least should have felt like *something*.

271

"Truly, I meant no harm," Ian said. "I don't know . . ."

"Then it's clear that you have to prove yourself," the Duke of Bight's Bay said. "All this talk of you being the Promised Warrior or not the Promised Warrior, of curses that aren't curses, and spell that aren't spells." He looked up and down the Table. "I . . . I find myself uncertain. I had no inclination to war with the Dominions, not now, not with—" He stopped himself. "Not with the present situation, by and large, as it is, by and large." He shook his head. "But I must say to my fellows that I'm torn. Putting a hand in the Wolf's Mouth has long been a privilege, not a right." He held up his metal hand. "We all have faced the Pain, but we faced it to prove ourselves worthy to lead, worthy to follow, worthy—not to prove ourselves not . . . untruthful."

He walked to the curtain behind the Table, and pulled it to one side. It moved silently.

Behind it lay a stone table, just short of chest high. And on the stone table was a stone sculpture of the head of some animal.

It took Ian a moment to decide it was a wolf; it was too large, the teeth too many, the jaw too broad, giving it an almost cartoony look.

A rack behind the table held what Ian at first would have guessed were a dozen lances. Instead of being tipped in a spearpoint, each was topped by a wooden disk, about the size of a dinner plate.

"Each of us has, like our Father Tyr, faced the wolf, and put our hand in his mouth, and gripped the Pain."

"And that's how you lost your hands, eh?" Torrie said, startling Ian. Torrie had been silent, which was too quiet even for him.

"No," the duke said. He held up his metal hand. "That is how we sacrificed our hands, demonstrating our worth and virtue." He took one of the poles down from the rack. "It is the right of those who think the candidate worthy to attempt to push him off, after he's gripped the Pain; it is the right of those who think him unworthy to block those attempts." He replaced the pole. "But the Promised Warrior, of course, will feel no pain when he grips the Pain; his hand will not wither and burn." He gestured toward where the spear Gungnir lay on the hard floor. "Just as you grip the spear of Odin without harm."

Bullshit. Ian had touched the spear while he wasn't wearing Freya's gloves. Just once, in his sleep. He rubbed at the still-sore spot on his left arm where the blister had been.

"And you're asking me to stick my hand in that statue's mouth, and grab hold of this Pain, while you stand around and decide if I'm going to die or not."

The duke nodded. "Yes." He sat back down, and waved a hand toward it. "That is precisely what we ask."

Ian swallowed, heavily, but it didn't remove the metallic taste of fear from his mouth. They expected him to burn his hand off—at the very least. And what if one of them decided that they were all better off without Ian?

"But what if he doesn't?" Maggie stepped forward. "What if he says, 'So be it, you've received the warning, do with it what you will—I'm going home.' What if we just turn our backs and walk out?"

The Margrave of the Hinterlands rose. "You have appeared in front of the Table by your own choice, all of you. Do you think you will leave without being judged? Do you think that we are helpless old men for you to taunt and then just walk away? Step forth and be judged."

Torrie's mouth was dry. Time had run out. "Wait," he said. "Wait." He took a step forward. "Judge me, instead. I'm his champion."

*   *   *

Arnie remembered a smile.

He couldn't, for the life of him, remember what village that crossroads was just outside of. But it was somewhere between Nam'po and Sindae-Dong. Dog Troop had been cut off from the rest of the Seventh. The Old Man—the captain's name was Young, and while he was really in his midtwenties, he looked like he was about eighteen, maybe; he was destined to be known as the Old Man, although not to his face—had gotten his orders over the radio, and had ordered what was probably officially called a strategic withdrawal, but everybody knew was a retreat down the road until they met up with some support.

The Old Man had left behind a two-man machine-gun team with orders to hold out as long as they could, and then get away, if they could. They'd probably slow the lead elements of the oncoming division for a few minutes, and minutes were in short supply.

The gunner's assistant was an acne-faced kid from somewhere in Georgia; he just nodded, once, his face white as a sheet. The gunner, though, was that loudmouth Petrocelli, from New Yawk, and for once Petrocelli didn't mouth off. He just nodded, said, "Understood, Cap'n," and smiled.

Arnie still remembered that smile, the smile of a man about to spend his life to buy his brothers-in-arms a few minutes, a distraction.

But shit, this wasn't that bad. Petrocelli had been a kid, maybe twenty-three, twenty-four. He'd thrown away maybe a half century of life.

But what did Arnie have?

Not a damn thing worth keeping.

Not his life. He wasn't afraid of dying. It had already happened, more than not. The best part of him had died in his arms not so long ago, and the only reason he hadn't gone along with her is that she made him promise not to, and Arnie wouldn't lie to Ephie, not on her deathbed, and not any other time.

Besides, he had been lucky. He'd had it all. It just hadn't lasted forever. You get lucky enough to live with a good woman for ten, then twenty, then thirty years, you get to the point where you can't even remember how long it's been that you've known that the old cliché about your "better half" was just the plain truth, no embellishment.

And then, after he had finally retired, and after he had just started to enjoy spending every remaining hour of his life with her, an old friend in a white jacket had called them into his office. He had known from the start that Doc had bad news: Doc only put on the professional look of concern when he had bad news.

But Arnie hadn't been prepared for how bad the news was. Nobody could be ready for that obscene, ugly word: metastasis. The pain got worse, and only ended with a needle that brought her, finally, easily, to the end of all pain.

Somehow, he had gotten through each day since then. And sometimes it didn't hurt for minutes.

So it was with not even the slightest twinge of regret that Arnie took a running start to leap to the surface of the Table, then jumped over an empty seat, toward the Wolf's Head.

He landed hard, and wrong, and pain shot through his left ankle as his left leg buckled beneath him; even as he sprawled hard on the marble floor, he was already forcing his right leg underneath him.

Arnie Selmo rose to a three-point stance like a runner would take, and then launched himself forward, toward the Wolf's Head, bouncing on his leg like it was a pogo stick.

It was like he had put a knife into his kneecap, but that wouldn't matter, not much longer, as he thrust his hand deep into the stone mouth. Stone teeth scraped against his arm, drawing blood, but that wouldn't matter, not for long.

There was what felt like a wooden bar at the back of the mouth, about where the throat should have been.

Arnie gripped it tightly, and waited for the Pain, and the end of it all.

But there was no pain. A distant humming filled his ears, growing so loud that he couldn't hear anything else, making his whole body vibrate like a guitar string. The pain in his ankle and kneecap vanished in that vibration, along with dozens of other minor pains that he only noticed by their absence.

He still lived, dammit. He should have been burned to a cinder in moments, but instead, he was still standing, still holding onto the wooden bar at the back of the Wolf's Mouth.

"No!"

Nobody would ever believe him, anyway, so he would never mention that it was with anger and disappointment that he gripped the wooden bar in the back of the Wolf's Head with all the strength he could muster, and yanked at it, shattering the stone sculpture into dozens of pieces, leaving him with what now was, inescapably, the handle of a war hammer in his hands, as he stood before the marble pedestal on which it had rested.

He was angry, angrier than he had ever been, so it was the most natural thing to raise the hammer above his head, and smash down, hard, on the pedestal.

It split in half with an almost unbelievably satisfying *crrack!*

And in the rubble lay a diamond the size of an egg.

Arnie turned to face the sea of faces, the rush of voices raised in shouts and cries, as he raised the hammer Mjolnir over his head.

The words came to him easily, as he faced the men of the Table:

"Does anyone," he shouted, letting his voice rumble and roar, "any one of you care to dispute the safe passage of my friends from this Hall?"

And then, only then, did the Hall fall silent.

CHAPTER TWENTY-TWO

A Farewell

Ian met her in the gardens, just as dawn was breaking. The walls of the Keep would block the sun for hours yet, but the sky was a royal blue, lightening by the minute, as gray masses of clouds whitened into cottony puffs.

He had tried to sleep, but hadn't been able to. Arnie hadn't had any difficulty falling asleep in front of the fireplace, Mjolnir lying on the floor next to where he put his blankets. Ivar del Hival and Thorian Thorsen had quickly retired to their sleeping rooms as well, but Torrie and Maggie hadn't been able to sleep either, and had one by one exited their sleeping rooms and joined Ian in the central salon of their suite in the Residency.

Another all-nighter. Well, somebody had to do some planning, some thinking ahead.

It was nice to be able to think beyond the Table. That felt downright luxurious.

Marta made her way down the path toward him, dressed in yet another variation of her traveling outfit of blouse and culottes.

"Good morning," he said.

Her eyes were red, and her smile sad as she took his hands. "Good morning, my Ian," she said.

He slipped his arms around her waist and locked his fingers together. "Am I still your Ian?"

She nodded. "Yes, if you want to be. If . . ." She shook her head. "But it would be awkward now, wouldn't it? You were part of the party that has shaken Vandescard to its foundations." She had to laugh. "No more Tyrsons? It would be hard to imagine a Vandescard without the Tyrsons."

"Oh," Ian said, "I figure they'll find sufficient excuses to chop a hand off the worthy, sooner or later. But I suspect that the idea of invading the Dominions will be put off, at least for a while, or—"

"Or until Odin actually sends us the Promised Warrior. Unless. . . ."

"If you're going to count on Arnie for that, I think you'll be surprised. And not pleasantly." What was it about Arnie that made him able to hold Mjolnir? The hammer's handle had burned off generations of hands among the Vandestish elite. What was it about Arnie that made it safe for him to hold it?

Ian thought he knew.

He'd known it every time that he had seen Arnie take down one of those little figurines of Ephie's, dust it, and then carefully, gently, put it back in its place. He knew it the day that Arnie had volunteered to come along. Not for his willingness, but for the glee in his voice at the prospect. At last, at long last, Arnie had found a way he might be able to kill himself without breaking his promise to Ephie, and he had seized on that chance without pause, without hesitation, without regret, until he found himself standing in the rubble that had been the Wolf's Head, holding the hammer of Thor in his hand, the Brisingamen diamond at his feet.

Arnie just didn't give a damn about dying. Was that what had saved him?

Maybe. Probably.

"If not him," Marta said, "perhaps there will be . . ."

Ian's jaw tightened. "I wouldn't count on that. Not real soon. We're going to go have a little talk with Harbard the ferryman, the six of us." It wasn't nice to play with people like they were toys. It wasn't nice to curse Hosea, or to—

But let it be, for now. The six of them, Ian carrying both Giantkiller and Gungnir, Arnie bearing Mjolnir, should be a match for the old bastard.

"You leave this morning?"

Ian nodded. "As soon as the old ones wake, we're going to, er, acquire a dozen or so horses from the stables here, and head off." Somehow he didn't think that Arnie would get a lot of resistance, and what the hell, they did have some good Dominion gold.

"And you were going to leave without speaking to me?"

He shook his head. "No. I'm not that much of a coward," he said.

"Then what of us? The idea of settling down to become the next margrave doesn't appeal to you," she said, shaking her head in amazement. "It really doesn't, and I really don't understand it."

Ian shrugged. "Maggie put it to me kind of bluntly, last night—she asked if I really wanted to spend the rest of my life squeezing taxes out of the citizenry in between bouts of political intrigue and the occasional battle, and the answer is no."

"But . . . but ruling the Hinterlands is what I was born to do," she said. "Even if you asked me to leave it—"

"You wouldn't."

Discussing it was hopeless, and useless, and what made it worse was that he liked Marta, a lot. She was gentle, and kind, and tough beneath the polished exterior. And truth to tell, he liked her just the way she was, even though that would pull the two of them apart.

He kissed her, hard, her tongue warm against his. After a long time, he pulled back, just a little. "So. What of us? Do we say good-bye here?"

"I think, perhaps, we should say 'farewell, until we meet

again.'" Her smile was both warm and sly at the same time. "Oh, if you don't mind, I'll still represent myself as your betrothed."

He chuckled. "And if you find somebody you'd prefer, well, it won't hurt his status much that you'd thrown over Ian Silver Stone, killer of giants, for him, eh?"

"Of course." She nodded. "Then again, he would have to be very special. And there is always the possibility that you'll come to your senses, isn't there? You know that there will always be a place for you in the Hinterlands."

"I hope I can stop by, often. Or at least, every now and then."

"That would be nice," she said. "I won't promise to wait, but ... as I say, he would have to be somebody special." She patted her belly. "You won't mind if I don't wait on having a daughter for you, I would hope."

The thought of another man in her bed bothered Ian more than he was willing to admit, but so be it. "No, that would be fine," he said.

"You lie," she said, laughing. "You're such a foreigner about some things."

"You'll miss that."

She nodded. "Well, yes, I will. And you will miss me."

He kissed her lightly on the lips. "That's certainly no lie."

"And perhaps I could remind you, once more, of all that you'll be missing."

"That would be very nice." Ian offered her his arm.

They walked back into the Residency, and up the stairs to the second-floor suite that Ian shared with the others.

The rest were all awake. Arnie and Torrie were busy packing the various bags, while Maggie, Thorian, and Ivar del Hival sat in front of the fire, each with a steaming mug of tea in hand.

"Good morning," Maggie said. "And good morning to you, Margravine." Maggie smiled. "I hope I'm not being too presumptuous if I suggest that you and I go off and take tea together this morning, before we leave. I could tell you some stories about your . . . friend there."

Marta smiled back. "That would be very nice."

"Please." Ian held up a hand. "Later," he said. "If you'll excuse us."

He turned and followed Marta into his bedroom, hoping that he wasn't blushing too much.

And then she was in his arms, and he couldn't have cared less.

As they reached the top of the road overlooking the Seat, a black bird spiraled down out of the blue sky. It startled Torrie's horse—Torrie had picked a high-spirited black mare as his primary mount—but Ian's somewhat morose bay gelding barely seemed to notice, even when the bird lit on a thick branch a dozen feet over their heads.

"Greetings," it said. "I've come to bring word to he who waits,

"For word of your victories, word of your glories,

"Tell me what I need to know, without hesitating.

"I'm always eager to hear your stories."

Ian looked from face to face among the others, and was surprised that they were all waiting for him. Even Arnie, who rode clutching Mjolnir as carefully as Ian used his free hand to hold Gungnir.

There was no point in lying. Hugin or Munin would surely be able to monitor their progress back to Harbard's cottage.

"I'm sure he'll have heard," Ian said, "that we've managed to survive. We're on our way to Harbard's Crossing now."

But it would be a mistake to carry the Brisingamen diamond with them. Yes, they would be hard to take on directly, carrying both Gungnir and Mjolnir, but stealth might succeed where directness would not.

"Can I bind you to take the diamond to her, not to him?" Ian asked.

"Thought and memory alone must we bring to him," the bird cawed. "Say: 'bring this to Freya,' and so I will do.

"I have long been an honest messenger,

"Long before you."

The bird cocked his head. "You might ask of your friend Hosea, some time. He—"

"Orfindel?" Torrie put in. "Hosea? The real one? You're sure he's alive?"

The bird ruffled its feathers. "No, I make no such claim,

"Though I saw him at work, but yesternight evening,

"Still, he may have curled up and died since,

"Though he showed no sign of such leaving."

Maggie cocked her head to one side. "We speak of our friend Hosea, not Harbard or anybody else in disguise."

"Ah," the bird said, cocking his head in perhaps unintentional mimicry, "you wound me, you do.

"I said that I saw your friend; and I

"Do not say what I do not know to be true."

So be it. "Bring this to Freya," Ian said. He flung the diamond into the air. If Hugin and Munin could be diverted by Odin from giving the gem to Freya, surely that would have already happened with the ruby.

The world was at times more treacherous than Ian would have liked, but you had to learn to trust who you could.

The diamond tumbled through the air, shattering sunlight into a myriad of bright colors, until the raven's feet closed about it with a loud click. Broad wings beat against the air as it climbed high into the sky, until the bird was only a dot over the trees.

"Well," Torrie said, smiling. "Looks to me we have some riding to do."

Ian nodded. "Let's go."

Maggie chuckled. "Always in a rush, that's the way men are. Can't just enjoy the moment. Hmm . . . maybe that explains the way you all—"

"Maggie." Torrie was actually blushing. "Stop it."

She laughed. "Now, now, now. I was just thinking that that explains the way you wolf down your supper, that's all."

Ian had to laugh.

"Well," Thorian Thorsen said, kicking his dun gelding into a walk, "the day grows no younger."

Ivar del Hival grunted. "Neither do I. Although I wish that I would, from time to time."

Arnie Selmo shook his head. "Not me," he said, quietly, sadly. He shook his head. "If I had a wish, that's not what I'd wish for, not for a moment."

CHAPTER TWENTY-THREE

Harbard's Crossing

Hosea was waiting for them on the front porch of the cottage, his long legs stretched out, the heels of his boots resting on the section of stump he was using as a hassock. He had been there since they had first sighted the cabin, more than an hour before, and he hadn't moved: he was whittling at a piece of wood, although it was too early in the process to tell what it would become.

He smiled and nodded as they rode up, but made no move to rise.

Ian dismounted, carefully, one hand on the grip of the saddle, another on Gungnir. He would not throw it. Thrown, it would return to Odin.

"He's gone. No need to be concerned." Hosea raised a slim hand. "It's really me," he said, an ever so slight slurring in his voice. "I understand that at least one of you was clever enough," he went on, his smile taking the sting out of the words, "to figure out that he was impersonating me, while I lay chained in the cave that he uses to stable Sleipnir. Used, that is. He and Sleipnir are gone."

"You won't mind if we check that out for ourselves," Maggie said.

Thorian Thorsen, Ivar del Hival, and Arnie made their way around the back in company. Ian was again impressed with how quietly Ivar del Hival could move; the big man made only a little more sound than Thorian, who walked silently, his sword out, and at the ready. Arnie brought up the rear, swinging Mjolnir one-handed, prevented from dropping it by the leather strap terminating in a wrist-loop that now wrapped its handle.

"No, I won't mind at all, Maggie," Hosea said, slowly. "How can I reassure you?"

"It is he, and only he." The voice from inside the cabin made Ian jump. He remembered that voice. "I assume you'll trust me with this, as you've trusted me with so much more." She stood in the doorway, looking almost exactly as she had the last time.

Her glossy white hair hung loose around her shoulders, although the bangs had been pulled back to either side of the part, held by a pair of golden clips. The creamy cotton shift she wore ended several inches above the knee, and was belted tightly, emphasizing her slim waist and the full breasts that didn't seem overly large for a woman with broad shoulders. As before, Ian was reminded of Rachel McLish, the body-builder— Freya was muscular, certainly, but there was nothing even vaguely masculine about the lines and curves of her body.

Her smile dazzled as she walked out toward them. "It's good to see you again, Ian. And to meet you, at last, young Thorian del Thorian. And you, Maggie Christensen."

Ian never remembered deciding whether or not to give her the spear, but moving neither quickly nor slowly, she reached out and then she had it in her hands.

Ian let out a breath he didn't remember holding. It felt good to have the spear out of his hands. He stripped off his gloves and flexed his fingers, working the knots of tension out.

Her smile broadened. "Ah. I see you do remember me." She beckoned at all of them. "Come into the house, please—Hosea? Would you be so kind as to invite the other three? Dinner waits, and we have much to discuss."

* * *

Crowding eight people around a table intended for four at most made dinner more intimate than Ian would have cared for; he found himself squeezed tightly between Torrie and Ivar del Hival.

But the stew was rich and meaty, the cider cold and sweet, and the apple pie that Freya took from the oven with her bare hands—it would take more than a hot oven to burn the flesh of an Aesir—was even sweeter and richer than he remembered. It was silly for a piece of pie to make such a difference, but each bite seemed to ease the road-weariness that had settled in each joint and muscle.

The conversation flowed around him, but he just sat and half-listened. Arnie, Thorian Thorsen, Maggie, and Hosea were headed back home. Freya had drawn a map toward a Hidden Way that would lead back to the Newer World, Maggie having rejected the first one she suggested, which terminated somewhere in central Europe. Yes, they had their passports in their kits, but the passports wouldn't show any entry stamp, and it was best not to draw any attention. And Hosea didn't have a passport at all.

This Hidden Way's other end opened up somewhere in Wisconsin, it seemed; it would be just a matter of hiking to the nearest town to catch a bus or plane, or to rent a car, to get home.

Torrie and Ivar del Hival were going to head up to the Dominions—maybe, accidentally, Odin had had a good idea by directing them toward Thorian del Orvald, and besides, Torrie wanted to see his grandfather again, and meet his grandmother. They assumed that Ian was coming with them, and he probably should, but . . .

Why did he feel so shitty?

It didn't make sense.

"Excuse me." He pushed back from the table, rose, and

walked out into the night. Out of the corner of his eye he saw Torrie rise to his feet, but stop when Maggie seized his arm.

"Leave him be," she said.

The night was just blackness, barely relieved by the twinkling of a canopy of stars above. He leaned back against one of the porch's support posts, and sighed.

Marta had pointed out some of the constellations, and Ian had pretended to make up some others. There was a ragged rectangle with a line of three bright stars perpendicular to it that she had said was called Thor's Hammer, and there was that lazy Z near the horizon called Ouroborous.

He wondered if she was looking up at the same stars right now, and if she missed him.

Slowly, gradually, his eyes adjusted, and the distant darkness took form and shape, the vague blur at the edge of the clearing becoming trees, the patch of slightly lighter gray becoming the road up to the cottage.

He walked to the far corner of the porch, and looked down the slope to where the river Gilfi rippled in the starlight, shimmering like a writhing metallic snake. It was pretty, in a cold, cruel way.

The door creaked open behind him, and Arnie Selmo walked onto the porch.

"I'm going to be turning in. You need anything?"

Ian had to laugh. "You can stop pretending to be my squire now, Arnie. We're done with that."

Arnie joined him in chuckling. "Well, to tell the truth, I was thinking like your landlord," he said, his tone half-serious. "Who you owe some rent to, come to think of it."

Ian nodded. "I'm good for it. I'll write you a check when we get back."

"Fair enough. And I do know where you live, eh?"

"There is that."

"See you in the morning. We got a long day tomorrow; let's get an early start."

The door opened and closed again. Ian leaned against the post.

Again, the door opened behind him, and he recognized Torrie's heavy footsteps.

"Well," Torrie said, idly tossing and catching the two apples he held, "Maggie said that I should leave you alone, but I figured you could tell me that yourself, if you needed to. Want me to go away?"

Ian shook his head. "No, not really."

"Care to talk about it?" Torrie asked.

"Nah." Ian shook his head. "I think I need to figure out what's bothering me before I go around talking about it."

"Heaven help you if you should expose some weakness without having it all thought out in advance, eh?" Torrie chuckled. "Yeah, well, it's up to you. If you ever need to talk, you know, well . . ."

"Yeah."

"I'm not the sensitive New Age guy type, but I am your friend," Torrie said.

"I sort of noticed that. At the Table." Ian shook his head. Torrie had been willing to step forward and face the Pain, rather than Ian. And it wasn't just an impulse, either; Torrie wasn't impulsive. He had thought about it, and decided on it well in advance. "Thanks," he said.

"Well, I do owe you one."

"You did."

"You can't give an inch, can you?" Torrie laughed. "Well, look," he said, lowering his voice, "Ivar and I've been doing some talking. If you want to come with us to the Dominion, that's fine. But if you don't, that's fine, too." He clapped a hand to Ian's shoulder.

"When are you leaving?" Ian asked.

"First light," Torrie said. "Maggie's agreed to go home with Dad; I'm going to slip away before she changes her mind. Let me know, either way, eh?"

"Sure."

Torrie tossed and caught one of the apples, then took a bite out of it. "I'd better go feed these to Silvertop," he said from around a mouthful, "like I said I would." He walked off into the dark. The sounds of gravel clicking and grinding under his boots diminished in the distance.

"Ian." He hadn't heard Freya's footsteps, or seen the flash of light from the opening door, but she stood next to him, Giantkiller in his scabbard in her hand. "May I?"

"May you what?"

She apparently decided to take his question as permission to belt Giantkiller about his waist. "The world's a dangerous place, Ian," she said. "You need to be ready for it." She patted at the hilt of the sword. "It's a good sword. You choose your companions well, perhaps better than you know."

"You mean Arnie."

"Certainly." She nodded. "In part. Among others. What did you see in him?"

Ian shrugged. "He was there, and he wanted to come along." He spread his hands. "I didn't have any idea."

Her laughter was quiet music in the darkness. "Ah, not an idea in your head. I don't think I would have believed that, not even when I was young."

"So how can he—"

"Hold Mjolnir without harm?" She shook her head. "I don't know. I know what the maker of Gungnir bound that spear to, but when he made Mjolnir, he was interrupted, and I don't know how the geas he laid on it ended up. I suppose you could ask him, but I doubt he'd remember. He's lost—no: he's given up much of what he knew, much of what he was."

Ian wasn't in the least surprised to hear that Hosea had made Gungnir and Mjolnir. "Happens when you get old, so I hear."

"Mmmm . . . so it does. And some is taken away from you," she said, "sometimes by those you trust." Her voice was colder. "I . . . am not used to living alone, and you have chased my husband away."

From anybody else Ian would have taken the words and the tone as a threat, but somehow he couldn't find it in him to feel that way with Freya. "You want me to fix you up or something?"

"No," she said. "And I'm not very angry; Harbard and I see some things, some important things, differently, and I think we need a short vacation from each other. Maybe only a few years; perhaps a few centuries.

"But right now, I don't want to live alone, either. I'm going to ask Arnold to stay here, with me, at least for a while. He will resist the idea at first, but he will agree, if I have enough time to persuade him."

"Fertility goddesses know much about men, eh?"

"Why, of course we do." She laughed. "Although only the important things."

At first, Ian was surprised, but he thought about it for a moment. Not a bad idea, really. Freya might be ageless in body, but she was almost unbelievably old. And Arnie was, well, Arnie was just about used up in some ways. "Feed him apple pie every day and slough some of those years off, eh?"

"Yes." She touched him lightly on the shoulder. "I knew you'd understand. Thank you."

"But . . ."

"But you don't think," she said, her hand sweeping up and down in front of her body, "that Arnie's really ready to take on a young woman. You think that how I look might scare him away." She caught his gaze and held it, unblinking, like a snake with a bird. "But I'm not a young woman, Ian. I'm older than you can imagine, and I don't mind looking it."

She looked away, releasing his eyes. She was now an old woman, body bent and skin wrinkled with age, her white hair limp, the shift that had clung tightly to her now hanging loose. "And I'm wise enough," she said, her voice ever so slightly weak and reedy at the edges, "to look nothing like Ephie Selmo at all."

Ian must have blinked again, because she was, again, as he had first seen her, as Freya would always be in his mind: young and firm, ageless.

"But Harbard. Won't he . . . ?"

"No, he won't." Her voice was clear as water from a mountain stream. "Arnie is perfectly safe. Harbard would no more want to face Gungnir in my hands than in yours, I assure you. And Arnie holds Mjolnir; he's no one to trifle with." Her smile was warming, reassuring. "Harbard has been known to stray from time to time, as have I," she said. "One gets used to these things."

"And the diamond? The ruby?"

She shook her head. "Where they are is something you don't need to know," she said, her voice icy and distant. "Just remember that I've vowed to keep them safe until the time is right, and that while I am older than the hills around us, Ian, I've never been known to break my word." She sighed. "But enough about me. What about you? You seem so weary, so tired in spirit."

"Yeah." Ian nodded. "That I am."

"Would you be angry with me if I offered some advice? Old heads are wise heads, sometimes. Would you be offended?"

He shook his head. "Nah."

"Then go back to Hardwood. Relax until you're tired of relaxing," she said. "Take some time to yourself. Study some more with Thorian del Thorian; he has much to teach you. Let

Karin Thorsen apologize to you, in her husband's presence. It will be good for her, and better for you. It will be good for you to hear an apology. You'll probably never get the apologies your father owes you, but . . ."

"I worked that out years ago."

She nodded. "I know." Her hand stroked his back once, twice. "So go back to Hardwood."

"I just might." Why did the idea of going back to Hardwood make him feel like he'd dropped the weight of the world from his shoulders? "I think I will."

"Good." She nodded. "And then, when you're ready, the work awaits. If that's still what you want. Do something for me, though, while you're in Hardwood, while you live in Arnie's house."

"Yes?"

"Pack up all the pictures, all the knickknacks, all the memories of *her*, and put them away. Do it gently, carefully—always treat them with respect—but put them away. Paint the walls; put in shiny new sinks and tile and a new kitchen. Make it yours, instead of his. It will be best for both you and him."

"I can't." He shook his head. "I couldn't do that without Arnie's permission." He wouldn't do that behind Arnie's back. Sure, the changes would probably be good for Arnie—it wouldn't shame Ephie's memory for him to have a life, after all—but Ian couldn't do that, not without asking Arnie.

"Well," she said, "then stay with us a few days, and I'll get that permission for you." She smiled. "I'm very good at that."

"I've noticed," Ian said.

"You could help, if you'd like."

"Oh?"

"You could use this." She tapped Harbard's ring, where it rode on his thumb, a perfect fit. "Believe, concentrate, and while you wear this, you'll find yourself more persuasive than you ought to be." She tilted her head to one side. "You don't have to lie. Don't you truly think that Arnie would be better off living here with me, in a world live with possibilities, than huddling in a musty museum dedicated to his dead wife, waiting to die?"

He fondled the heavy ring for a moment, where it rested on his thumb. He removed it, and slipped it on each finger in turn, and without seeming to change at all, it fit each finger in turn, as though it had persuaded both the fingers and itself that it would always fit. It would pulse only when he was trying hard to persuade somebody.

No.

Ian removed Harbard's ring from his thumb and tucked it in his pocket. He would surely have use for it again, but not here, not now. It would be a good thing to keep, yes; but Ian knew somebody who sold his soul for a ring, once.

Ian shook his head. For the first time that he could remember, Ian found himself pitying his father, and not just hating him.

Freya was waiting for his answer.

"Yes," he said, "I do think Arnie would be better off here, at least for now. And I'll be happy to tell him that," he said, slowly, carefully, knowing that he was probably about to give offense, but not caring. "But I'll only do it with my own voice, my own persuasiveness, whatever that is. And that's all I will do."

"Ah." She smiled. "I knew you would say that, Ian. I did, after all, say that you *could* use the ring, not that you *should*." She leaned over and kissed him on the cheek. "Come back into the house when you're ready."

"Sure."

She turned away.

"Freya?"

She stopped, turned back to him.

"Yes?"

"Thank you."

She nodded. "You're most welcome, my Silver Stone."

And then she was gone, and he was alone, again.

He took the ring that Count Pel Pelson had given him out of his pouch, and slipped it on his ring finger.

It fit well, but not perfectly, as Harbard's ring had; there was, after all, nothing magical about it.

But Ian looked again at the way that the ring's two inscribed hands supported the round green stone. A reminder, perhaps, that the fate of the world is supported by many hands, and held in each of our hands. That was a good thing to keep in mind, and maybe it would be a good idea to keep that reminder on the ring finger of his left hand, the hand nearest the heart.

Just a little more time, he thought.

Just a little more time to himself now, and a few days here, while Freya worked on Arnie. Then Ian could leave for the Hidden Way, perhaps managing to spend another night on Bóinn's Hill en route. He still had the apple seeds in his pouch, and perhaps Bóinn would appreciate him planting a nice apple tree or two. He'd have to ask her.

"And then," he whispered, quietly, to himself, "and then, then I can go home."

Author's Note

A couple of real people appear in this book. Greg Cotton is a pilot and a friend. Once, while flying a borrowed Lance from Minneapolis to Winnipeg, he and I set down at the tiny airport outside of Northwood, North Dakota. Rick Foss, of Ladera Travel, has been my travel agent for years. I thought it would be kind of fun to share him with Torrie and Maggie. The shooting-the-burglar story Arnie Selmo tells of Bob Adams was told to me, almost exactly that way, by the late Robert Adams, on more than one occasion. Any errors in the retelling are mine—or maybe they're Arnie's.

With those exceptions, the usual disclaimer applies: this is a work of fiction, and all the characters portrayed in this novel are fictional.

Going to Northwood, North Dakota, the town on which I've modeled my Hardwood, North Dakota, to find a Hidden Way, would be a real bad idea.

Particularly if you found one . . .

During the writing of this book, I got a lot of help from Jim Drury; Beth Friedman; and, particularly, my wife, Felicia Herman, who is always willing to chase down some obscure fact that I need, and usually comes up with half a dozen more that I needed but didn't know I needed. Jeff Schwartz was kind enough to go over the fencing and swordfighting scenes, and give me the benefit of his knowledge of both the broad and fine points of both, which is pretty darned encyclopedic. Lisa Freitag, M.D., gave me a much needed lecture on the nature and treatment of epileptic seizures; and Elise Matthesen spent many hours running her sharp eyes over the whole thing.

I'm always grateful to my agent, Eleanor Wood, for things both obvious and subtle.

Needless to say, many things right about the present work are due to their efforts; the blame for any and all things wrong should be laid squarely at my feet.

One of the many nice things about this job is the people you get to know. Sometimes, in publishing, there're more of them than you can count, but I'd like to thank the folks now and formerly at Avon Books for their patience, confidence, and support during the writing of this book and the one before it.

I think that sounds kind of maudlin, but if so, it's maudlin that's been come by honestly.